"You won't hurt me?"

Pure willpower kept her voice from sounding shaky.

He was too damned close.

"Actually, I don't say that to anyone at all. I rarely issue promises," the vampire replied in a soft, deadly voice.

If dead things were so damned cold, Jesse reasoned, why did she feel heat coming off him? Why did she feel as though he was touching her?

There was no way she'd face him or look into those drowning blue eyes. Eyes were mirrors of the soul, and vampires didn't have souls. Would his eyes be empty?

It doesn't matter, she thought, *I'm taking you down.*

Books by Linda Thomas-Sundstrom

Harlequin Nocturne

*Red Wolf #81
*Wolf Trap #83
† Golden Vampire #110

*Wolf Moons
†Vampire Moons

LINDA THOMAS-SUNDSTROM

author of contemporary and historical paranormal romance novels, writes for Harlequin Nocturne. She lives in the West, juggling teaching, writing, family and caring for a big stretch of land. She swears she has a resident muse who sings so loudly she virtually funds the Post-it company. Eventually, Linda hopes to get to all those ideas.

Visit Linda at her website, www.lindathomas-sundstrom.com, and the Nocturne Authors' website, www.nocturneauthors.com.

GOLDEN VAMPIRE

LINDA THOMAS-SUNDSTROM

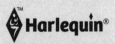

TORONTO NEW YORK LONDON
AMSTERDAM PARIS SYDNEY HAMBURG
STOCKHOLM ATHENS TOKYO MILAN MADRID
PRAGUE WARSAW BUDAPEST AUCKLAND

Recycling programs
for this product may
not exist in your area.

ISBN-13: 978-0-373-61857-6

GOLDEN VAMPIRE

Dear Reader,

Vampires. Tall, dangerous, gloriously sexy immortals with enough worldly and otherworldly experience to knock your socks off. What's not to love?

For those of us addicted to that little kick of adrenaline a gorgeous vampire can provide, I dedicate Vampire Moons. My new series features an international quad of atypical vamps—who are loyal to a cause and to the women they desire.

When those qualities are mixed in with words *sexy* and *forever*, well…I'm hooked. Hopefully, you will be, too.

First up in this series: *Vampire Lover,* a Harlequin Nocturne Bites ebook novella. Followed by *Golden Vampire.* After that, stay tuned for *Guardian of the Night* in the Harlequin Nocturne line and then a final unnamed Harlequin Nocturne Bites ebook novella.

And yes, I'm also a werewolf lover. So my sexy wolves always make unscheduled appearances.

Please do check out my website and let me know what you think of my vampires. I'd love to hear from you.

Linda

www.lindathomas-sundstrom.com

To my family, those here and those gone,
who always believed I had a story to tell.

Chapter 1

The man was running for all he was worth—flat out, effortlessly, over snow-dusted ground. He was, Jesse Stewart decided, idiotically underdressed.

His riding breeches, or whatever they were, were beige and formfitting. He wore black boots to his knees. A white shirt, long-sleeved, composed of some kind of soft fabric, billowed as he moved, stretching out on either side of a wide-shouldered torso, no doubt rippling with effort.

Jesse adjusted the binoculars.

From a distance, the man was a speck of movement in a green landscape filled with old shapes—mountains, forests, vast stretches of meadow sprinkled white for the winter. Tall trees formed stark canopies to the north and east, lush against a gray sky streaked with the pink of an approaching European sunrise.

Jesse manipulated the lenses to get up close and personal.

The guy's hair was a shoulder-length, silky curtain of gold, at least six or seven inches longer than her own hair. Automatically, Jesse's free hand went to her somewhat dark, damp and matted locks. She couldn't remember the last time she'd brushed; maybe the day before. Primping wasn't her forte.

Once upon a time, she'd worn her hair long, as most young girls did. But long hair was trouble, and high on upkeep. Long hair gave the bad guys something to hang on to in a fight—although her fighting days had been over for some time now. For the most part.

Lowering the binoculars, adjusting her headset, Jesse frowned. The running man moved as gracefully as an animal. He was a thing of beauty, a bit of tension both at odds with and somehow wholly a part of his surroundings.

Did he chase the clouds? Outdistance a storm? Did he run for the sake of running? For the sheer exhilaration? Had he lost his horse?

Who was he?

Why did he run?

Trained to take in details, Jesse couldn't seem to break the habit, even on a routine helicopter flight. She held tightly to her binoculars, knowing on some internal level that though this guy presented a pretty picture, something about the scene down there seemed *off*.

Give or take the possibility of the man losing his equine pal, it had to be thirty degrees outside. The guy wasn't wearing a coat. In thirty-degree weather, the great breaths he had to be taking would be painfully icy. He'd be a freaking ice cube by now. Yet he ran with a certain joyousness that Jesse thought she could perceive. Her own legs were antsy from being cooped up. She could have used a jog.

Another interesting point, she noted, was that the guy on the ground didn't seem to be following any visible track, path or road. They were a hundred miles from the nearest city of merit, and a distance from the closest village. The only thing near this place, so the map beside her suggested, was an old castle, long since fallen to ruin. Nothing else. No dot of civilization bigger than a pinprick.

"Hey, Stewart. What are you staring at?"

The air in the chopper stirred with the question. Jesse's concentration shattered.

"Earth to Jesse."

Jesse turned her head. "Stan, can you note this place? Exactly?"

"This isn't anywhere near where we're heading," her pilot said. "It's just an isolated spot in the middle of nowhere."

Then why would *he* be in it? Jesse continued to wonder. Where would the guy down there be headed? It seemed the old adage was always true—that the devil was in the details.

"There's a castle here." She again hoisted the binoculars, hating the way her pulse thudded as though she were the one in that landscape moving faster than anyone had the right to move. She could hear her heartbeat drumming in her ears beyond the *whop-whop* of the chopper's blades. Fast and irregular.

Interesting. Vicarious running, maybe? The desire to be out of this flying tin can and stretching her cramped muscles? Even on a private jet the long trip from Los Angeles to Europe always took its toll. The chopper was icing on being stuffed into a tiny space.

"Castle?" Stan snorted. "I wouldn't call it that. More like a pile of rubble right out of a scene from *Frankenstein.*"

"You've seen it?"

"Only from up here. We're talking isolated and none too inviting. Picturesque though, if you're a horror freak."

Stan might have said something else; Jesse didn't listen. Through the lenses she watched the man on the ground slow, and knew the chopper would soon pass him by.

She didn't take her eyes off him when she turned her head and the binoculars bumped against the window with an intensity she figured might cause a black eye. The guy had stopped right in the center of a snow-covered field, his upright body looking like an exclamation point. An eerie chill slid up the back of Jesse's neck. More chills followed, and a need to speak.

"Take her down, Stan. Please."

"We're going to be late as it is," Stan protested. "We have an assignment, remember? They're waiting. It's almost full daylight."

"Take her down. Just for a minute. Circle if you have to."

Heavy sigh from Stan. "Okay. You're the boss."

Yes, she was the boss. The assignment was waiting. Heads of state, no less, requesting her personally for this one. She'd actually been recommended by the FBI.

"Hang on," Stan said teasingly, as if a chopper harness would allow for anything more than the slightest movement in any direction.

Jesse pressed her forehead to the Plexiglas, curious about her reaction to the scene below. She'd always trusted her instincts. She'd built her business around those instincts. You couldn't find missing people for a living and be on top of that game if you lacked fine-tuned abilities.

Right now, she could feel Stan eyeing her warily. Rumors resurfacing, she guessed. Rumors that had rippled through the old precinct labeling her "psychic." What a crock. Anyone with half a brain knew there was no such thing as powers derived from the cosmos. Intuition, yes. Hard work and good resources, yes. Cosmic connections? Hell, no.

"Down we go," Stan announced, circling the chopper in a wide arc, coming up on the target from behind.

The target remained still while the wind assailed him from all angles. Jesse's heart gave a lurch, having nothing whatsoever to do with the copter's movements. An odd few seconds of dizziness came and passed. The golden hair, the breeches, the way he stood there, seemed so strange. Almost…erotic.

A punch of anxiety made her hands shake and her heart rate spike. Suddenly, Jesse wasn't sure about harassing the man. She wondered what he might think. A chopper coming from nowhere and then almost chasing you down when you're minding your own business had to be some sort of rude awakening, especially out here in the middle of nowhere.

She repositioned the binoculars, feeling a bit like a voyeur. With the subject in full view, she sucked in a breath, rolled her tense shoulders and fended off another jolt of anxiousness that read like honest-to-God discomfort. She wanted to shout for Stan to lift the bird, though for the life of her she didn't know why. She even opened her mouth to issue the order. But then, in that same moment, the man below looked up.

The chopper shot past, flying low like a pestering bee.

Jesse had to turn her head again to see the guy brush back his hair. She got a brief glimpse of a pale, chiseled face, expressionless, for all the predictable irritation of the grass and twigs the chopper was kicking up.

"Back," she barked to Stan, chills now covering both arms beneath her jacket, her tongue feeling heavy in her mouth.

Another look was what she needed. Not because the guy down there, when viewed full on and in the quickest glance, had been shockingly handsome, almost godlike in a European-nobility kind of way, but because his chest, seen through the unbuttoned shirt open to his navel, wasn't heaving from the effort of all that distance, and the speed with which he'd traveled it.

He had to have run a couple of miles at least since she'd first sighted him.

More than that. She had to double back because of the way he stood there, motionless. Because of the way her blood ran hot beneath her chilled skin over the entire ordeal. The guy didn't flap his arms to keep out the cold. He hadn't raised a middle finger in any kind of universal sign language that would tell them to buzz off. He hadn't flung any expletives their way that she could see. He just stood there, waiting.

She could hardly breathe.

Stan banked in the air and returned for a second pass. Jesse's stomach dropped along with the descent.

There he was. Unmoving. Still as a statue, and looking, in his open-legged stance and white shirt, like a candidate for Adonis status. The closest thing she'd seen to something like him had been years ago in Paris, at the Louvre, carved in marble.

Hey, bud, Jesse wanted to say. *Looks aren't everything.*

Looks could, as a matter of fact, be deceiving. Usually were.

More shivers rocked her, the closer they got. Bone-deep shivers. The man was actually brutally handsome. Yes, that was the right description. *Brutal.* So inhumanly gorgeous, he hurt the eyes.

A second round of dizziness hit her, making it difficult to focus her eyes, let alone the powerful lens. The rolling sensation in her gut turned queasy.

Did she want to remain here?

Did she want to get closer?

Yes.

No.

Why not?

The shakes were always precursors, forewarnings, of her internal alarm system kicking in. This one cried out *Red Alert!* But it was too late. They were floating now, hovering some twenty feet above him. Jesse didn't reach for the speaker controls. She maintained a stranglehold on the binoculars in her lap.

"You do know how rude this is?" Stan's voice was loud in her earphones.

Sure she knew it. She wasn't an imbecile, and hadn't gotten to lead this particular crime-busting unit due to charm alone. Or looks. The perception of her actions just didn't matter at the moment. Guilt didn't enter the picture. Only one question remained to be answered. *Who was this guy?*

He looked up.

Jesse looked down.

Her eyes met his through a full quarter inch of windshield.

Time seemed to stop.

Breathing stopped.

The chills on the surface of her skin solidified. The noise of the chopper's blades faded into a distant thrumming sound as Jesse's heart sputtered, suspended, as if she was about to free-fall. As if she had somehow slipped into those incredible blue eyes boring into hers and...

As if she knew them, somehow.

As if she knew *him*.

Captured. She was captured, the victim of a gaze so intensely piercing, so all-consuming, that Jesse couldn't pull herself away or utter so much as a single syllable of protest. Though the chopper was holding her up, the man's blue eyes dragged her down. She felt so very cold all of a sudden, and needy. She felt as if those eyes of his were touching her all over, with open access to her most private places.

Vertigo hit as she squeezed her thighs together, accompanied by a stupid desire to go down there and view those incredible eyes up close. Ask him what the heck he was doing, and why she felt as though she might have known him in the past, somewhere. Find out why his gaze was...intimate.

Moisture gathered on her brow in direct contrast to the chills. Jesse watched, mesmerized, horrified, as the man's lips upturned at the corners in an arrogant half smile. She watched his beautiful mouth form a silent word.

Jesse.

A knee-jerk reaction lifted her butt off the seat, harness and all. The chills became waves, hitting, moving, hitting—sensory bombardment of the cruelest kind. Every one of her nerve endings tingled. Every cell screamed.

There didn't seem to be enough air.

But he couldn't have said her name. He could not have known it. She'd allowed her imagination to run away with her reasoning skills. She was jet-lagged, that's all. She hadn't slept more than two hours at a stretch in the last week. This slipup was a rare one. She was nothing if not diligent. Notoriously diligent. Anything less and she'd have been dead long ago.

Fact. The distance between them did not close. That was a physical impossibility. Yet damned if it didn't seem to close. Damned if that guy down there wasn't a creature of nearly heartrending beauty. And damn it to hell if he wasn't also some kind of discernible omen.

Out of the corner of her eye, Jesse noticed Stan lifting a hand in greeting, or perhaps in apology. The movement, so close beside her, snapped her back. She caught Stan with tight fingers on his sleeve. After a shake of her head, she looked back at the man on the ground and inhaled a breath of stale air to get herself together.

"Got the hots for guys in period costume, boss?" Stan asked, obviously amused by her behavior. "Think how far info like that might go in the unit."

Stan, slightly rotund and visibly rough around the edges, had always been good for a laugh. But not this time. Jesse was trembling—arms, legs and everything in between. Her heart couldn't have pounded any harder. Her face was numb. Beneath her frozen skin, her blood boiled in her veins. Her thighs quivered with an unmistakable desire to be down there, next to a man she couldn't possibly know. She'd just experienced heart-stopping desire for a stranger! A damn marble statuelike man whose arrogant upturned lips had given her the weird sensation of having formed her name.

Ridiculous.

Insane.

"Out of here now, boss?" Stan asked. "If it's a guy you want, I'll volunteer. I'm pretty sure there are boots somewhere in my closet."

Stan was speaking. She needed to listen. But the man down there just wouldn't let up.

The man was...

Jesse sat back, absorbing what now felt curiously like a wave of panic that brought on another stomach drop. A word struggled to the forefront of her mind that might finish her dangling sentence. That word was blinking brighter than a traffic signal. Etched in a laser beam. It was a word to explain the inexplicable. A reason for the sudden, unwarranted desire, and also for dispelling any urge to see *him* up close.

It was the reason for not finding out firsthand what kind of long pointed teeth no doubt lay hidden behind those arrogant lips.

Feelings of rightness poured over Jesse, rerouting the cold. She knew the answer to her question suddenly in a burst of insight. One word explained all the rest.

Her whole body cried out. Terror, hatred and disgust bubbled up from her throat with a taste of oxidized iron.

"What is it?" Stan asked, eyeing her with a swinging sideways glance.

"Vampire," Jesse whispered, her mouth exceptionally dry.

Lance Van Baaren stood his ground, staring up at the disappearing helicopter as if his race against the rising sun didn't matter.

But it did, of course, matter. The warmth rising over the mountain hissed along his skin like small licks of fire; uncomfortable, but tolerable. Familiar, yet always obscene.

Though he had long since surpassed the need for surviving solely in darkness, a trait relegated to others of his kind, he found shadows infinitely easier to navigate. He found sunlight disturbing. Too warm. Too bright. Too much of a reminder of the brilliant parts of his past.

Besides, humans existed in the light, coveted it, and he had no right to share their space. Yet the prickling sensations of the breaking dawn on his skin brought with it vivid memories of the color, sounds and scents of life. And now, also, the disturbed atmosphere of a nosy whirling bird.

He still heard the sounds of the helicopter's blades, though they were diminished. He heard the heartbeat of the woman inside the flying machine. As if its rhythm had been transferred to him through the meeting of their eyes, the irregular thudding of her heart now beat against his neck.

Some called this *bloodlust*. Indeed, it felt to him as if the blood inside *her*—the woman in the helicopter, the woman who had recognized him for what he was—was calling to him. His own blood was moving closer to the surface of his skin, as if leaning toward *her*.

Her knowledge of him made her dangerous, of course. But she'd been sidelined by the immediacy of the connection between them. The meeting of their eyes had also caused a secondary effect. She would return. He knew this in a jolt of precognition. She would come back for him, whatever reason she chose as an explanation. She couldn't possibly understand why. She'd be groping for the source of the connection between them.

What were the odds she might know everything?

Then again, Lance mused, what were the odds she'd be here at all, after all this time? That he'd see *her*?

Such an event was highly unusual. Intriguing.

Still…her eyes were the same, unchanged. He'd have recognized them anywhere. Those brown, amber-flecked eyes that suggested introspection and hidden depths had met his once before, pleadingly, trusting him to make a bond. A bond she had used today to name him, if not place him.

"Indeed. What are the odds?" Lance whispered.

Golden feelers of early-morning sun danced along his shirt like sharp, slender knives needling, but now the sensation seemed more a herald of things to come than discomfort.

A little girl had been in that helicopter. Here. Now. Only she wasn't so little anymore. Hair the color of shadows. Eyes like a dove.

No, he corrected. Not the eyes of a dove anymore. Wiser eyes. Hardened eyes. The eyes of a woman grown from a girl who had seen the viciousness of the world firsthand. A girl who had barely survived her own personal hint of what hell on earth might be like.

He knew this, knew her, and what lay behind the quickness of their connection.

"Jesse." Saying the name aloud made him take a useless breath. "Do you know that my blood runs in your veins? That it remains there today, and after all this time? That the little girl from a Los Angeles alley, now grown to womanhood, has been called from the sky because of the blood I once gave her, in order to save her life?"

Pressing the hair back from his face, Lance looked mountainward. The helicopter was heading for the castle. Jesse would know where to find him, all right. She would come calling. He'd seen that in her.

Then again, perhaps those brown eyes of hers were like a dove's eyes. Perhaps the little girl he'd once helped hadn't been tainted too much by the hand she'd been dealt. There was a chance she wasn't too far gone. Just as there was a chance he wouldn't wait for her to arrive.

In all the world, in all its limitless time, he'd never run across one of *them* before. Had he not removed himself from the world, hid himself here, far from the madness, from the despair of a civilization plagued by others identified with his kind?

He'd once tried to save as many humans as he could. He'd spent centuries doling out justice. But he'd grown tired, weary. The world had become so large.

Giving the gift of life back to little Jesse had been his last good deed.

The girl in the sky.

The woman with the blazing brown eyes.

"What have you done with your second chance? Why are you here now? What has brought you all this way?"

She had been so very small in his arms when he'd held her. She had thought him to be an angel. Maybe her perception of him as an angel was why he had chosen to help her in the first place, and why he'd made her his last.

Lifting a hand in a gesture of parting, or maybe mere acknowledgment of an imminent problem dropped into his lap, Lance gazed at the yellow cast of sunlight on his palm, noted the steam rising from his pale skin, then took off at a sprint—not for the cover of the nearby trees, but in the direction the helicopter had taken.

Chapter 2

"No shit? Vampire?" Stan said, eyes wide. "I've heard about those things before, but I've never seen one. And," he added, "you're kidding, right, boss?"

Jesse pressed herself rigidly against her seat, wishing she had been kidding. Wishing for anything other than for that man to have been what she thought he was.

That glorious piece of flesh down there was a vampire. Not a man. In no way a man. His molded flesh was dead flesh; nothing more than a walking pile of dust that evil had rearranged into the semblance of a human being.

Fighting evil is what she did for a living.

"How can you tell?" Stan asked, turning his New York Yankees baseball cap around backward. "Except for the getup, I mean?"

"I can't explain it," Jesse admitted, wondering about

that very same thing, reluctant to try to define the vibration going through her body.

How many times had she felt this vibration before, when she had brushed up against such creatures by accident on a busy city street, and then had been left to wonder what had brought her to a stop, shaking? How many times had this happened prior to gaining a clearer picture, before she became more adept at recognizing the feeling?

But this brush had been different. Startling. Sensual. Not just that, but overtly sexual.

Oh, yes. She knew this golden man was a vampire, much in the same way some people recognized an oncoming storm system by experiencing pain in their arthritic knees. In a similar way to animals sensing earthquakes. Vampires were like that for her. Seismic. The ultimate nightmare. Creatures no longer alive, but not completely dead.

"Really, boss?" Stan said in an obvious attempt to lighten the atmosphere. "I guess I actually would be the better choice, then. You know, between me and him?"

Stan was offering a toothy smile when Jesse looked over. His green eyes were positively merry. Of course, he had to believe she was kidding. He wouldn't know any better.

"An infinitely better choice," Jesse agreed, faking a smile, feeling like hell. She'd just wanted to jump out of the chopper for a few seconds back there, headfirst. She found that momentary loss of control disconcerting. She needed control, had to get it back. Control is what kept her together, had kept her together since…way back.

In order to regain her equilibrium and make sure that no one could rob her of her most precious trait again, she'd have to come back here, to this remote place, without Stan. She'd have to plan what to do when she caught up with *him*. *It*. She wasn't a vampire hunter, but had made it her business to learn a thing or two. To ease the nightmares. To try to cope.

"All that charm of yours is why your girlfriend made me promise to keep my distance," she added. She needed to talk, needed to put the compulsion to hunt the bloodsucker aside for now, even while knowing she wouldn't sleep until she dealt with it.

"Carol? Naw, she wouldn't make you promise that," Stan said. "She knows—"

Stan's sentence dropped away unfinished, and too late. Stan had no doubt realized he'd made a mistake by merely thinking about alluding to Jesse's past, and to the fact that she had never, as far as anyone in the unit knew, ever gone on a date.

No one brought up this loner thing. Not to her face, anyway. But that didn't mean she hadn't heard the things said behind her back.

For the most part, she was glad to have the comments remain out of earshot and out of focus. Her mantra was to let the guys in the unit wonder why the little woman was so tough on crime, and even tougher on men. Uncertainty meant they would keep their distance.

"However," Jesse said into her headset with a manufactured lightness, "a compliment won't break my promise to Carol, I suppose. So I'll say that I don't know about the boots in your closet, but I do like your cap."

Stan smiled wider, appearing comfortable with their usual pass-the-time game of unrequited, never-in-a-million-years kind of flirting.

"E.T.A.?" Jesse asked.

"An hour at most."

An hour. Too much time to think. Bad stuff was

sitting beneath the surface of her skin, with a bitter tang best left to nightmares, monsters and dark alleys.

Too many nightmares.

Stan was peering at her.

"What?" Jesse managed to say.

"That thing down there put some kind of whammy on you, boss?"

"Maybe."

And wasn't that truth revealing? She had, in fact, felt the damn vampire's stare all the way to her bones. She'd known better than to look into his eyes, but had done so anyway, unable to help herself. Admittedly, she was the idiot here.

A leftover shiver, not quite dispelled by the distance, shook her. The vow she'd once taken as a teen came rushing back, repeating over and over in her mind.

Find them. One at a time, if need be.

Show them what the word dead *should mean.*

But she'd grown up. Finding *them* wasn't her job. Finding missing persons was. Missing humans. The instinct to take the missing persons gig to the next level, secretly, still burned her insides, though. One denizen of the "next level" was down there on the ground, somewhere near that old castle.

Jesse looked across the trees, thinking that Stan had been right in the description of the ruins, though he had it associated with the wrong monster. It wasn't Frankenstein's castle down there. It was Dracula's.

"I hear over in Germany guys wear cute little shorts. With suspenders," Stan said. "I could fly us in that direction."

"You just want a beer," Jesse retorted.

"Carol doesn't like me to drink beer." Stan offered up a shrug as if to say: Sometimes a man has got to do what a man has got to do. Then he added, "I'd kill for a beer."

Jesse laughed and rested her head against the seat, thankful that Stan and the others didn't know about the monsters, and that their dreams could remain safe. Also thankful that her own dreams would remain a secret shared with only one other person on this wide and lonely planet, and that person would never talk, gagged by patient-doctor rules of confidentiality.

She'd had enough of being labeled certifiable. Ten years was enough. Ten lost years.

"There it is," Stan announced in a hushed, conspiratorial whisper.

Jesse follow the direction of his hand gesture.

"The castle. Ain't she a beaut?"

Jesse could not reply. The sight of the great pile of stone sitting atop the hill, nearly as white as the dusting of snow clinging to its turrets, produced a second stab of anxiety in her.

These were gothic environs for the living dead. As far from Hollywood as possible but the vamp wore breeches and a billowy shirt, like in the movies. Stereotypical stuff—the clothes, the hair, the chiseled features, the body *and* the secluded castle.

Shouldn't there be something wrong with monsters looking like Greek gods? What kind of omnipotent deity allowed for discrepancies like that?

Were vampire looks the source of their allure? Like perverts holding out candy for children? Because that's exactly what vampires did. Prey.

This one…

This one had been…

Jesse again hid her shaking hands from Stan, and kept her expression neutral. Inside she was screaming.

Her heart continued to race. She had to look to make sure Stan couldn't hear the turmoil of her thoughts.

Go back! Go back there now!

This creature is special.

This blood drinker is powerful.

Her mind was reeling, pressurizing. Past, present and future were rolling together, becoming muddled. She had to retain control, knew the routine.

Concentrate. Separate the threads.

Put everything in perspective and in its place.

She was the force to be reckoned with here. She was the director of an elite missing persons unit sanctioned by both FBI and CIA, and was good at her job. More often than not, she found the people she was hired to find, most of them alive. She brought people back, offered closure and collected huge sums from families and governments alike—and all the monies were channeled back into her business to keep it solvent. All of it—the helicopters, the assignments, the training, the job—were to help keep families together at all costs.

Could she now add to that objective killing vampires?

No. Must stay sane. Vampires will tip me over the edge.

Yet how could she stay sane when she'd found one of them? With a pair of blue eyes haunting her, taunting her? *His* blue eyes.

He had been interested in her.

Correction. *It* had been interested.

Pile of dust. Dead Adonis.

She had brought this about herself. She had given the order to take the chopper down. He, *it,* had not known her name. That wasn't possible. Just as so many things about bloodsuckers weren't.

What kind of two-legged creature lusted for human blood? What sort of two-legged creatures savagely killed those they fed upon?

Jesse gnawed at her lip to keep the screams at bay. Images were rushing at her. Bloody pictures bathed in red. She blew out the air she'd been holding, told herself to calm down and acknowledge the pictures and move on. She went over things again, clinging to a fringe of hope.

Yes, she had been there when her parents were killed. She had witnessed the freaks of nature tearing their throats out and then lapping up their life's blood. The monsters had turned on her, had nearly killed her as well. She'd be dead now if a couple of L.A. cops hadn't turned the corner and found her.

The pictures in her memory overlapped, changing, morphing as though someone shuffled a deck of colorful playing cards.

Blue eyes. Pale skin. Golden hair.

Deceitful beauty. Hurtful. Dangerous.

A tunnel of darkness…

Blood.

Her parents had been tangled up in a bloody heap. Her mom had been barely thirty, just two years older than herself today. Her brave father's efforts against the monsters had done nothing. The alley had been too dark, too isolated, the event impossibly quick.

And herself? Young Jesse Jean, just ten years old, had been panic-stricken. At ten years old, she had lost everything, except her life. She'd been shut away for ten more years, unable to process the brutality of such an attack. Closed off. Committed. Until she'd gotten better, a recovery due in part to her secret objective, the only reason for which she could possibly have been spared. *Kill them all.*

There. Compartmentalized.

Okay. Jesse found that she could breathe again. Her rapid heart rate was slowing. She opened her mouth, unhinged her jaw. "I'd like to see that castle sometime," she said as casually as if she were a tourist looking at sites.

"Yeah, I thought you might," Stan said. "But that's another day, boss. And trust me, there's a better one at Disney World."

Chapter 3

The city was like all cities to Lance, cold, dirty, overtly noisy and smelling of ripe human flesh. He had not missed these things, and regretted being immersed in them now.

People swarmed, though the sun had long since set and the night was chilly. So many people. So little space. It was a miracle that disease and illness didn't take more of them, these walking creatures in such proximity to each other. He dreaded stepping into the flow of moving bodies on the sidewalk, dreaded even a single touch.

Watching from the corner of the Grand Hotel Beaumont, a building nearly as old as recall, Lance waited, arms crossed, posture adapted to mimic those of the men loitering near the traffic light beside him. Buses, automobiles, some of the cars so large as to be buses, flashed past in unending lines of lights and colors as he stared. The sight was disappointing.

Horses had once ruled the streets of this place. Elegant animals, graceful, alive, much more to his taste. Elegance was a concept lost in the twenty-first century. He didn't want to adapt to changing times that ruled out beauty, quiet and the artist's touch altogether, in favor of the odor of gasoline and oil, concrete and asphalt. For these reasons and others like them, he wasn't sorry he seldom ventured far from home.

Leaning back against the building, Lance closed his eyes and sent his mind outward, then became suddenly alert. He felt a ripple in the air, an atmospheric gasp, as though the world itself had held a breath.

He turned.

She was there, emerging from the hotel lobby, surrounded by a small group of men and women, all of them silent, purposeful and directed.

Jesse. She stood out from the crowd, and would have risen like cream to the surface anywhere, in any surroundings, in any circumstances.

He had eyes for no other.

She wore dark blue, the color of modern business dealings, striped vertically with thin white lines, and a white shirt beneath, its collar showing, the top button open. She wore pants, and a dark blue overcoat that reached her ankles. Her shoes matched the clothes, low heels, though not so sensible in the snow. A briefcase of black leather with a combination lock hung from one of her hands. No purse. No jewelry, outside of a watch. He could hear her watch ticking.

For an instant, Lance couldn't move, wanting to take in more details, knowing time was scarce. He recrossed his arms and stared at her beautiful face as she intercepted a question from a woman by her side.

"Yes," she said.

Only one word, followed by a slow blink of her eyes. Large, round, wide-set eyes. Except for a trace of black makeup, these were the same eyes that had found him and recognized him from the air. Not registering surprise or fear now, but steely and fixed. Little softness in them. Jesse's brown eyes were as businesslike as her suit.

His survey continued in a lavish sweep. High, prominent cheekbones gave Jesse's face a lean look, with a hungry edge. Her nose, narrow, and quite possibly handed down to her by aristocratic ancestry, guided him to her mouth.

Ah.

Here was the anomaly in the features of her face. Something noteworthy. It was as if all the femininity of her other features had slipped and been manifested into full, moist, luscious lips. Ripe lips, perfectly shaped, uncolored and in no need of embellishment. She left them slightly open as she listened to the woman beside her, as though by utilizing a seventh sense, she might taste the variances in her surroundings in the way most people tasted food.

Lance's arms fell to his sides, a very small movement, but enough to cause her shoulders to twitch. This pleased him.

She turned her head, her dark curls scattering across one cheek with the swiftness of the motion. A wave of smells floated to him, as though borne on a breeze. She had taken the time to wash her hair with a fruit-scented shampoo, which meant that she had recently been naked, in a shower or bath. Water had caressed her, dripped over her skin, beading in hidden places.

Ignoring the pulse of excitement this thought brought with it, closing his lips over his extending teeth, Lance stepped back into the overhanging darkness. It wouldn't really matter how far he removed himself from her, he supposed. The woman who had known him from the helicopter, from afar, would not miss him here.

It's in her blood.

Still there.

Jesse.

Thinking her name, he watched her carefully. She lifted her head. With a glance in his direction, she held up a hand to excuse herself from the woman speaking to her in a polite gesture that meant "please wait." She took a step backward and rotated, needing to face the disturbance she had noticed, dialing up her intuitive powers.

Her skin glistened, as if each cell in her body strained to capture and name the disturbance she'd felt. Undeterred by the peripheral movement near the hotel, the people on the sidewalk passing between them and the noise of the cars, Jesse, now full-grown, focused her eyes on the darker bit of night wherein he stood. Her heartbeat signaled her alertness, thudding inside her chest with a burst of adrenaline that echoed loudly inside his head.

"Blood to blood," he whispered.

She twitched again. Her lips closed. Though her hold on her briefcase tightened, she said nothing, did nothing. Just stood.

"Miss Stewart?" the woman by her side said after a full minute had passed.

"Jesse," Jesse corrected without moving. "Please call me Jesse."

Jesse. Lance mouthed the name.

Again a twitch, there, along her shoulders first, and down her spine.

"Jesse, yes, thanks," the woman continued. "You've had a long trip, so we should be going. Is there anything else you need?"

"I'll see to it she has everything," a stocky man answered for Jesse.

Sans baseball cap, this was the man who had shared the helicopter with her. He had traded in his sweatshirt for an ill-fitting suit, and looked uncomfortable.

"Very well. Tomorrow, then? At eight?" the woman said, half to the pilot, half to Jesse's back.

"Eight," Jesse repeated.

"Eight it is," the stocky pilot agreed.

"You won't change your mind about coming to dinner? It's just down the street," the woman persisted.

"Do they serve beer?" the pilot asked, seemingly jokingly, because Jesse turned back to the others with a smile playing on her mouth.

Was that a joke between colleagues? Lovers?

A flare of heat seared through Lance's torso in reaction to the smile she had offered to another man. His fists clenched, unclenched. *She* felt this, too. The woman once so little and afraid of the dark leaned over as though to set her briefcase on the ground, a ruse to lift her head and again look straight at him.

Her smile dissolved.

Lance's chest tightened. *Won't you smile for me, Jesse?*

But she would not, of course, do so, no matter how much he wished it. A few drops of his blood, back then, dribbled into young Jesse's wounds, prevented this. A near-fatal attack in a brutal alley prevented this. The blood he had given her, old as he was, strong as he was, had provided her with an edge in a world filled with so many dark, beastly secrets.

It had also, unfortunately, provided her with a key, a connection, to him.

Well, he amended, *perhaps not so unfortunately.*

"Jesse," he said quietly. "I'm here."

Could she hear him?

He watched her straighten so quickly that she turned on one heel. Bright spots of pink tinted her cheeks. Her chest rose and fell, straining at her buttons.

Lance's gaze fastened on those buttons. Then up to the white collar surrounding a slender neck marred by a jagged white scar of puckered skin that ran nearly full circle from front to back, much like a necklace of woven white thread.

Still there. The scar. Openly visible. Uncovered by a scarf or high-necked sweater. The remnant of a terrible, life-threatening wound, and worn uncovered as what? A badge of courage? An indication of the secrets curled up within her incredibly honed, fighting-fit body?

The scar as a talisman? A remembrance?

Below Lance's waist something long dormant stirred for the second time in a hundred years. His incisors extended in direct correlation. He ran his tongue over his teeth, felt the familiar razor-sharpness, then blinked slowly, noting how everywhere else his muscles again stretched toward *her,* as if recognizing a piece of himself.

"I'm waiting," he said, his voice throaty with greed, lust and longing—for Jesse; sensations he hadn't experienced since he'd lost his only love in that awful swirl of time gone by. *Gwen.* Lost to him because he'd refused to bring her over. He'd refused to make her one of what he was, though she had begged.

And now Jesse. What was she to him?

Although caution had prevailed with the injured girl

in the dark alley, and though he had been careful with the extent of his gift to her, he had ensured that her little life would continue. He had kept Jesse alive by giving her a few drops of his own ancient blood.

"I can taste you now, on my lips. I know your scent, your sound, the texture of your skin and what races though your veins. I know those round brown eyes," he said to her from his distance. "There is no mistaking the power of this recognition, or the longing it evokes."

"Boss?" the stocky helicopter pilot and possible partner called to Jesse.

"Carol isn't here," Jesse said. "Golden opportunity with the beer, don't you think, Stan?"

Stan. A base name. A commoner's name, Lance thought. A peasant's body with a peasant's need for yeast drinks.

Not Jesse's lover.

Surely not.

"Jesse," Lance whispered to her again, wanting to touch her, repressing the need to do so. But this time she was ready, Lance saw. This time, Jesse held up a hand—to him. *Wait,* the gesture implied, begged, proposed. *Not now.*

Her lips formed a straight line. He wanted to kiss them open, part them with his tongue, indulge his sense of taste. This woman would not be fragile, weak or easily distracted. She had determination, fire, an edge.

It had been such a very long time since he had felt these things, or allowed himself to feel anything at all.

"Come with me," he whispered to her.

Her shudder shook him. The becoming pink flush drained away from her cheeks as she retrieved her briefcase and spoke to Stan.

"I'm tired," she said. "You go along with them. Make them buy you a round."

Stan studied her intently.

Taking a step in Jesse's direction was involuntary. Lance's feet moved independent of his will. Jesse shuddered again. He could sense her fear, manifesting in the air as a metallic cloud, acidic in taste, mingling with the fragrance of her freshly washed hair.

A groan stuck in his throat.

"You sure?" Stan pressed. "What'll you do?"

"Sleep. Glorious sleep," Jesse said. "It might be the last chance."

"I hear you," Stan conceded. "Eight o'clock will come early. There's a job to get started."

Stan had missed her meaning, Lance saw. The daring, deathly double entendre. Last chance to sleep? Did Jesse assume he was here to finish what his brothers had started that night so long ago?

"Yes," was all Jesse said.

Lance's head came up.

"Well, then, maybe just two beers, to make sure I sleep," Stan proposed, again wearing a conspiratorial grin. "Who knows? Maybe three? Then it's off to what I'm told are four-hundred-count sheets. Whatever the hell that means."

Stan headed after the others, but stopped once more to look at Jesse. "You sure, boss? You'll be okay? I won't be long."

Jesse nodded, tossed her hair and offered a smile that wasn't genuine.

"Can I ask you a question before I go, boss?" Stan said.

"Shoot."

"Is a four-hundred-count sheet a good thing?"

"The best," Jesse replied.

"Something to tell Carol about?"

"Carol will be envious."

"Right. Good." Bolstered by this information, Stan waved and turned and disappeared into the night.

Leaving Jesse to *him*.

Jesse stayed still, her pulse continuing to race.

She said aloud, ignoring every other person within hearing range, "Why are you here?"

Chills leaped up and down her spine. Her overcoat felt heavy, awkward, and might slow her reaction time, she supposed, but she didn't dare remove it. It took effort just to speak.

Scanning the dark, she was sure she saw him. A blur in the shadows. An unmistakable presence. The pounding of her heart told her so.

"Why did you let your friends go?" the voice asked in turn. The vampire's voice. Smooth, deep as a well, infinitely alluring. She'd known it would sound like this, grate on her like this, haunt her like this.

"Chances are they don't know about monsters, and probably wouldn't be happy to find out," she replied.

"Monster? Is that what I am?"

"You hide in the dark."

"Merely to ease your fear."

Jesse opened her mouth to reply to that, but couldn't. She was so far beyond fear she'd forgotten what fear felt like.

"You knew me," the deep voice said in a tone that was both frighteningly eerie and mesmerizingly soft. The voice of darkness itself, spoken from its very soul.

Like velvet sliding over her skin, his presence poured over her. Her trembling returned. With the consistency of honey, the vibrations he caused melted downward, over her stomach and her hips, toward the space between her thighs.

He was doing this to her on purpose. *It's what they do.*

"Why are you here?" she repeated in a stronger tone, inching one leg closer to her other to quell the sensation of his fingers drifting across such an intimate place, setting her posture for action. "What do you want?"

"I want to help you."

"Help me? Are you insane, as well as inhuman?"

A man bumped her elbow. Jesse shook off the touch, only to find a hand firmly gripping her upper arm. Her body reacted with a sway. *God...no!* She hadn't even seen him coming.

With trepidation, she looked at the hand on her coat. Gloved in black leather. Long fingers. Wrist covered in black wool. Fine coat. Fine fabric, well-cut and expensive.

Her glance moved upward, even as her other hand reached into her coat pocket. There wasn't time to get around to the gun nestled against the small of her back.

More inventory. His shoulders were wide. He was very tall, at least six-four. How was it possible for vampires to fuel or maintain muscle growth, or possess all those glossy, golden curls?

She regretted not joining Stan and the others. She thought about shouting, calling them back, warning them. Closing her fingers around the Taser she kept in her pocket, Jesse drew the weapon upward, determined to use it the first chance she got, not knowing if a Taser would do anything to a vampire. Was there anything inside a vampire that could be scrambled by a sudden dose of voltage?

"I won't hurt you," the vampire murmured, moving again.

Shocked, Jesse found him behind her, his body pressed to hers. She felt the hardness of him through her overcoat, and sensed the unusual stirring of the air between them.

He had removed his hand from her, didn't hold her in any way now, having already exhibited the blatant display of what a vampire could do.

No looking at him. Never look at a vampire.

Looking up would mean exposing her neck. In no way was she going to serve up a snack to this freak of nature. Using a Taser might give her time to reach the gun. The revolver would do enough damage on the spot to make him run for cover at least. Lick his wounds, maybe.

"Won't hurt me?" she said. "I'll bet you say that to all the girls." Pure willpower kept the tremor from her voice.

He was too damn close.

"Actually, I don't say that to anyone at all. I rarely issue promises," the vampire replied in a soft, deadly voice.

If dead things were so damn cold, Jesse reasoned, why did she feel heat coming off him? Why did she feel as though he was touching her, when he wasn't?

There was no way she'd face him or look into those drowning blue eyes. Eyes were mirrors of the soul, and vampires didn't have souls.

What she needed to do was hit him with the Taser and run, without so much as a single glance in his direction. No last look that said, *I'm taking you down.*

"Jesse." The vampire whispered her name like a caress. "I do not lie about this. I am here to help."

Jesse felt a tug on her hair. The goddamn vampire had touched her, had taken hold of one strand.

Freak!

The Taser was at the level of her hip. Two more inches and she'd have him. If the weapon had no effect, at least she would have tried. Maybe she'd gain precious seconds in which to get away.

Her head arched back, pulled gently but insistently against the vampire's sturdy chest. Jesse's hand fumbled as he spoke into her ear.

"Help you," he reiterated.

But he didn't mean what the words implied. He meant something else entirely, Jesse was sure. The touch on her hair was sensual. He'd pitched his voice lower yet, and it passed through her like the shot of an electric arrow. His hips were pressed against hers. His heat rushed at her with the force of a tsunami.

"Help with what?" Her question emerged as a faint demand. "What could you help with, other than the possible exception of mentioning where all the other vamps are in this city, so that I can find them all once this assignment has concluded."

"So." The vampire sighed. "You hunt. I thought as much."

His breath moved the hair near her right cheek, pulling her internal heat upward. That was another thing, Jesse reminded herself. Vampires weren't supposed to have breath.

Again, the huskiness of his voice drifted over her, definitely like velvet—thick, dark, rich. Wrong.

In a moment of near panic, Jesse felt a gathering of

moistness between her legs, and wanted to Taser herself. Shock some sense into her treacherous body.

Why hadn't she already zapped him? He was way too close and too freaking nervy.

What was this *thing* doing to her?

"If it's a promise you want, I'll make it." The vamp's suggestion rang with earnestness. "Perhaps we could go somewhere more private and talk things over?"

"You don't like crowds?" Jesse spoke to get hold of herself. She had to zap him. Any more heat, and her legs would grow weaker than they already were.

"I'm thinking of you," he said.

"If you were thinking of me, you wouldn't suggest such a thing."

"Your face is flushed, yet you're cold."

Words spoken like a kiss, like a further promise, so close to her face. So close to her neck.

Fire seared through Jesse's rigid body. She swayed, caught herself. Snapping her head away from him, she positioned the Taser against his thigh.

She was flushed. She was shocked shitless, but not so very afraid. She'd already knocked at death's black door and it hadn't opened. Any time on earth she might have had since that night in the alley when her parents were murdered was not only torture, but stolen. Her mother and father had paid for her extra time with their lives.

Was she frightened of this vampire and his kind? Yes.

But she was not afraid to die.

"It will not harm me, you know." The vampire caught her hand, closed his gloved fingers over hers and over the Taser. "Save yourself the trouble. Come with me."

"Where? Hell?" Was that her voice? Didn't sound like her.

"I was thinking of someplace more comfortable, like your room," he said.

"Over my dead—" Jesse closed her mouth.

"Or mine?" the vampire suggested.

"Aren't you already dead?"

She had turned her head, was looking at him now. Her body followed, still connected to him by his hand on hers.

The vampire was smiling fully, gloriously. His beautiful mouth was full of white teeth, two of them longer than the rest and as sharp as stakes. All of a sudden Jesse wasn't so sure about the *dead* part. How could he be dead? This was the golden-haired runner, now dressed in black, who looked at her. The creature with a face so handsome, her eyes ached.

A wayward pulse ricocheted through her arms, legs and nerves, ending where no pulse should end. Where no thoughts or feelings or sensations, even those gone astray, should ever dare to tread. The barriers of which no man had ever dared to penetrate, and sure as hell no dead thing ever would.

Jesse tugged her hand free of his grasp and heard the crack and buzz of the Taser going off against his hip. Nothing happened. The thing, creature, bloodsucker, didn't even flinch.

The sound of the Taser hitting the sidewalk at their feet seemed important somehow, and tinny.

"Perhaps you're tired," the arrogant vamp suggested. "It's obvious that you're not thinking clearly. I did warn you about the weapon."

"And I'm thinking maybe I won't sleep tonight. Maybe I'll work all night and sleep during the day, when you can't find me."

The golden vampire smiled again, as if he thought

her statement funny and her threats benign. He grinned casually, as though he wasn't one of the walking dead, as if his presence wasn't threatening and as if this unusual connection that had brought them together might be fate instead of lust for American blood types.

Tomorrow, Jesse thought, she'd be gone from this place.

"Oh," he said casually, as if he had read her last thought. "Never fear that I can't find you, Jesse, if I try."

She stared openmouthed, unable to respond, knowing deep in the pit of her stomach, if not the depths of her own soul, that he meant this. He could find her anytime he chose, anywhere. Hadn't he already found her here?

Probably it would be a waste of time to wonder how he'd accomplished this. He had just offered up a threat. A warning. A promise.

And then he was gone.

Poof.

Vanished.

In the space of a blink, a skipped heartbeat, a sharp intake of air and the sound of the useless Taser settling on the sidewalk, he had left her.

The air settled back to chilly. The fire beneath Jesse's skin flickered out. She waited two full minutes, counting each second, refusing to shout, then she turned, walked back into the hotel's opulent lobby and sank onto the closest chair.

Chapter 4

Lance doubled back, needing to return, unable to let Jesse go. From a place near the hotel's tall, leaded windows, he observed her sitting in the lobby chair, saw her rest her head in her hands and was cognizant of the despair she must be feeling.

Jesse'd had a shock, but had been trained not to show it. She'd been in possession of both Taser and gun, the outline of the gun discernible against her back. She had tested her "monster" theory by using the Taser.

And now? Head in her hands, in the lobby, alone.

If only he could go to her, make her listen. Those wise eyes of hers had indeed pegged him. *Monster,* she had said. He was all that and more. But her eyes had told him something else—that she didn't remember him from the alley, so long ago. She'd known him only from the helicopter and their brief encounter there.

Jesse would be thinking he was after her. Yet she

hadn't wanted her pilot to know. She'd gotten rid of Stan before confronting the monster.

Just who was guarding whom?

Placing one hand on the glass, spreading his fingers as if to touch her through the pane, Lance watched Jesse get to her feet. She checked her hand for the Taser she'd picked up off the sidewalk, glanced at it behind the fold of her coat and tucked it inside her pocket. She rolled her shoulders back, hesitated and turned to glance behind her. Seeing nothing, senses probably on overdrive, she headed for the elevator, moving as steadily as she could, refusing to create a scene.

Lance walked back through the doors, straight to the elevator, and watched the numbers light up. Tenth floor. She had gotten off on the tenth. He stared at the number ten until the elevator started its descent. Nine, eight, seven...

Then he made a decision.

He'd let one woman slip away, but he didn't have to be alone now if he could convince Jesse he wouldn't harm her...further.

Still shaking, Jesse stood with her back to the door of her suite, listening, gun in hand, senses open.

The only worth the damn gun would have would be if a neighbor heard the shots and called for help. It wasn't loaded with silver bullets. She didn't usually load those or carry a set of sharpened garden stakes when meeting the local law enforcement in a foreign country, but she'd make damned sure she wouldn't make that same mistake again.

She hadn't been wrong. This vampire was powerful. He was old, possibly as ancient as she'd first guessed. She had never stumbled across anything like him. The experience had left her feeling as though she'd been run over by a truck.

The bloodsucker had followed her here; why? Due to brief eye contact from the chopper? On a whim?

God, she should have known better.

So why had his presence triggered such a chaotic response in her? Even now, small licks of fire were moving back and forth across her skin, singeing, burning, warning. A terrifying dampness in her private places signaled a stimulation brought on by the monster's closeness. The rich timbre of his voice had been like a stroke of his hand across her breasts—highly personal, intimate, extremely provocative.

It was the Dark Seduction. She had read about it. A look, a word, a whisper, and victims fell into line with a vampire's wishes. That's what she had read. That's what she had been told by those who professed to know about such things. But no one could have actually believed it. She hadn't. No one in their right mind could have. A person's mind was their own.

Nevertheless, this vampire's body had radiated heat, not cold. She'd felt his breath, though he couldn't have been breathing. His nearness had left her damp, fevered and interested. His touch had left behind tingling sensations that persisted even now as she tried to steady the gun.

Jesse jerked away from the door, ignoring the ache of her old neck wound, preferring to concentrate on what a fool she was and how stupid her actions had been so far. She had allowed a vampire near enough for a nibble. His lips had been dangerously close to her throat. This kind of mental slippage could not happen again, ever. She'd all but deserved a bite.

Just how he had known where to find her was the

question she had to answer. Also, why he had come. She'd been in the city one day. How the blazes could he have found her so easily?

If this vampire dared to roam the city, and in particular this hotel, as though he owned it, how many other monsters were doing the same thing? How many of those people in the lobby were *people?*

The gun in her hand wavered.

What would he do to Stan? He'd seen her with Stan. Should she go out and find her pilot? Then what? Explain that she truly hadn't been kidding in the chopper, and that vampires actually did walk the earth? Explain how she knew this? Explain about her past?

None of those things were options, as she saw it. People didn't believe in monsters, they merely watched them on TV. Stan had assumed she had been playing with him in the chopper. The unit thought her odd enough without bringing the threat of vampires into the mix.

But vampires existed. They did. And this one was her problem.

Her mind raced on.

Maybe this one didn't want Stan. Maybe he only wanted her. Maybe she was some kind of vampire magnet. Should she be flattered? she wondered cynically. Maybe change her perfume?

It wasn't funny. Not remotely. This sadistic levity was fear talking. Panic whispering. No matter how much her mind wanted to make light of the situation, this foreign gig had turned dangerous. She had somehow been marked.

Her eyes went to the window. Night out there. Brown silk drapes tied back. Window closed. There was a balcony beyond the window, as if the window might have once been a door. She'd noted this earlier, as she always did when taking stock of her surroundings, foreign or otherwise.

Room scan. Beige damask sofa. Gilded chairs. Heavy picture frames and glass cocktail table. Very old, faded and pricey Aubusson rug on the patterned parquet floor, the kind found in mansions and expensive European hotels like this one.

They'd put her up in luxury. In a suite. Not the usual Motel 6, but good old-style European hospitality.

And she just happened to have a box of silver bullets in her luggage. In the bedroom. Twenty paces away.

She raced there, glanced behind the door, under the bed, in the closet and expansive bathroom, with both hands on the gun. There was no shower curtain to hide behind in the bathroom, only a glass enclosure still damp from earlier use. She could have used another shower, she thought. A cold one. Maybe bathe in ice.

Her hands were still shaking as she moved back to what served as a living room to check the connecting door to Stan's room. *Locked.*

There wasn't anything else to hide behind here, though she doubted this vampire would try to hide behind anything. This one was brazen, intelligent, used to getting his own way. And he was sensual. Like golden velvet.

She had made a mistake, and had to get over it. He absolutely would not catch her with her pants down again. She'd need coffee, plenty of it, to stay awake and on guard. Fabulous hotels had room service…

Her hand stopped halfway to the phone. Before anything else, she needed another stern inner chastisement. This so-called Dark Seduction was no joke. The vampire's pulse-scrambling routine had just about been her ruin. His throaty, suggestive voice was a ruse, nothing more. His soft touch was a lure. And his hard body? The golden hair that surrounded him like an aura? The blue eyes she just knew were the color of shallow lake water?

Holy hell! The vampire looked like a freaking angel, instead of the demon he was.

Head cocked to the side, Jesse lowered the pistol and stood a minute more, blinking back the shakes, reasoning herself into a practiced state of calm while staring at the door.

"Ghosts come and go through closed windows and doors, not vampires," she said aloud. "A vampire would have to knock."

When the knock came, seconds after the thought, Jesse jumped. Gun pointed and ready, hair on her arms standing straight up, she opened her mouth to speak.

Perched in his boots atop the railing of the balcony, knees bent in a squat, coat blowing in the wind, Lance watched Jesse sweep through the suite.

Like a professional, she moved quickly, agilely, until she was satisfied no one would jump out at her, at least right then. Was she a police officer? Something similar? Is this why she had come here to help rescue the American senator's daughter?

He watched her whirl to the door, gun in hand, and heard her chopper pilot call out from the hallway, "Boss? You in there? You up?"

Her relief was obvious when she heard who stood in the hallway. Noting this, Lance experienced what felt like a bullet piercing his flesh, but was in fact something else altogether. Jealously? Lust? Hunger?

The warm scent of a woman after all this time in

limbo was an indulgence, and intoxicating. Jesse was soap and oranges and silk. She was pink flushed skin and musky feminine dampness. Soft curls danced over her collar. Those same dark curls, the color of night, curtained her graceful, scarred throat.

Turning his face into the wind, Lance tried not to think about her throat or the veins beneath it. Tried not to let his thoughts linger on all that heat bubbling beneath the surface of Jesse's skin.

Closing his eyes, he again caught the scent of blood, heard a little girl's cry, tasted fear in the old alley. Her cry. Jesse's.

Having once rescued her, it appeared now as if he might have saved her for himself. As if destiny might have played a hand. Yet his dilemma was a troublesome one. Was this attraction merely bloodlust, having tasted Jesse in the past? If not bloodlust, would he be able to bring her to him in the end? Bring something so alive, so beautiful, over, forcing her to give up everything she knew?

Did he dare to find out if he could love Jesse, knowing he might lose her, as he lost Gwen?

He'd vowed celibacy. He'd lived like a monk ever since that night in the Los Angeles alley when Jesse had thought him an angel. A very dark angel. The moment had opened his eyes.

He'd been a Watcher. A Guardian. A purveyor of justice. An immortal set to keep other immortals in line. He had given it all up because of Jesse. Because of the bloody night they'd shared in that alley and the look in her eyes when she'd asked for his help.

He closed his eyes now to block out the memory.

"Stan?"

"Yes, boss."

Jesse yanked back the bolt, lowered the pistol and threw open the door.

Stan caught sight of the gun right off. His gaze rose to meet hers. "Room service that bad?"

"Yep. If it was the maid, I was going to ask why she didn't leave more towels."

"Yeah? Well, the gun might have gotten you towels, for sure. Maybe even two chocolates on your pillow."

"You think?"

"I know."

Jesse motioned for Stan to step inside. He obliged.

"You went for beer?" she asked, gun dangling at her side.

"Had one, but was tired, so I came back. Thought I'd check in before hitting the sack. I'm right next door, you know."

"I know."

"If you need anything…"

"I'll shoot."

Stan grinned. "Now, that's the boss we all know and love."

"Yes, well, I aim to please."

Stan stifled a chuckle as he gave the room a cursory glance. "Big and drafty," he said.

"Good sheets, though," Jesse reminded him.

"Wouldn't want to get spoiled, would we?"

"You imagine this will ever happen again?"

Stan shook his head. "You're right. I doubt it would. So I should probably savor that piece of chocolate on my pillow. Take small bites."

"If the maid shows, I'll send over a case."

"You do that, boss," Stan said, turning toward the hallway. "Eight o'clock?"

"Eight it is."

Stan spoke over his shoulder. "You don't suppose they'll give us coffee?"

"I'll bet they would if we were going to be around long enough to drink some. They might toss in a couple of gold watches."

Stan waved a big hand in the air. "Okay. I hear you loud and clear. And I'm not spoiled. No sirree. Not me."

With that, Stan disappeared.

Jesse closed the door, took a breath that filled her lungs, spun with her pistol raised and pointed, and said to the presence she felt like a draft creeping along her skin, "How the hell did you get in?"

"Why didn't you tell Stan about me?" Lance asked in turn, from his position against the bedroom doorjamb.

"Don't ever say his name again," Jesse snapped.

"Are you lovers?"

"That's none of your business. You have no right to be in my room."

Lance nodded solemnly. "It's a hotel," he said. "Not your home. You might want to note that, because if it's not personal space, I need no invitation."

Jesse's body, he saw, went stiffer.

"You'll need my help on this case," he said over the audible boom of her heartbeat, witnessing how wide her eyes had grown.

"Now you think you know why I'm here?"

He observed how Jesse kept her wide-eyed gaze below the level of his neck. *Neat trick.* He wondered where she had learned it.

"You're here to find Elizabeth Jorgensen, are you not?" he asked her.

"How could you possibly know that?"

"I watch and listen," Lance said, doing just that by watching Jesse's lips close, tighten, open again.

Those lovely lips quivered as she spoke. "Is it a fight you want?"

"Far from it."

"Then what is it you do want?"

"To see you," he confessed.

Her gaze lifted slightly. Her pistol leveled at his heart.

"Silver bullets," she said.

"Resourceful."

"Leave now," she directed. "The way you came in."

Lance shook his head. "You can trust me, Jesse. You need to trust me."

"Right. And I'm just a stupid, brainless woman who would fall for such a line. I know what you are. I know what you can do."

"Agreed, you are not stupid. But you will learn, perhaps the hard way, to accept help when it comes, in whatever form it takes. You are in need of help on this one."

Her finger was squeezing the trigger, and Lance didn't blame her. Unwanted attention, however, such as a gunshot in a busy hotel, was not to be condoned. Neither were silver bullets.

In a flash he had a hand on her weapon. Another second, to her like a blur, and he had taken the gun from her while encircling her waist with his right arm.

The sharp elbow to his side was a surprise. As was Jesse squirming free of his hold. She ducked beneath his grip and gave him a solid punch to the stomach. Then she turned her shoulder into him and pushed off for a potentially lethal roundhouse kick.

Lethal to a human, that is.

But he was so much faster. He caught her ankle before it struck his back, and sent her spinning. Jesse had better reflexes than the average human, he had to note, and a more sinewy strength than her size suggested; signs that her body still held secrets only he might know she possessed.

Quickly back in balance, she came at him again with a sharp kick to his left thigh. He felt this one, and winced. With his hand on her knee, Lance pulled upward, sending her toward the floor, but he grabbed her by the arm before she hit the parquet, wrenching her elbow forward. Using his free hand, he gave the closed window beside them a shove.

In a single powerful retraction of his arms, Jesse was lifted, struggling. She was a hellion, twisting, fighting, refusing to give up or give in. But he had years on her. Centuries. And the unearthly power of an immortal.

He had her out the window before her second startled breath, and straddling the balcony railing—ten floors above the ground, in the darkness, with lights and city sounds all around and nothing below but a sheer drop to the pavement.

Jesse stopped struggling.

"You must trust me," he repeated.

"Go to hell."

"You'd rather die than trust me?"

"Go to hell!"

Lance offered Jesse a disappointed shake of his head, then let her slip from his grasp.

Chapter 5

Jesse felt herself slipping and scrambled for a hold.

There was no hold.

All sounds ceased except for the great intake of air that would very possibly be her last. The city lights, the stars overhead, the vampire's white face, whirled in abstract patterns through her vision and through her mind as her hand slid over the vampire's sleeve in what felt like slowed motion. As her body dangled precariously above nothingness.

So, it has come to this.

With every bit of energy she had left, she fought the stark realization of her predicament. Her fingers clutched at the vampire's gloved hand, then felt even that tiny bit of security go.

She was falling.

Contrary to near-death coda, her life didn't pass before her eyes; only that speck of it when things had changed for her. When she had cheated death.

Parents. Alley. Monsters. Blood.

Maybe she couldn't have helped her parents, but hopefully the things she'd done since then would help herself, somehow.

Red. Slashes of it. Sprays of it. Across my face, drenching my coat.

White. A flash in my peripheral vision. Angel? Tunnel? My brain calming down to accept its fate?

What would a ten-year-old know of such things? Of blackness, darkness, night and finality?

Jesse closed her eyes against the sensations of frigid air on her face and the rise of bile in her throat, and let her body go loose. What use was a struggle?

Then she felt something close over her wrist.

Abruptly, and with a bone-wrenching pain in her right shoulder, she stopped falling.

She opened her eyes.

A hand had caught hold of hers, at least temporarily. A gloved hand was wrapped around her right wrist. She hadn't fallen far, but was dangling by one arm over nothingness, legs heavy, her overcoat weighing her down.

Afraid to look up farther than the hand clamped to hers, Jesse knew it was the same creature that had let her go in the first place who now, oddly enough, had tossed her a lifeline. Unable to help herself, she tilted her head back, absorbing the pain in her shoulder, clenching her teeth against a scream.

It was the vampire, all right. Jesse could see that his knees were bent, and that his legs were folded beneath him. He was perched upon the narrow iron balcony railing as though he were some sort of bird comfortably resting on an alarmingly thin ribbon of metal. He looked to be in perfect balance. He wasn't straining. How he'd reached down to catch her, she didn't even want to think about. The hold on her wrist was tight, but it was, after all, just one arm, one hand. Five fingers, belonging to a vampire, stood between herself and certain death.

Staring up, refusing to cower, ignoring the straining ligaments, she said, "What are you waiting for?"

The vampire's face was pale and solemn. "I'm waiting for you to come to your senses."

"Do it," she said.

"Drop you, you mean?"

Jesse's gaze almost met his. She watched his mouth open as he spoke again.

"I told you I wouldn't hurt you."

"That's funny," she countered, "since I seem to be dangling off the side of a building."

The vampire grinned. At least it appeared that he did. Jesse's world had begun to fuzz around the edges. The searing heat in her arm and shoulder were barely tolerable.

"This was the easiest way to get you to listen," he confessed.

"Listen?" Jesse echoed breathlessly. "Listen to what?"

"Elizabeth Jorgensen is no longer in the city."

Maybe, Jesse thought, she was dreaming this. Maybe she had fallen, and this was a last few brain cells working overtime.

"Trust me, Jesse. I know this," the creature above her said. "I have ways of finding things out."

Swallowing a groan, Jesse glanced down, below her feet. Hadn't she always figured she would go like this? Some final dramatic moment sufficient enough to beat out the time she had cheated the dark?

"I will not let you fall."

The vampire's voice was deep, toneless, nothing like

the dance of light she'd seen in his eyes in the frosty meadow. His voice willed her to believe what he was saying.

"I have no intention of letting you go," he clarified.

Jesse blinked back the pain. Her shoulder hurt like a son of a bitch. Her muscles couldn't stay attached much longer. She wasn't sure about retaining consciousness.

"This is your idea of fun, then?" she asked, clearly enough, she thought.

"You must admit that I have your complete attention," the vampire replied drily.

"And you want my attention because…?"

"Let's just say I have a desire to help, whether you want my help or not."

Damn shoulder. God, it hurts.

Damn frigging vampire, bloodsucking…

Another shallow breath accompanied still more pain. Her thoughts had turned staccato. Her head was beginning to whirl.

"You mentioned Elizabeth Jorgensen," she panted. "How do you know about her?"

"I overheard some things and guessed that's what might have brought you. An American senator's daughter disappears while traveling with her famous father, the government here calls for help from the States, and you fly overhead in a helicopter."

Jesse felt like screaming. The shoulder was red-hot, dangerously near to irreparable damage. Through clenched jaws, she managed to say, "I could be a tourist."

"Yes, most of the tourists who come here wear guns and carry Tasers."

"If they don't, they should." Her head felt light. She could no longer feel her fingers.

"Just as all of them should meet with the aides of our top officials," the vampire continued. "In hotel lobbies."

What was he? Some kind of monster detective?

How long before she passed out from the pain and became vampire dessert?

"You live in a castle!" Jesse charged, as if that fact should either make some sense or negate what he knew of her assignment.

"Yes," he admitted. "I live in a castle. However, I do get out now and then."

"Just my luck." *God! This hurts!* "What do you actually want?"

One more minute was all she needed. One more minute of consciousness to get this straight.

"I want to be near to you," the vampire said. "For a while."

"Go fuck yourself."

"Such language, Jesse. Have we been around bad elements too long?"

"And the wild horse you rode in on," Jesse added.

"Perhaps Stan is a bad influence," the vampire suggested.

This shut her up. Would he hurt Stan next?

"You have the exterior of a woman," the golden predator went on, staring down at her intently. "And the verbiage of a cop. I'm assuming you are one? Cop, I mean?"

"This is the deduction of a guy who wears puffy shirts and breeches? Excuse me. Not *guy*. Monster."

The vampire laughed aloud with a sound that wasn't wholly evil, and more like an acknowledgment of a comment well aimed.

"Will you listen?" he asked.

"Do I have a choice?"

"Are you in pain?"

"I've been better."

"I'll pull you up if you promise to behave."

"It's not my gun hand that's injured. And I won't promise anything. I'd rather you drop me than to owe my continued existence to something like you."

Now the sucker did smile. Fully. Inappropriately.

Damn him. What had he done with her gun?

"I wonder if that's true," he said softly. "Death being preferable to life, in any case?"

"Shouldn't you be qualified to answer that question?"

"Perhaps."

The vamp gave a tug of his arm. Jesse swore she heard her shoulder tear. She bit back every obscenity she knew until she found herself on both feet, if barely, on the balcony railing. In *his* arms.

The terrible truth of a mind in turmoil was that this monster felt like a man. He felt solid and strong.

"See?" he told her. "You're safe."

Jesse didn't want to close her eyes, but she did. The relief she felt was overwhelming. If it wasn't for the fact that she couldn't move her arm and couldn't feel anything outside of the raw pain engulfing her shoulder, she might have been glad to be where she was. The question now, if she could focus on answering it, was why the vampire hadn't let her die.

"I guess you don't like roadkill," she whispered. Which is what she would have been, had she fallen. "You prefer juicier fare? Live bodies to taunt and victimize?"

A bullet to the chest would have been preferable to a ten-story drop, she acknowledged. Both bullet and drop would have been preferable to the damage a vampire could inflict. She'd seen the carnage.

But, her mind nagged, if she were to die here, who would find Elizabeth Jorgensen? How would another life be saved, and the Jorgensen girl reunited with her family? No one deserved the darkness, the sadness, the loss of being separated from their loved ones, or of being cut off prematurely from life.

Forcing her eyes open, Jesse scanned the dark chest in front of her, thinking, *Yeah, right. A truthful monster. What next? A vampire with a conscience? A soul?*

Should she cast stones, a more distant part of her brain queried, when she'd lost her own soul long ago?

The fact was, the broad chest she had her head against didn't rise and fall quite as a human's should.

"I'm afraid I don't care much for human fare these days," the vampire said, sounding completely truthful.

Senses beginning to fragment, Jesse inhaled the scents clinging to the monster. *Leather. Wool.* Alongside those smells lay something more elusive that she couldn't put a name to, and maybe shouldn't try to classify. Vampires were evil. There was no such thing as a good one. How could there be? Everything she had ever learned taught her about predators pursuing their own bloody agenda.

This one hadn't killed her for a reason known only to himself. Maybe he just wanted to toy with her a bit longer. Darkness loomed in the pit of Jesse's stomach with that thought. She ached for vengeance, figured she must have five lives left after he'd tried to take this one from her, if in fact there were nine to begin with.

One vamp less would make for a better world. She had to see to this, personally.

And he had asked her to trust him?
Where is the goddamn gun?

Lance smoothed the wind-whipped hair back from Jesse's face. The thrill of touching her rippled through him, resonating deep inside his body.

Defiant, she was. Willful. *Special.*

How many of those traits were due to her tiny infusion of vampire blood so long ago, and how many were determined by genetics alone? As he recalled, her father had been courageous. Her father and mother had fought bravely for their lives. They'd fought for hers.

He shouldn't have been holding her. Shouldn't have gotten this close. The need to possess her for reasons other than thirst was called the *blood lure,* and driven, he supposed, by centuries of leftover emotion. He was titillated by the recognition of what she was and could be if she survived her task. It was a case of like calling to like, in its extreme, no matter how minuscule the amount of an immortal's cells remained in her veins.

Desire was already curling through him, along with feelings best left in the past. It had been so long since he'd held a woman, immortal or otherwise.

His mind brought up the picture of a lifetime he had tried to forget. Memories filled with both sweetness and sorrow. Beautiful Gwen, as fair as Jesse was dark, had been filled with sunlight and surrounded by flowers. He could still smell Gwen, feel her, hear her, if he tried. The agony of their union haunted him; a kind of sweet torment he could never forget.

But that was another lifetime. A memory. *Dust.*

Nothing of springtime clung to this woman in his arms. No wildflowers and sunlight made it past her stern resolve. Jesse was composed of energy in flux;

edgy, lean and raw in spots. The air around her swirled with action and concentrated agitation. The slight space between them crackled with electricity.

Still, somewhere within the package was a woman. The dark curls she refused to tame were an indication of a softer side. The soap and citrus scents drifting from her with a maddening allure bespoke the fact that somewhere inside Jesse a piece of the gentle girl remained, hidden, lost. He wanted very much to find that girl, see again the innocence in her brown-eyed stare.

"Why me?" she asked, her voice muffled by her position.

"In time I'll tell you," he replied.

"Why?" she pressed.

Blood. It's the blood, he wanted to say, but repeated, "In time."

"Are you going to kill me?"

Taken aback, Lance studied the top of Jesse's head. She had asked this same question all those years ago, waiting for death to strike. The woman had guts to have survived. He had to give her that.

"No," he replied quietly. "Haven't I convinced you?"

"It's what your kind does!"

"Some of us, yes."

"Some? There are *kinds?*"

"It would seem so."

"Maybe I lucked out and you've already had your dinner? Maybe you killed someone else tonight?"

"I've killed no one, Jesse. As I said, I have no taste for humans."

Jesse twisted in his grasp over the use of her name. "Like that's comforting?" she shouted. "Okay. I'll play. So where has Elizabeth Jorgensen gone?"

"She was taken," he told her.

"Abducted?"

"Yes."

Lance felt the minute Jesse began to weaken. Having straddled death's threshold, and in spite of her dribble of ancient blood, her strength was waning. Her body would fight her will, and lose. But in the hours ahead, she would need every ounce of strength she possessed, and more. If she went after the Jorgensen girl, she would again confront the nightmares.

Was she ready for that?

"You are brave," he whispered to her. "Yet you are also vulnerable. I've come to warn you about this."

"Is someone else going to dangle me over a balcony? If so, I think I'll move to the ground floor."

Lance slid a hand beneath Jesse's chin to tilt her head upward. She closed her eyes, refusing to make eye contact.

"You are out of your depth if you imagine you might rescue Elizabeth Jorgensen on your own," he cautioned. "I wouldn't count on the government or your senator's aides in this instance."

Tough and resistant as she was, Jesse felt good in his arms. Her closeness screamed at him, provoked him. Leaning forward, Lance brushed her mouth with his—just a wayward slip of his lips across hers, the slightest of actions—and he was sure he had found her hidden softness, her weakness. In his illicit action, he had perhaps stumbled upon the key to Jesse.

The hard cop wanted to be loved. She wanted to be saved. Not in any physical way, it was too late for that, but at the level of her soul.

Jesse felt unworthy of her continued existence. She was afraid of being vulnerable. He saw this quite clearly now. Her mouth was made for taking, yet had probably never been taken. Her body, lithe and strong, would have never been shared. No man had been allowed into her inner sanctum. She had never offered herself up to anyone.

The sadness of this insight made Lance tighten his hold on her. The loneliness she must have endured. The pain. All this time, alone.

Just like him. *All this time.*

He feathered his mouth over hers, found her lips closed to him. She may have been beyond caring what he did, but the effect on himself was immediate and startling. His muscles seized, squeezing the breath from his captive until her big eyes opened. Her brown gaze met his. Without warning, he was thrown back in time to the meadow. He saw himself looking up at the helicopter, and felt her looking down.

Amber-flecked eyes.

Amber. Flecked.

The eyes of a hybrid.

Yet she didn't know. Hadn't guessed. She didn't realize how close she was, in this city, to danger. She'd have no idea how easily she could be found by others she'd count as being of his kind when her blood would be the greatest enticement for them all.

Her gaze streaked through him with the force of a lightning strike, hard and swift. Her face was ashen, completely colorless around those incredible eyes. Her body continued to vibrate. She had called him a monster, but he wanted to protect her. This was a stunningly new sensation. A regenerating goal. Suddenly, he wanted to always protect her, always be her champion.

Yield, Jesse.

He pushed his will into her, then rested his mouth on hers.

Yield.

He urged her lips to open, knowing she had no choice, taking advantage anyway. He met with the heat and slickness of her mouth, ran his tongue over her teeth. He stroked her arms with his hands, inhaled her groan of pain and called to her from deep within himself.

"They can hurt you, Jesse. This kiss proves that you are susceptible to their will. I cannot have that."

Hating what he was about to do, knowing she would despise him even more for this, trust him less for this, he bit down on his own lower lip with his razorlike teeth. Feeling the rush of blood rise to the wound, he tipped Jesse's head back and held her there while he allowed several drops of his blood to flow onto her tongue.

She choked, coughed, struggled, writhed in pain. Her shoulder was sorely wounded, he knew with his lips still on hers. She no longer had the use of that arm. But coughing made her swallow. When she did, her eyelids fluttered. She made a sound like a lost soul searching for light. Still, she was no match for him, and she knew it. She had fought as much as she could have, and had precious little left to fend off the beast.

With a quick sweep, Lance lifted her into his arms. Even then she groped for a way to resist, feeble now, exhausted.

He brought her pale face close to his, whispered to her, "My blood for your own good. Remember this."

Jesse went limp. Her head lolled back and her legs dangled uselessly over his biceps. He'd taken the fight out of her. He had taken it all. Her body would be assimilating a monster's blood, needing what remained of her reserves to do this. She would need to drink more in a while.

Back through the open window Lance jumped, then turned for the bedroom. Gliding soundlessly over the carpets, he laid Jesse carefully on the bed and leaned down to run his fingers over her face. She stirred, choked again, but she could not open her eyes. The slightest movement was beyond her.

Rest, he sent to her in a silent command. *Sleep now, Jesse. Sleep while you can.*

Fitfully, she turned her head from side to side, perhaps seeking the coolness of the pillow, perhaps trying to negate what had happened to her. When she paused, her neck and throat, covered by a faint sheen of sweat, lay exposed. There before him spread the intricate network of white lines that crisscrossed the skin beneath her chin.

"God's blood!"

Lance's pulse thudded. A tidal wave rammed his arteries, moved his ribs, causing him to tense. The sheer magnitude of his reaction to her necessitated his getting away.

He placed a finger over her jugular vein, so blue against the whiteness of the scar. Tracing the pathway of blood, his finger dipped to her collarbone, then to the first button of her white blouse. He slipped the button from its hole, pressed back the two halves of silk and lowered his lips to the V between her delicate bones.

Smooth skin. Unblemished. Soft.

"Perhaps not composed of sunlight," he mused, "yet something else equally as potent."

Something that moved him.

He kissed her tenderly, there, and again at the corner of the old wound. His insides began to churn. Not soap and oranges now, he thought. The scent clinging to Jesse was blood. All that blood right beneath the surface of such fair, fragile skin. Within reach. There for the taking, just because.

His teeth were already extended. The hair on his arms was standing on end. Gently, he took the flesh of her throat between his lips. He'd smelled her from the ground, while looking up at her. He had recognized this, known this, known her.

Lightly, he sucked inward. With his tongue against her thrumming artery, he whispered silently to her.

"Jesse."

Not a woman, really. Nor a monster. Jess was nothing quite so easily defined. Nothing so clear-cut. Maybe knowing this would help her in the end. Save her in the end?

Jesse hated the bloodsuckers. Yes.

Jesse wanted to kill them all.

But sooner or later, Jesse would have to know the truth.

About herself.

Chapter 6

Nothing. No movement. Not even an unnecessary breath.

Still as stone, Lance tried to rally himself as his body spiraled into chaos. It was time to go, leave her, and create some distance. Jesse's sudden vulnerability would have been dangerous for a male of any species.

If he broke her skin after his little blood donation, even with a fingernail, she wouldn't stand a chance against him. One bite with his teeth, and with his blood already in her veins, and Jesse would lose her fierce, hard-won free will. One bite, and she would bend if he called, no matter where she was, no matter how far away.

Blood calling to blood.

After all those centuries of his existence, Lance found it odd to suddenly be confronting the ultimate test, to have the things he stood for in jeopardy—chief amongst them the concepts of honor, loyalty and adherence to a vow. Would those things win out, as they always had, or would those things go by the wayside when confronted with a life of isolation and loneliness?

Jesse would never agree to a bond between them. The exchange of blood between two willing beings, one of them immortal, was a ritual more sensual than anything or anyone living or dying could conceive of. Much more than a merging of body parts, blood sharing resulted in a fusion of souls known as the Dark Surrender. The giving up, or surrendering, of each individual soul to the union, to the whole. To some, this was considered the death of the individual. Indeed, if a human, a mortal, was involved, that mortality died out. But it was replaced by another spark, an everlasting energy that would continue in a new way.

So the rumors foretold.

He'd never come close to such a thing, himself.

He had been mortal once, in what seemed like another lifetime. It was hard to recall that time, though, other than remembering how he had been chosen for the job of Guardian. He had accepted immortality and the governorship of his kind, but had never passed his fate along to another living being.

He had never participated in the Dark Surrender. Had never sunk his teeth into a human vein. In all this long time, he had regretted his decision to remain alone only once, when he refused the one other woman he had loved her own immortality.

Had that been wise in retrospect? Immortality was as much a curse as it was a boon. Maybe more of a curse, actually. Humans were born, they aged and then they died, while he stayed the same. *Always the same.*

His plan, in the beginning, had been to keep immortal

populations down and the ancient blood untainted. If he had changed a female, ever spontaneous as they were, and without one of them being chosen for this gift, there was a chance she would have created more harm than good. She might not have been able to control her hunger.

Accepting his own fate as a Guardian had necessitated leaving human emotions and humankind behind. *Until now,* he inwardly conceded. Because he couldn't make himself leave this room, this bed and the woman in it. Helping Jesse in that alley long ago had brought the emotions back. Ruined him, to some degree.

Anger, rage, hope and loneliness had tainted him since that night. Jesse, the girl all grown up, continued to affect him in ways he'd never have foreseen. The little girl, now a full-grown woman, had brought the old longings back. Given her history, she would never choose to follow his path, nor would he dare to ask it of her—not if he adhered to his own rules about justice and preserving human life.

Holding back wasn't easy. Jesse was pale, still and completely helpless on the bed. After this night she would hate him doubly for pointing out her vulnerabilities and for letting him gain the upper hand. This might very well be the last time he'd be able to touch her. The last time he'd get close.

He had given her his blood, twice, in order to help her, perhaps sensing something special from the beginning. Even knowing nothing about his actions and his reasons for helping, she'd wonder what she might offer him in exchange for his information about Elizabeth Jorgensen. She would fear what that exchange rate might be.

He had told her the truth about the senator's daughter. Jesse was out of her league. She might be stronger than a normal mortal, but against a nest of the entities she called bloodsuckers, the fools he was sure had taken Elizabeth Jorgensen, Jesse would end up as liquid dessert.

The city was infested with lesser beings the humans called vampires. Tainted blood had been tainted further with each new generation of them. They bit others in anger and self-defense, on purpose and by accident, for pleasure, and out of the ever-present excruciating hunger that overcame them. Sometimes they bit down on human necks for the sheer godlike ability to create more creatures like themselves.

Perhaps, way back, the first shared blood between the creatures had been for want of company, for remembered closeness. But as the gift of immortal blood diluted more and more, those memories, along with all remaining humanness faded. Vampires had become the bane of the East.

Lance Van Baaren. A being apart...

Those emotions he'd thought lost with time's passage were blatantly in the forefront here. For this one moment, suspended in time, he remembered what it felt like to be human, and in need of something.

Running the points of his teeth across the intricacies of the threads of Jesse's old wound to make sure his blood had dispersed, Lance felt a second explosion rock his insides, so powerful that it also shook the bed. He didn't need human blood to survive. He'd told her the truth about that. This didn't mean he didn't hunger for it. It didn't mean he was immune from the desire for a taste. Blood, not for sustenance, but more as a way to experience the closeness he lacked.

Desire for the blood of the woman whose vein lay beneath his lips, while hoping to keep tethered to an ancient oath that meant never craving that very thing, was a peculiar dilemma. A new one.

His options?

Jesse might actually survive this case and her search for the Jorgensen girl if he gave her more of his blood, whether or not she agreed to it. Without another infusion, she'd be nearly as helpless as she was that very minute.

Nevertheless, he could not force her to accept this gift. He could not give her more of himself unless she agreed. More blood meant there was a possibility she would turn. He was, in fact, and in spite of his hunger for her, held by that vow of blood celibacy.

He had reinforced her on the balcony so that a useless arm would not trip her up. In doing so, he had made things worse than they already were. Because he'd gifted her, he had made it easier for the others to find her. The monsters. Jesse's freaks.

"Perhaps…" he murmured to her with his mouth against her glistening skin. "Perhaps someday I will taste you, touch you again. Right now you are in danger. My blood is both a curse and a blessing, you see."

Sliding his arms beneath Jesse, Lance pulled her forward, cradling her head against his shoulder. The closeness was pain, a dark, circling need. He placed a lingering kiss in her dark curls. *So soft.*

An immortal's senses were acute. For one as old as himself, senses were also an obstacle. He was aware of every part of Jesse. His body, long ignored, had suddenly come alive, burning, hardening, with arousal.

But daylight wasn't far off. The hotel had grown quiet. Stars still shone outside the window, tempting his eyes that way. Out there, for him, was endless night.

Perpetual darkness. It wouldn't snow again; a calmness rode on the wind for the time being.

When morning came, Jesse would start her search for Elizabeth Jorgensen in spite of his warnings. He'd had a hand in shaping that defiance, too, he supposed. He could keep her in a sleep-induced state, but knew in his soul that if he took her from here, carried her away and hid her, Jesse would remain his mortal enemy. She would never understand his reasoning or be able to sift through the forces driving her anger.

The only acceptable action was to let her go. Keep watch over her. Be there, near her, and hope to eventually win her trust.

"Trust," he whispered, and carefully, with tender fingers, he tugged Jesse's arms from her overcoat. He repeated that word as he removed her damp jacket, fighting the sheer savageness of his longing.

He removed her silky white blouse, finding beneath it a fine, delicate wisp of lace that was a notable contrast to the businesslike cut of her dark suit. Another clue to Jesse lay in this discovery. Her tough exterior, like her suit, covered a feminine interior. As hard as Jesse might fight with the world, the pretty lace lingerie meant that she liked the feel of the feminine against her skin.

Lightly gilded skin.

Lance moved his gaze over flesh that stretched across honed planes of lean muscle. She had a striated stomach and defined upper arms and shoulders. Her breasts filled the fine white lace harness. Through the pale weave, rosy-hued nipples lay like unbloomed roses behind a lattice border. A delightful sight. Almost a shock. Delicious. Achingly appealing.

He had to touch her. Even the strength of his will couldn't prevent it. Against his principles, knowing it to be wrong, Lance pulled his fingers free of the black leather gloves.

Just this once, Jesse.

He laid his cool, bare palm against her stomach. Fending off the riot of sensation accompanying the gesture, his senses scrambling, Lance closed his eyes to soak it all in…realizing, as he emitted a groan of pleasure, that he had crossed over the forbidden barrier separating his existence from hers.

Jesse woke to a sound. She sat up, endured a brief wave of vertigo, and as the room righted itself, realized she was alive.

It took a minute to orient herself. She had to regulate her breathing, find out where she was.

Rarely in her own apartment these days, she allowed the standard recognition of a hotel room to fill in. The framed watercolor pictures on the walls weren't hers. The fussy silken drapes at the windows wouldn't have been her choice. Only a lamp and a telephone sat on the bedside table.

There was no gun beside that phone. And no vampire in residence.

Her heart beat faster with each section of the room she surveyed. As she looked to the doorway, her pulse thumped audibly in her neck. Hands flying to encircle her throat, the events of the night came hurtling back with stunning severity. Balcony. Vampire. The excruciating pain of her shoulder all but torn from its socket. Those things had not been part of a dream.

She felt along her neck with frantic fingers, finding no puncture marks. Relieved, Jesse moved her wounded arm, expecting the worst. But her arm felt normal, didn't hurt at all.

"If last night wasn't a dream, then what was it?"

Tumbling from the bed, backing herself up into a corner of the room on unsteady legs, Jesse again surveyed the scene.

No vampire.

No gun on the table.

She could move all ten of her fingers.

But she was shaking, head to toes—no doubt part freak-out, part cold. Glancing down at herself, Jesse found a whole lot of nakedness, skimpily covered.

She dived for her bag, open on the floor. Rifling through the contents, she fingered a slim wooden stake, originally placed in there merely as a reminder of her future goal. She clasped the handle of her pistol the vampire must have tucked there.

"Damn freak!"

She looked to the window. *Closed. Locked.* Which meant the vampire had used another exit.

And locked the window? Why would he do that?

Why didn't she ache?

Why didn't her shoulder hurt like hell?

Why didn't her neck?

By all rights, she should have been in need of meds and a good stiff drink, no matter what time it was.

"What the hell happened to my clothes?"

She grabbed her robe. Ten steps later, she was in the front room of the suite, gun in hand. *Nothing out of the ordinary here.* This window also was closed and locked. The drapes were open, the sun was already up and the day looked dreary.

Her focus slid to the door. The monster must have exited that way, like a lover leaving his mistress's room in the middle of the night.

Again, she glanced down at her nakedness.

"Fucking vampire!"

Yeah, she had a mouth like a cop. "So what?" That's exactly what she'd been for four years before this current job. As all cops knew, swearing helped to ease pent-up tension sometimes, even if it didn't seem to help much now. Anger, fright and frustration were tangling within her, making knots, with anger sifting to the top.

She'd been compromised. Maybe even violated, though she didn't think so since she was still in her underwear. However, there was no doubt as to how she'd gotten undressed.

"Bloody freaking bloodsucker!"

He'd done something to her that caused her to black out. Did that something also include the ability to heal her arm miraculously? Was there a chance he had merely made her think she'd been hurt?

Opening her mouth to utter another curse, Jesse hesitated. *Bad influence,* the arrogant vamp had said.

"Stan!"

She raced to the door connecting her room to Stan's with fear in her throat. Fingers trembling, she tore at the lock, yanked the door open and stared into the dark space between her door and Stan's. Applying knuckles to wood, she rapped, called out and swallowed back the rising panic. Would the monster have done something to Stan?

She kicked at the door with her bare foot.

"Okay. All right, already," a voice called out from the other side of the door. It was Stan's voice, registering surprise, but not in the least panicky.

The door opened wide. Stan filled the doorway, his body blocking out the weak daylight displayed in the windows behind him. He was dressed in a white button-down shirt, brown socks and a pair of patterned boxer shorts. Jesse could have kissed him, she was so relieved.

Stan said inquiringly, "Boss?"

"You all right?" Jesse knew her voice sounded winded.

"The question is, I think, are *you* okay?" Stan said, with no hint of his usual grin.

"Yes. Of course. He—"

Recognizing the question in Stan's raised eyebrow, Jesse stopped talking. It would be quite obvious to Stan that she was only partially clothed.

Jesse waved at herself. "Sorry. I thought I heard something over here." The lie would have to do. No way she could explain anything that had happened to her. She wasn't all that sure herself about what had occurred.

"Everything here is okay," Stan said. "Maybe you heard the TV."

"Yes. For a minute I thought you… That you… What time is it?"

"Seven-forty." Stan eyed the gun in her hand, though her arm was lowered. "You been holding that thing all night?"

If she had the nerve, Jesse thought, she'd have slumped. Instead, she fastened a grin to her face. "Yeah. The maid never did show up. See you downstairs in ten?"

Carefully, she closed the door. To ease the panic tightening her stomach, she said aloud, "God, Stan. How could I be so careless? Forget about the monster, Carol would have killed me if I let anything happen to you."

Turning a full circle in the center of the floor, Jesse made a new vow. "This will not happen again. I swear it on my parents' grave."

Then, unable to balance the fear and the emotion

any longer, feeling uncannily unprepared for what she'd found in Slovenia, she sank onto the couch with her head in her hands.

"Boss. You truly are looking like those sheets didn't do much good after all."

Stan sidled up to Jesse in the lobby carrying a brown paper bag. Bless him, he also handed her coffee in a plastic cup. After waiting for her to sip, which she wasn't yet able to do without showing him how badly her hands were shaking, he rustled the bag.

"Muffins," he said. "Carrot and blueberry. Totally healthy."

Jesse gave him a sideways glance.

"Sugar is one of the main food groups, right?" Stan went on. "Do you think there are any foods that taste good and don't have sugar?"

"Broccoli," Jesse said.

"I mean that we actually might eat."

"You got me there." Jesse drank the coffee using both hands, found it hot and absolutely necessary to her well-being.

"Did you sleep at all?" Stan pressed.

"Soundly. I don't even remember taking off my clothes."

Well, at least that was the truth.

"I only had one beer, so I remember taking off mine," Stan said, pointing outside. "Here's our ride, I'm thinking."

A black Jaguar sedan had pulled up at the curb. Its finish was a shining ebony despite the weather. Its windows were dark-tinted. Jesse headed outside with Stan in tow, anxiously searching the street, telling herself that vampires couldn't appear in daylight, so she didn't have to worry about meeting up with any nocturnal monsters anytime soon. According to her wristwatch, it was a couple minutes to eight.

An expressionless, dark-haired, liveried driver emerged from the Jag. Jesse looked him over twice to make sure he wasn't the vamp in disguise, though her gut told her it wasn't possible. When he opened the door, a wave of leather smells hit Jesse. Her feet faltered on the curb. An ounce of coffee spilled.

That smell.

Like him.

She felt herself whiten around the edges.

"You didn't by any chance hit your minibar?" Stan queried.

"Was there a minibar?" she quipped, sliding onto the backseat.

"I wouldn't know, I'm sure," Stan said. "Drinking alone is prohibited. Mind if I have one of these muffins?"

"Go for it."

Jesse rested her head against the beige leather seat, trying not to breathe too deeply, afraid she might start quaking all over again if she did. In what had to be the hundredth time in twenty minutes, she thought back to the neat pile of clothes she'd discovered on the bedroom chair, and wondered if the evening could have been a dream, after all.

She moved her arm. *No pain.* But she was almost certain she'd been on the balcony with the vampire, a monster who had nearly killed her, then asked for her trust. He had dared to put his mouth on her, and his mouth had tasted like blood.

With a stranglehold on the coffee cup, she let a

"Fool!" slip out. Stan looked over, a muffin pressed to his lips.

"I think Elizabeth Jorgensen may have already left the city," Jesse said.

Stan bit into the muffin, not wanting, Jesse supposed, to comment on her statement by asking how she knew this. Maybe he believed those psychic-powers rumors.

"It stands to reason that whoever took her would get her out of sight fairly quickly," she continued.

"That's logical," Stan agreed, brushing crumbs off his chest. "So, you want me to fly you someplace?"

Yes. To the damn castle. Dracula's castle.

And then what?

She could not form those words.

"The officials we met last night may have something for us this morning. A place to start, hopefully," she said, instead.

"This isn't Los Angeles." Stan took another bite of muffin, gesturing as he spoke. "It's a city, only much smaller. Someone will be bound to know something."

"I meet with the senator at nine."

"You want me along, or warming up the bird?"

"Bird."

"You want to tell me where we'll be going?"

"Do you really want to know?"

"That depends. Does it involve the letters ESP?"

"You have been listening to the rumors?"

"Well…"

"What? Spit it out."

"I'm thinking you may be acting a bit odd this morning, and that it's most likely due to the fact that you're not telling me something," Stan said, spitting it out quite nicely, Jesse thought.

"I don't always wake you up by flashing myself half-naked, you mean? That kind of odd?"

Stan nodded. "Precisely."

"I had a bad dream, that's all."

"Did it involve guys in white puffy shirts and black boots, by any chance?" Stan queried.

Jesse took a few seconds to figure out how to reply to that, and gave up. "Unfortunately, it did."

"That's funny, boss, because I also had a dream about that very thing."

Jesse shot forward on the seat, her body alert, her eyes glued to Stan's ruddy face.

"And I swear to you right now that I am not gay," Stan went on, popping the rest of the muffin into his mouth. "Nope, not a gay bone in my body."

Jesse waited for more of an explanation, feeling dreadfully unbalanced.

Stan swallowed. "It's just that I dreamed that the guy was there, by my bed, looking down at me." Seeing the concern Jesse knew must have been on her face, he concluded, "So don't I feel like an ass for mentioning it, or how odd you're acting?"

Screaming would have done nothing for either of them, but Jesse wanted to scream. The monster had been in Stan's room, as she'd feared. His visitation hadn't been a dream. It was no coincidence that both she and Stan had envisioned the vampire in their hotel rooms.

Was this a warning? A monster letting her know he hadn't been kidding and that he possessed superior strength and cunning? How was she supposed to get around that?

"Okay." Stan was eyeing her soberly. "I'm starting to think the ESP thing might be contagious. I think I know where we're going in the chopper. Am I right?"

"Probably," Jesse admitted, holding the coffee cup tightly.

"The dream about the guy was an omen, or something equally as inconceivable? And strange, since we both had it?"

Jesse nodded. "I'm not sure what that means. I'm flying by the seat of my pants here. But I think, because of these dreams, the guy we saw may be connected to this case."

"Okay." Stan sighed, looking not at all happy about this new development, and also as if he had a lot more questions that he was reluctant to ask. "I sort of understand the concept of hypnosis. But I don't know how he could have put the whammy on both of us."

"Maybe I just solidified the idea of him in your head by telling you what I told you about him."

"That's likely it." Stan looked somewhat relieved as he added, "Jesse?"

"Yeah?"

"I'd prefer you didn't tell Carol."

Jesse glanced up. "About the dream?"

"About the boxers. Carol buys me little briefs. I'm definitely not a briefs kind of guy."

Jesse fell back against the seat after briefly meeting her pilot's eyes. "Mum's the word," she agreed, glad that Stan had the smarts not to press her about this. At least not right then.

"Maybe we can work out some sort of deal with the ESP stories, Stan," she said, her mind racing beyond the conversation, trying to forge ahead. Had the vampire planned on attacking Stan and changed his mind? Had the creature put thoughts into Stan's head about himself as a reminder for her to beware, and because he thought she might accept his help if a mention came from Stan?

Just as likely, the vampire wasn't above blackmailing her into accepting his help, by showing off his nebulous talents.

He was, perhaps, warning her to back off, and leave his "kind" alone. He might be trying to frighten the daylights out of her as payback for interrupting a good sprint to his ghoulish castle.

In time, is what he had whispered to her on the balcony, if the event had actually taken place. He would make his purpose known to her *in time.*

Well, she couldn't afford to wait for those answers. She was thinking about a meadow, tall white turrets and the monster's hand on her wrist, when she should have been laying out a plan for retrieving Elizabeth Jorgensen.

She kept seeing two blue eyes, with the fires of an inferno dancing behind them. Looking into his eyes had been stupid. Dracula now loomed large in her mind when a girl had been missing for a few days. Elizabeth Jorgensen might possibly be the bait this monster dangled in front of Jesse to get her to come to him, for whatever nefarious reasons.

Maybe the creature knew about Elizabeth because he'd taken her. It wasn't a big leap to see how he might be involved.

"Bait acknowledged," she muttered into her coffee cup. "Game on."

His castle would be the first place she'd look for the girl, along with an explanation for her own lost hours. Odds were that the golden monster would be waiting for her there and that she was playing into his hands. Still, she had to take the risk.

Why, though, her logical brain kept asking, would he want her out of the city, when he could have bitten her on the balcony, or in her hotel room, with no one the wiser?

Stan murmured something as he brushed more crumbs off his sleeve and offered her the brown bag. Jesse shook her head, tuned in to her own thoughts, thinking that she felt like crap already, and the day was just beginning.

Chapter 7

The advantages of being an old vampire were few. Being able to tolerate the light filtering through the tinted windows next to him came in handy at the moment, Lance decided. Not having to return to safe ground every twelve hours was another nod in his favor.

He couldn't imagine having to repose in dirt, underground, or inside a coffin like the lesser beings he sometimes thought of as the spin-offs. And he had intuition enough to realize that the sensations beating at him as he watched Jesse exit the hotel were more than mere hunger.

He was able to follow Jesse this morning because his Guardian status elevated him so far above Jesse's monsters as to be another race altogether. Yet in her eyes, he remained a freak.

Because of his blood in her veins, he had a connection to her that meant he could easily find her, keep an eye on her, as he'd tried to tell her last night. This was an aspect of guardianship he had not anticipated, but one that currently suited him. The perks of a blood bond between them made the disadvantages of being what he was almost worthwhile at the moment.

A weak cop was a dead cop, he knew. If Jesse wasn't in law enforcement, she had a similar profession. Beyond that, she was filled with a longing for revenge that would see her set up as a hunter, though it was obvious she knew little about the creatures she sought. He didn't need to examine this particular assignment of hers, and what could happen to her if she pursued it. He could see the outcome easily enough.

Wrong job this time, little one.

Then again, why should he care?

Here he was, in the city, acting like Jesse's jealous lover by waiting to see what she might do next; knowing as surely as he was beginning to know her that Jesse would be scenting the direction of the abducted girl as she sat in the car. The honing of her senses was a gift he had provided her with, though he'd offered it so that Jesse would at the very least see her monsters coming. The problem with such a gift was that it had also brought him closer to her.

He hadn't planned for this unusual side effect.

Had he?

He felt her thinking, heard her breathing, knew how frightened she was. The pull she created in him had become stronger than his vow of self-imposed exile, and serious enough to make him step outside the car, in a crowd, if he had to.

Today he would approach Jesse and try to make her see reason. She might view things more clearly in the daylight. He needed to convince her to leave before the others found her. Jesse was intelligent and, hopefully, logical. She'd have to realize she needed his help without his tipping her fear right over the edge of the abyss. But he had to be careful. Jesse Stewart carried around a blight on her soul, much like a chip on a shoulder, only deeper and much more unsettling.

Perhaps rightly so.

Staring at her car, feeling her presence inside it, Lance easily discerned her turmoil. With empathy, his own hands fisted. Would she realize her senses were on overload this morning, and that something inside her was different? Did she feel him there, watching?

If her car turned left, he thought, he'd feel somewhat relieved. A left turn would take her to the people waiting for her at the government offices. He'd try to speak to her there, in some hallway or another. If she turned right, she'd be trespassing in the city's danger zone. She might find her wretched vampires a dime a dozen there, and he'd be forced to point out her vulnerabilities yet again.

His guardianship had indeed, it seemed, stretched in scope. Not only was he watching the vampires, but the humans as well. A willful hybrid female loose in this city would make his task all the more difficult right out of the gate.

All vampires knew of him instinctively, of course. Up against him, they would perceive his position of power, his superior strength and will, even if they were ignorant of his history. Knowledge of him ran in their veins, no matter how diluted their blood had become, although this didn't mean a contemporary gang of them wouldn't try to take him on if the stakes were high enough. Stakes like cornering a hybrid female who smelled like food.

There weren't many female vampires, since they were

far outnumbered by lusting males of the species with little or no self-control. Females were in high demand. The vampires in this city would be after Jesse in a heartbeat. As no doubt they had been after the Jorgensen girl.

It might already be too late for Elizabeth Jorgensen. But he was Jesse's only hope. If there had been others like him here, things may have been different.

There had been others, once upon a time, Lance reminisced. He'd had friends until they had dispersed around the world in search of their own destinies. Perhaps they were also, for all intents and purposes, as monklike as himself. Celibate, lonely, monotonously continuous, disgusted by the way things had turned out and secretly desirous of company.

Were those things the reason he had become interested in this female, blood bond or not? Someone he had touched, twice. Gotten close to. *Not entirely human.*

Last night he'd wanted so much more from her than a sparring partner. Last night he had wanted everything. All of her. He had wanted to be a man, proving to her that he could act like one. If Jesse hadn't ever hosted his blood, that scenario may have had a chance. Then again, if he wasn't what he was, he'd never have known her at all.

It was a dangerous attraction. He was all too aware of that fact. He could manipulate the blood bond if he chose to. He could force her to his side. If he asked it of her, she would tilt back her head and offer her scarred neck to him.

Though he had never drunk from a mortal, with Jesse, the temptation hovered like a continuous rush. A long-dormant thirst lay twisted throughout his being.

His attention jerked back to the street, drawn by movement. He sat forward. As Jesse's car drew away from the curb, her heartbeat thudded beneath her pert, pink-tipped breasts, trapped by frilly white lace. He perceived this as though her life's pulse had indeed become his own. As if her spark had reignited his own flicker of life. The awareness, the closeness, the intimacy of being so close to a flash of life kept his attention riveted on her car.

Then he tightened his grip on the steering wheel, nearly breaking the wheel in two. "Damn her hide," he whispered as her car made a sharp right turn.

Chills drizzled down Jesse's back as she stared out at the passing buildings, attempting to get her thoughts back into some sort of reasonable order. The chills just wouldn't let up. She felt cold from the inside out, and somehow, as she jostled her thoughts toward Stan's side of the car, her attention kept being pulled past him to the window.

A white van cruised by. Relieved to note that the driver of the van wore a hat and a uniform of some kind, she let out a sigh. The driver had red hair and wore glasses. Not her concern.

So, where was he, then? Her new nemesis. In some dark basement, recouping his strength? If tucked away, why then did she sense his presence? His nearness ran across her nerve endings, doubling the chill factor, presenting as anxiety run amok. She actually felt his gaze, even though she couldn't see him, knowing he was close by.

None of this made sense, really. Maybe it was just her imagination running overtime.

The sky was a dark, dull gray. Jesse turned her

focus to the people on the sidewalks. Compared to Californians, Slavs seemed muted personalities in their black, navy and charcoal layers. Although the clothes were chic enough, the drabness of the city carried over on the busy walkways, making her long for the colorful glare of L.A. The hot pink of sunburned skin. The bright hues of sun and sand and ocean.

She craved a warmth she barely found these days.

Exhaling a stuttered, surprised breath, Jesse glanced past Stan again, her attention virtually yanked that way.

She saw it. A dark shadow slipping between the buildings.

Her pulse exploded, as if that shadow had been some kind of incendiary device. She knew exactly what it was, and what it meant.

"Pull over!" she snapped so curtly that Stan jumped on the seat. "Here!" she directed, and the driver did what he was told without question.

"I'll be a minute," she said, addressing Stan's inquiring gaze. "I have to make a personal call. Need privacy. Wait here for me, Stan, please."

Out of the car before the driver could step out to open the door, Jesse hopped to the curb. Hugging her coat tightly to her, and with her boot heels clacking loudly on the concrete, she approached the place where she'd seen the shadow and whispered in horror the word "alley."

Terror gripped her. There were so many reasons not to go into this alley. Too many to count. The atmosphere in there virtually rippled with the monster's presence. The air seemed to buckle. Cracks between the buildings in old cities provided plenty of dark spaces for night-loving creatures to infiltrate, and one such creature had melted into this one.

A tingle ran through Jesse's body. She went to full alert, with the outer layer of her skin covered in ice crystals. This wasn't her golden nemesis, she knew from the vibe. A cousin, maybe.

A murky space like this would suit a monster nicely. Near to a busy street, this would be a perfect spot for a filthy bloodsucking fiend to pick off a meal. Maybe even a senator's daughter.

And my family.

The tingling in her limbs became an insistent buzz she likened to pressing on a booby-trapped doorbell. A vampire had gone into this alley and she had to follow, though terrible, unspeakable things happened in places like this one.

Hell, she wasn't even sure if she could actually go in there. Already, the familiar vertigo was taking her for a spin.

Inhaling the fetid air, Jesse looked hard at the opening, trying to decide what frightened her the most, the monster or its hiding place. Damn, though, if she wasn't angry this morning, and anger was calling the shots. One tall piece of velvet-voiced, arrogant vampire scum had already gotten the better of her. She refused to upgrade that number to two. Not today. The tall vamp had told her *they* had Elizabeth Jorgensen, and one of *them* had scuttled into this hole.

Confront your fears.

You can do this.

The space between the buildings was narrow. Swallowing a blasphemous oath, Jesse squeezed through, entering a hazy world of moist stone and grimy asphalt.

She was in. A couple of steps in, anyway. The odor of the place hit her like a billy club in the face—awful, more nauseating than the leather in the car. But she had to face this alley. She had to start somewhere in addressing Elizabeth Jorgensen's kidnapping, and would begin by confronting her own personal fears.

Every fiber of her being demanded that she enter this alley, knowing what had gone in before her. She'd avoided this moment for years, had panicked more times than she could recall. After last night's show of weakness, however, her ego needed a boost.

Time to move on.

Make a leap.

Jesse took five more steps. As the hazy light from the street dimmed, she became even more certain of the presence of a creature inside. Her pulse rocketed. She heard nothing over the thundering of her own heart.

Maintain control.

But maintaining was difficult when the dank odor confronting her was disgustingly that of mold, mildew, age and grime. Fighting off a gag reflex, she inwardly chanted, *It's only an alley. Alleys aren't alive, only the things that roam in them.*

There was no room for cheating on this test. All six senses were required to catch a beast, and all six were necessary to face down old fears. She had gotten this far. Only a few more steps remained.

"I can do this."

It was a long, narrow space, four shoulders wide and looking more like a tunnel to hell. As far as Jesse could see, there appeared to be no break or turn. No trash cans lined the asphalt. There were no visible doorways.

"So, where are you hiding?" Jesse murmured, flexing her fingers inside her coat pocket like a gunslinger cracking knuckles before a showdown.

The buzz in her body had intensified with each step,

and now centered in her hands and feet. Her right cheek twitched. She felt *it,* all right, here somewhere in the periphery, its feel wrong in the dank darkness.

Encapsulated in the alley's dimness, Jesse paused. Her nerves continued to tap out a warning. *A test,* she told herself. *A beginning. Pass this one and go directly to Boardwalk.*

"Can I do you something?"

The thing had the audacity to address her, and in a voice teeming with unrepentant hunger and a heavily accented Eastern-European sprawl of syllables.

"Just an alley," Jesse whispered, her fingers closing around the wooden stake she'd brought with her today, in case just such an occasion as this one presented itself. "Not a gateway to hell."

"Well?" the creature pressed. "Cat got your tongue?"

Did it assume its lure had worked, that it had gotten some poor unsuspecting soul to follow it inside? The hair on the nape of Jesse's neck raised. Her nerves were red-hot, despite the chill. This vampire gave off the stench of moldy parchment paper, saturating the close, damp air.

Although fear edged her ability to speak, Jesse forced herself. "What," she said, "are you doing here, in the daylight? Has your watch stopped?"

Her surroundings oscillated in a crest of frigid air. *Movement.* The vamp had relocated to her right in that fishy way they had of suddenly appearing where they were least wanted without actually taking a visible step. Maybe, she reasoned, because they were neither dead nor living, the laws of nature no longer applied.

Nasty thought.

Drawing the stake out of her pocket, Jesse jumped toward the opposite wall. Her head felt light, her body moved between cold and hot. But it was too late for retreat. The thing had a bead on her and was no doubt waiting to pounce.

Up.

With a shocking bit of insight, Jesse looked up, managing not to hurl the coffee she'd ingested. The freak was there, above her head, hanging by its hands from a drainpipe. Like a bat.

Run, Jesse's warning system screamed, though she knew she couldn't escape this meeting, important on many levels.

"I wasn't sure about the bat part," she remarked, drawing on the false sense of calm cops had to adopt in life-and-death situations. Focus was everything. All senses had to remain on alert while adrenaline slammed through her.

Incensed, perhaps unused to its breakfast talking back, the vampire dropped to the ground in front of her. Landing with barely a sound, it straightened its gaunt body.

The thing was short, maybe five-six, tops, and all bones. A walking cadaver. Its white face shone like a circus clown's, its eyes black holes of nothingness. As discomfiting as those things were, they alerted Jesse to the exact spot where his withered, useless, unbeating heart would reside.

Down and to the right.

The vampire hissed, bared its teeth and moved in another blur of speed. But Jesse'd had enough of being paralyzed. Elizabeth Jorgensen was waiting to be found. Stan waited in the car. The wooden stake in her hand awaited a target, and she just happened to have one. If she didn't do this now, she might never have the nerve.

She scrambled to the side, anticipating where the vamp would end up, without thinking. Spinning on her heels, she breathed in more stagnant air, perceived a softer hiss in the silence and straightened with an adrenaline rush that made her hair stand on end.

The freak was on her before she blinked.

Terrible sucking sounds came from the vicinity of its mouth. A drip of hot, sticky saliva hit her chin as it whirled. Jesse swore, ducked again and lunged to the side. She rose to her full height, with the stake positioned in her hand, its sharp point facing out.

"Elizabeth Jorgensen," she said as the vampire grabbed hold of her coat. "You know the name?"

"Death to all foreign bitches," the vampire snarled.

"Not today," Jesse hissed back, driving her body forward with the gathered momentum of nerves working well beyond their limitations.

"Elizabeth…" she said again, without finishing the sentence.

A startled gasp came from the beast, then a curse uttered in a foreign language. Both those things were followed by a sudden burst of frigid air.

Silence fell.

Jesse stood, stunned, stake still poised in her hand. Pure unadulterated fright closed her throat as the smell of decay turned into the smell of ashes.

The stake wavered, though she maintained her grip. She stared into the dark, anticipating that the monster might rise again, not quite believing that a vampire could be killed by the force of thought alone. Because the tip of her stake hadn't touched it.

So what just happened?

"That was quite a show," a deep voice reproved, jamming her attention in another direction.

The velvety voice did not belong in the darkness of an alley, but in a bedroom. Soft-spoken, low on the register, exceptionally rich, it floated to Jesse as if on a stray breeze, bringing a familiar heat.

She spun, stake poised. A hand caught hers as she bumped into something solid, teetered sideways, then quickly regained her balance.

God, did she have the strength for round two?

"Although," the smoky voice went on, "this creature was new, and too hungry to control himself."

Jesse stood, frozen. *So, he had been watching.*

"How does it feel?" her nocturnal companion asked, stepping closer to her, his wide shoulders outlined by a ray of passing overhead light. "Being so close to a kill?"

"I didn't kill anything," she said.

"You hold a weapon."

"For self-defense." Jesse couldn't keep her hands from trembling uncontrollably. The truth was that she hadn't been prepared for one vampire, let alone two. Especially this one.

"But you would have killed him?" the golden vampire asked, his tone unemotional, smooth.

"If I had to." *And it would have removed one parasite out of how many? Hundreds?*

Thing was, she hadn't touched the gaunt monster.

"You did this," she charged, her attention on the creature whose face seemed to glow eerily in the alley's dimness.

"I didn't want such a thing on your conscience," he admitted.

"I was doing fine on my own. I had questions for it."

"And if *it* didn't answer? I wonder if you were you

planning on keeping a death count? Painting notches on the side of Stan's helicopter, perhaps?"

Jesse had to blink. In that one brief second, the vampire disappeared, glowing aura and all. Rounding on a premonition, she found him behind her.

"Now, that's just creepy," she said, holding the stake rigidly in both hands. "And the stake is still sharp."

"I'm afraid I am not so new, or hungry," he said.

Again, shadows coalesced in the space where he stood, as if filling in a deficit. As if he was an illusion after all. A dream. Some kind of terrible fantasy.

His voice, coming from Jesse's right, brought with it another shot of adrenaline. Jesse couldn't possibly have been any more alert. She pivoted and the stake bumped against his chest. He did nothing to restrain her this time and just stood there, quietly watching her with eyes she knew were light blue and deadly dangerous.

Her fingers quivered on the stake. She had a thought to drive it home, sink this big splinter into the place where the vamp's heart should have been, but wasn't. Nevertheless, she did not apply pressure. She didn't so much as poke a hole in his immaculate black overcoat, distracted by the scents of leather and wool—calling cards that didn't speak loudly of the word *undead*.

For the second time in just a few hours, she noted how something indecipherable hid behind those scents that she was unable to pin down. Indecipherable and intimately familiar.

Her thighs picked up the quiver. Deep down inside, all the way to her bones and extending to the ultrapersonal, unmentionable spaces in between, her body reacted to this vampire's scent with longing. Unwelcome. Sexual. *Vile*.

She groped for an answer to this new puzzle as her

stomach churned. He had to be doing this to her—making her perceive him in a different light. Vampires were notorious for this sort of thing. Then again, this one was out in the daylight, too, so it was pretty obvious she hadn't gotten some facts straight.

Furthermore, it didn't help that golden boy beside her didn't in any way resemble the other creature in the alley. He was way too solid and completely fleshed out. His bearing was regal, superior. Power radiated from him, carefully maintained and cultivated. Did vampires have kings and princes, or was he merely older and more experienced than his cousins?

Maybe he had recently fed on some poor unsuspecting soul, in order to look the way he did.

Thinking to take a step in the opposite direction, instinct warned that it was questionable whether she'd be able to get back to the car. Her feet weren't responding.

"Get away from me," she ordered.

"I believe you may be in need of further assistance."

"Not from you."

"Do you think you can make it out of this alley on your own? You are tilting on your feet."

The richness of the vampire's voice made Jesse's knees weaken further. Such a mesmerizing voice also went against nature, surely?

"I'm fine," she declared.

"I'm holding you up," he corrected.

He was holding her up. His shoulder was touching hers. The acknowledgment of his nearness produced a current of electricity that sparked through her body like a loose live wire.

"Are we to fight today? Here? After all?" Jesse

planted her feet in a wider stance and drew back. "Now that I have the use of both arms?"

"No fight. I told you I'd help and I meant it. I'm an ally, Jesse, not the enemy."

"How many times do you have to hear my answer on that subject?"

The vampire followed when she backed up a step.

"Damn you," she swore as he took a firm grip on her shoulder, the unexpected heat from his fingers streaking through her skin beneath her coat sleeve, waltzing along overextended nerve fibers.

"Stop it," she whispered.

As the demand left her lips, and in an exact contradiction of her thoughts, she leaned toward the warmth. Toward him. Automatically. Insanely.

Gritting her teeth, unable to comprehend why she might break her own rules, she allowed her focus to travel up. She found his mouth closed, with no evidence of vampire trickery confronting her at the moment, and no sign of fangs. His lips were full and closed tightly in his pale, chiseled face. Was the set of his mouth meant to insinuate concern?

Anomaly, big-time. A beautiful predator.

An urge so foreign hit that Jesse rocked against it. The urge was to touch him, explore, delve into his warmth. Those thoughts were more frightening than the idea of dealing a gaunt vampire a final death blow. No matter how long it had been since she'd felt completely warm or comforted, this was a false sense of those things. Trusting a vampire would be the epitome of the word *mistake.*

"Like you'd let me walk away from this," she said.

"Of course I will," he returned, as a flash of memory hit Jesse, there and gone in another passing bit of overhead light. This memory centered on his voice. She might have heard his voice before last night, in another dark place.

Where?

More memories struck with the force of an unanticipated blow. Recent stuff. This vampire had carried her to the bed, leaving a lingering perception of him as manly and strong. Leaving her with the inconceivable idea that he would be a capable, virile lover. If he were human.

Sacrilege!

Yet surely he'd had his mouth on her body. She could almost feel it there now, whispering along the curve of her neck.

Ignoring the urge to swipe at her throat, Jesse continued to hold up her hands as she retreated another pace. The vampire had to be exerting some sort of mind control, and she was caving, because the desire she was fighting was not to kill him, but to get closer to him; to tilt back her head and expose her neck. Her scar throbbed in anticipation, as if this would be a good thing. Her heart beat out a frantic refrain.

Stop! God. Stop!

"You won't be able to help anyone after I've put this stake in you," she shouted, in spite of the fact that the stake was now dangling from her fingers.

The memories were becoming jumbled. His face. His scent. Those things wrapped around her like an invisible blanket of uncertainty. Where had she heard his voice? Why did she want to trust him, when she knew better?

"You're making me weak," she charged.

"You've had a fright," he said. "Weakness is normal."

"Who are you?" Jesse realized she had only moments of strength left before she crumpled in a heap. She wasn't fast enough or strong enough to kill this vampire; that fact had become obvious. The alley was closing in on her. Without her mission to kill the vampire, the alley became a living, breathing entity, with this creature at the center of her personal storm.

She had to work for each new breath.

Instead of taking further advantage of her weakened state, the vampire maintained the small distance separating them. Jesse saw the street beyond him, and couldn't make herself move toward it. Blackness was settling over her. Too much nerve burn. Anxiety out of control.

Alley... Red... Blood.

She was dead. Just like her parents. Her time had come.

Concentrate. Separate the threads.

Put everything in perspective and in its place.

"Jesse?" the golden vampire called, his voice skimming the perimeter of the blackness closing in. "It's all right. Today, it is all right."

What was he talking about? The world was turning inside out, taking her down with it.

"Why don't you just kill me?" she said weakly in a repeat from the night before. Raising the wooden stake took every bit of strength she possessed. She concentrated on the length of wood as though it were the focus of her life.

"We've been through this, Jesse. The thing you chased in here knew nothing of the Jorgensen girl. He was little more than a pathetic scavenger, unlike the others who have taken the girl. You're not ready to face those others. Let me help you to the car."

"You really know who has Elizabeth?"

"Yes."

"Then where is she?"

"When you're ready to accept my help, I'll provide the answer. You'll know where to find me."

"You'd keep that information from me, possibly at the poor girl's peril?"

"On the contrary, I'll tell you everything when you're ready to do something about it."

The blur of the golden vampire's sudden movement merged with the blur of Jesse's surroundings. He pried her fingers from around the wooden weapon and tucked it back into the pocket of her coat. Then he dared to take hold of her again.

A stab of sensation, like hot coals on vulnerable flesh, accompanied his touch on her elbow, at once painful, scintillating and suggestive. His heat was disarming. Jesse's muscles contracted. She drew in an unfulfilled breath.

"You undressed me." She tried desperately to compartmentalize the growing desire to give her trust to this beast, fending off the idea that she'd end it all here, at last, with a creature like the ones that had brought her parents down. Not dropped from the roof of a building, but confronting a vampire on her own two feet.

"Your clothes were wet and your arm useless," he said by way of an explanation for his behavior.

"This arm?" she shouted, lifting it. "You made me think so, but here it is!"

He did not reply.

"You had no right to touch me in that way. In any way at all," she said, knowing she had to get to the car before the desire to give in to him became reality. No matter how loudly she shouted, his flame was calling hers, somehow. She was arguing, but wanted to stop. She was icy on the outside, while her insides burned… for him.

"You are stubborn. Not making sense," the vampire pointed out. "Without my help, you'll get nowhere, and may wind up dead."

The monster was benevolent now, and speaking with true earnestness? *Doubtful.* This had to be another trick. Of utmost importance was for her to remember that this was a vampire, not a man. A dead thing, not a suitor. Never an ally.

Never a lover.

This was a monster, not a savior. A thing composed of dead flesh molded to resemble a man…although he felt like a man.

"Why don't you want to hurt me?" She was torn by the rise of conflicting emotion, and in need of answers.

"Can it be something as simple as sensing a kindred spirit in you, Jesse?"

Don't say my name!

On your lips, it's sickeningly provocative.

When the vampire inched closer, his golden curls fell across his features like wings of sunlight in the dark alley. Strong arms encircled her, while Jesse's arms again hung uselessly at her sides.

Kill…him!

The directive dispersed as Jesse closed her eyes. The throb in her neck increased as wave after wave of longing, sexual, personal, made her shudder as the blackness of her surroundings faded to gray, to beige, then to white. Not the white walls of a room in an asylum—God no, not that—but the blistering whiteness of a singed soul. A damaged soul. Hers.

And in the white weightlessness a face appeared. The very pale face of an angel.

In distant memory, Jesse felt a prick. A coppery taste slid through her. A rush of liquid filled her mouth, thick, awful, difficult to swallow. She shook her head to negate the memory…and found herself waking, pressed tightly to the vampire in an unwanted embrace. A puzzling funnel of vagueness beat a path through her mind, blackening everything, including a good chunk of her former resolve.

This is wrong. All wrong.

The heat was addicting. In a perverse way, his arms felt strong and secure. The old wound on her neck blazed, and Jesse wanted to tear at her neck with her hands as she used to do, so long ago, in that white place.

No one there, back then in that hospital, had been able to douse the fire, she recalled. For years, she hadn't allowed hospital personnel to touch her. She had wallowed in the coldness of sorrow, mindlessness and regret, with her insides taken over by the flames.

She'd eventually found a way to calm those inner fires, a feat accomplished through the struggle and honing of her willpower. But she'd never been able to stand intimacy of any kind after that night in the alley. Intimacy led to sadness, pain and loss. The fire presently singeing her neck was a reminder, a throwback to everything that had come before. If she didn't move quickly in the direction of the street, she'd be unable to control what might happen.

"Lesson one," the vampire said, his tone dragging her back to him. "A hungry vampire can be ruthless. However, they are not all young and inexperienced. Rarely do they travel alone."

Jesse's stomach roiled. Beyond the scent of leather

and wool lingered an odor of ashes that had once been a monster. A creature unlike this one beside her, maybe, but how many definitions of *monster* could there be in a dictionary of the undead?

"Yes, and here you are," she choked out.

The golden head shook. Jesse thought she heard him sigh. She swore she felt a hand on her face, not leather-covered, but bare. Not the cold grip of death, but warm. In this vampire's fingers the familiar fires lapped, just like the fires of old, as if he wielded power over them, and thus over her.

She had to look up.

Had to.

She had to see exactly what she was up against.

Uttering a groan of shock, she met the intense blue gaze suggesting this vampire could drink her up by the meeting of their eyes alone. Large, beautiful eyes, topped by long, gold lashes. Endless, fathomless pools of blue, with something darker swimming behind.

Around her, the alley's dark edges disappeared as more fire, red, hot, molten, came on. Her chest imploded in an internal blaze of heat. Moisture gathered on her upper lip and between her legs.

The chilled air in the alley met her overheated skin with a hiss. Jesse swayed when she heard it. The word *run* rose from the furnace as if some external source had better sense than she did and would encourage her to get away from him, from this.

But the warnings came too late.

His eyes.

Blue eyes.

His face. So pale, and...

Familiar.

The vampire's hungry stare held her a breathless

captive. His mouth, hovering above hers, moved to form words she'd have to heed, but he didn't speak. Instead, Jesse's fleeting impression was that he was about to kiss her again. Or more likely, he'd bite her with the lethal set of canines his kind possessed.

He might prefer his meals struggling.

So then why, her mind asked, hadn't he bitten her last night, when he'd had the chance?

Her lips trembled with the strain of her internal fight versus her external motionlessness. She knew with certainty that he was going to touch her mouth with his, and that she was helpless in stopping him.

When his lips, with a blistering imitation of tender, did that very thing, Jesse tensed against him, unable to assert herself, cocooned in an immovable body for what seemed like an eternity before his fire swept her up.

Untethered, and without her anger to ground her, she thought her feet left the earth. It felt to her as though she and the vampire rose upward, above the grim alley.

His lips rested lightly on hers—hardly a touch at all, really—but she hadn't been mistaken about this last night. There was breath in him.

Breath in the dead thing.

Again Jesse thought to struggle. She was of a mind to use the wooden stake and get rid of his perfect golden carcass once and for all. Yet with the pressure of his mouth came a series of strange sounds that crippled her.

She heard flapping noises, reminiscent of banners or flags whipping in the wind. Behind her closed eyes, flashes of color accompanied the sounds: bright green, brilliant blue, electric red, and a gold that was a near-perfect match to the vampire's halo of hair.

Pungent odors arrived, very different from the wet

pavement of the alley and smelling more like straw or moist grass over muddy earth. Nothing like city smells.

The vampire's supple lips feathered over hers without resting in any one place, and the fact that she stood there became a reminder of his superior will. Jesse's reluctance slipped another notch. No one had ever kissed her, breathed on her face, dared come this close. Was this the kiss of death? Would she give in to that, too, if he asked it of her?

The meeting of their mouths brought something else with it besides turmoil. Despite the confusion and the immediacy of his closeness, Jesse heard a voice. Far off in the distance, seeming to come from the vampire's mind, a voice shouted, *"Help them!"*

Her ears rang with the stark terror in that plea until she was sure she was going to be sick. The earth seemed to revolve…

The golden vampire, the creature who held her and whose mouth had trespassed against hers a second time, quickly drew back. He turned his head to look beyond her, leaving Jesse gasping, and wondering if maybe he also had heard the voice and the panic in it.

Without the vampire's kiss, the mesmerizing inferno fizzled. Her surroundings spiraled out of control, making her a leaf in an eddy—twirling, twisting, sinking beneath the outermost levels of herself.

Green. Blue. Gold. Green. Blue. Red. Faster and faster the flashes of color and light spun…until they merged into a bleak, muddy gray. When the spinning slowed, the gray world drained, as if it were made of paint, now wet and dripping down the alley's walls. Light went out. Darkness returned.

Jesse was aware of her feet again on solid ground,

felt the crunch of grit beneath her shoes. She blinked back tears, afraid to face what had just happened.

"Jesse."

Stumbling back, she hit the wall of the closest building. Her breath whooshed out, but she held on because she was still breathing, still alive.

"Who was that?" Her voice was throaty. "Who called?"

"Your car is waiting," the beautiful, complex thing beside her announced, failing to address or acknowledge either her question or what had just passed between them. Stranger yet, his voice rang with audible sadness.

Was she supposed to speak? Hell if she could. She could barely stand, lost in the sense that she was still dreaming, and dreaming him. She was lost in the realization of just having defiled her parents' grave by finding anything redeeming here.

"Come," he said, holding out his hand for her to take.

What she needed was air, along with the reminder to continue to breathe. She needed a wheelchair and a more cooperative pair of legs. She needed to chant her mantra about control and mean it. She had picked up on something in the vampire's tone that she had missed before. A lilt. The slightest rolling of syllables. This vampire had a French accent that echoed softly in her mind. That accent meant something, was important somehow. It seeped into her consciousness without taking shape; another piece of a puzzle she couldn't grasp.

"Stan will be worried," he told her, his hand still raised.

"Stan?" Jesse massaged her temple with shaky fingers that felt as surreal as the rest of this. God, Stan would be more than worried. How long had she been in this place?

"Can you walk?" the vampire, the enigma, asked.

"I can run," she replied.

The smile he offered her was tinged with concern as he dropped his offered hand and stepped aside. His graceful movement sent another round of shivers through Jesse, and she knew unequivocally that she was screwed. This vampire had gotten to her twice. He'd had his mouth on her twice, and her body had responded to him favorably, bypassing her brain altogether.

She had allowed him to get close. She had been bent on destroying his kind and had been mesmerized by the beast's glittery bag of tricks. He was right. She wasn't ready to tackle a vampire. She had a lot to learn.

"Go, then," he whispered to her. "But remember what I've said."

Before she could tell him to jump off a tall bridge, before she could get hold of the weapon in her pocket, another voice called out, breaking the silence as raggedly as if the air and the spell that had bound her in place had been slashed with a serrated knife.

Chapter 8

"What is this?" Stan queried, marching into the alley with the brown bag still clutched in one hand. "Some sort of cell-phone hot spot?"

Stan. Wearing a scowl and his wrinkled suit jacket. Just about as far removed from vampire challenges as could be imagined, and seeming to Jesse like a knight in shining armor as he waded noisily through the dark, dead silence.

"Stan."

"You expecting somebody else, boss?"

Jesse stumbled forward, using the wall for support. "He... I—" Reaching Stan, breathing a sigh of relief, Jesse turned her head to gaze back at the alley—to find that it was completely empty.

Her heart gave one last thud.

"Jesse, I think we should go. You don't smell that? It stinks in here," Stan said.

"Yes. Go." Her tongue felt thick.

"Shall I ask what's up now or later?" he said.

"Later."

Crinkling the empty bag, Stan looked around for a receptacle. Unable to find one, he shrugged. "I would have figured piles of trash. Like a dump."

He followed Jesse to the street, walking as slowly as she did, scuffing his feet. "Sorry I ate the muffins," he said. "You shouldn't have left me alone with them, because you look hungry."

Hungry? She couldn't make sense of the term. But her treacherous body had seemed to hunger for the man…no, the *creature* whose lips had trespassed against hers.

"Can't eat," she said, tasting *him,* the handsome vampire, knowing he hadn't gone and that he was watching. His closeness rode her skin like a nonexistent breeze.

I know you're here, she thought.

"Yes, well, you're probably famished, all the same," Stan insisted, unaware of her panicky inner dialogue. "The bakery is two doors down. So what if we're a bit late to the gathering? They can't start without you."

How long? Jesse asked herself. *How long was I in that alley?*

She was so unbelievably stupid.

Choking back a cry, she jumped when Stan encouraged her forward with a supportive hand on her back. Stan, serious-faced now, steered her into the press of people on the sidewalk, where he waved for the driver of the car to wait before maneuvering her inside an open doorway.

She allowed Stan to guide her, needing time to regain her sanity.

Oddly enough, her stomach growled at the sumptuous

smell of freshly baked bread, though she still felt queasy. Stan sat her down on a stool in a room glowing faintly with fluorescent lights and lined with floor-to-ceiling windows. The lights buzzed softly overhead. Anxious, Jesse searched the street through the glass.

"Be right back," Stan said, heading for the counter to order. Then he pulled up a stool and sat down beside her. He removed a silver object from his pocket, which he carefully set down on the table between them.

Her satellite phone.

"You left this in the car," he said, placing a croissant on a napkin beside the phone and inching the napkin toward her. "I'm thinking you couldn't have made a call without it. So, do you want to talk about what's going on?"

Jesse stared at the phone. Telling Stan she had to make a call had been her excuse for going into the alley.

"Okay, eat first," Stan said, thanking the waiter for the coffee just delivered. "You're looking pale."

Jesse had to pick up the croissant, but didn't know how she'd swallow after being such a fool. It was a miracle she had made it out of the alley alive. If she'd been killed, Elizabeth Jorgensen didn't stand a chance of being found. She'd taken an unnecessary risk. She should have known better.

"Let me see," Stan began, eyeing her inquisitively. "Not the minibar, and not the hotel maid or the lack of chocolate on your pillow, so let's talk about the dream, shall we, boss? Is the dream what's eating you?"

Stan deserved the truth, of course. He was an ally and unenlightened. He might be in danger riding shotgun on this one. Also, she knew she had to talk because it was clear she couldn't be trusted on her own. Someone else had to know about this vampire in case she veered off track again. But her past was locked away tightly and not open for inspection. She wouldn't know where to begin, even if she could have.

"He's here," she said.

Stan took a moment to process her cryptic remark, but catching on didn't seem to be a stretch. "Are you saying that Mr. Poofy Shirt is actually here, in this city?"

"Yes." She found no relief in the answer.

"For real? He was in our hotel, in person? Not a dream?"

"Yes, to all of those."

Her hand flew to her neck. *No punctures.* That made two times he'd touched her without leaving a mark. He wanted to help, he had said.

No f-ing way that's going to happen.

Stan's eyes narrowed. "He was in that alley, maybe?"

She grunted a yes.

"That's why you went into that stinky hole? After him?"

Jesse's reply stuck in her throat. Stan might think she'd gone off the deep end if she admitted to anything so absurd.

He let out a thoughtful sigh and tapped the table with the fingertips of his right hand. "To what do we owe the honor of his presence? Filing a complaint maybe about the chopper breaking in on his privacy?"

"He followed me here."

Stan's eyes widened. "Okay. That's not good."

"You have no idea." Her words were whispered.

"Why did he follow you? Is he a stalker? Do we need to tell the authorities about this?"

"I'm not sure what they can do."

"We know where he lives. We can tell them."

"Again, I'm not sure how much it would help."

After a sort span of silence, Stan said, "There's something else you're not telling me."

Jesse looked into his creased green eyes. Human eyes. Fleshy, and expressive. "Yes," she conceded. "I'm sorry."

"You're not going to say he's a vampire again, are you?"

She mulled over the end results of an honest reply.

"Well, are you?" he persisted.

"Not unless you want to hear the truth."

Stan sighed again, thoughtfully. He'd be trying to rationalize this. The coffee cup he'd just twirled clattered on the table as his big hands stilled. "Puffy Shirt is a vampire, like in the movies. That's what you're telling me."

"Yes. You can go home if you want to. You can believe it or not, but in either case, he knows something about Jorgensen, and he is dangerous."

She waited for a big blowup. None came. Stan showed surprise over the fact that she might suggest such a thing as him leaving in the middle of a case. Seeing this, Jesse's heartbeat slowed slightly. Her pilot was going to give her a chance to explain, and what would she say?

"What does he know about the girl?" he asked, skipping over the other stuff, maybe not believing the vampire theory, but sensing trouble from some angle and getting right to the point.

"He said that Elizabeth has been taken out of the city, as a hostage. He said a nasty bunch has taken her."

"A nasty bunch of what?" Stan's forehead furrowed, then he said, "Jeez." Several seconds later, he spoke again. "Why do you think he's a...what you said he was?"

"I've been reading up on them. I've made it a point to know about them."

"What would make you read up?"

"There are things in my past that you don't want to know about."

"I don't doubt that's true, boss, but I need to know something, don't I, if I'm to believe this. If we're in danger in more ways than one, as you're suggesting."

Jesse nodded, swallowing back a knot of fear. "I had an experience with creatures like this once before, when I was young. The experience hurt me." More words of explanation wouldn't come. "I don't know why this one followed me or provided the information on Elizabeth Jorgensen, but he has had two opportunities to kill me, and didn't."

"Two?" Stan stood, looked around at the other people in the bakery and sat heavily back down. "He could have killed you? Does the creep have Jorgensen, himself?"

"I don't think so. He says he wants to help us find her."

Then again, Jesse thought as some semblance of reason returned, the golden vamp had taken the other vampire out before she could get any news about Elizabeth Jorgensen out of it. Was this to help her? Maybe the blue-eyed vamp had an agenda of his own for staking one of his own kind. In that case, what would his agenda be?

Stan shook his head, which looked naked without his baseball cap. He'd slicked back his usually untamed shock of wavy brown hair. "You're telling me there are people who believe they are vampires, meaning they're so bad and heartless, they're like monsters? And that some of them aspire to being helpful?"

"There are monsters. Believe that, if nothing else. Real monsters." Stan could think of her explanation any way he wanted to, as long as he realized the danger.

"So, you believe that this guy, whoever and whatever he is, knows who has taken the girl?"

Jesse found herself standing and didn't remember getting to her feet. She held on to the edge of the table with both shaky hands and glanced down at Stan, ready to scream if her neck didn't stop aching. Every time she thought of *him,* the scar tissue lit with a fresh burst of fire that inexplicably brought dampness to all the wrong places.

He had caused this sensation of lust in her. His presence stirred up an unacceptable longing buried so deeply within her that she'd thought it nonexistent. And on some level of awareness, she knew that he was gone. Finally, gone.

She sat back down. Horrified that she'd been thinking of the golden vampire as a he, instead of an it, she said, "I'm hoping this isn't some kind of sick game. On the other hand, his information might be all we have to go on."

"What if we ignore the bastard and get on with our job?"

"Is ignoring a lead an option?" Jesse knew damn well that it wasn't. Still, she wondered if the vampire was going to haunt her until he got what he wanted, whatever that might be, and whether she actually could afford to play his game. She'd had a taste of what he could do and had come up lacking. The simmering fires beneath her chin, and between her thighs, was a sign that he knew very well how to toy with her.

Or maybe she was just turned on by the challenge.

She searched Stan's face carefully. For the first time in her adult life, she felt the need to confide in someone. She wasn't sure she'd have the strength to face this arrogant vampire on his own turf, and whether she'd be able to ask a monster for help of any sort. If she stayed alive until then. However, if he spoke the truth about knowing the whereabouts of the Jorgensen girl, she'd have to take that risk.

"Let's go," she said, glancing away from her pilot, unwilling to see signs that he might already think she was as strange as the rumors suggested.

"Okay." Stan got to his feet and waited for her to rise. "It's going to be Dracula's castle, then, or does this guy have a penthouse suite nearby?"

When she said nothing, he nodded. "Dracula's castle it is."

Stan picked up the untouched croissant and wrapped it in a clean white napkin. "In that case, and if it's true what you say about this guy being bad news, do you think we might rent an armored tank? Is that in the budget?"

Jesse's heart ramped up its beat as she moved her shoulder without the slightest trace of discomfort. A thought nagged. If last night hadn't been a dream, how had her arm healed? If it wasn't a dream, then the arrogant vampire had actually dangled her from a balcony, for real, and after using his eyes to mesmerize her, had stripped her down to her underwear.

It just wasn't possible. Yet her head felt light and fuzzy thinking about it, and about being unconscious in the same room with a...

Stumbling toward the bakery's door, frantically sending her senses outward in search of a disturbance that would have the feel of vampire written all over it, Jesse was glad to see daylight, however meager, and the crowds on the sidewalk.

He isn't here.

Okay.

Breathe.

Snapping her spine straight, Jesse reset her resolve. She had a job to do, and by God she would do it, no matter who or what stood in her way. She would find Elizabeth Jorgensen.

"Alive," she muttered as her heels hit the pavement.

"Run, little dove."

Lance leaned against the wall with his hands behind his back so he wouldn't be tempted to pull Jesse back.

He had gone too far. Hoping to ease her nightmares about the alley, he'd nearly allowed her to see into her past. Her young voice called out to him, as it had, over and over, since his first sighting of her in the helicopter— only this time, she'd heard it, too. Ten-year-old Jesse's voice had come between them, dug up from wherever it had come from, pleading for him to help her parents, and for him to reverse the carnage.

It was a close call. He should have figured Jesse'd be tapping into her new senses already, and by doing so, have an open line into his own thoughts.

After such a mishap, she needed space. He'd have to be more diligent in the future about engaging her too eagerly, when all he could think about was the power of the moment when his mouth had touched hers, and the responding rush of the blood beneath her luminous skin.

She'd felt it, too.

Lance shook his head to clear it. Already he had

crossed the line. Pursuing this case further meant danger on all counts.

He didn't have to help Jesse; didn't have to place his own existence in jeopardy, or return to the world he despised. The blood would help her. Their encounter in the alley would alert her to how unprepared she was. He could walk away, go back to his domain and continue, as always. Being near Jesse meant confronting emotions long ago shoved aside, and best left there.

She was right to think him lethal. But then, he thought with regret, the others, those who had the American girl, were so much worse.

He shoved off the wall.

Surely it was possible for an immortal as strong as himself, and as disciplined, to leave this woman to her own fate, despite the fact that he had already, in essence, tromped all over it?

He shook his head again, harder this time, realizing it was too late. Jesse's heartbeat had become his. Her pulse resonated inside his chest. His blood mingled with hers, inside her.

She is my responsibility.

The woman who wore a scar at her throat like a trophy, a reminder that she had passed through hell and back, equated him with the species she despised. Yet he was a part of her, and had been for a while.

"Angel," he whispered, heading for his car. She had called him that once, and it had changed him. Had she been so wrong?

He hadn't been able to save her parents. It was far too late by the time he had arrived on the grisly scene. But he had taken care of the bloodthirsty scavengers, and one little blood-soaked girl lived on, believing for a few moments in angels. A little girl, feeble, and near to her own death, had known the difference between himself and the others on some subconscious level.

Maybe she would see this, because it seemed that he was going to be her guardian angel again, whether she liked it or not.

Jesse would come to him. She'd arrive on her own, seeking answers for his crimson kiss and for the reason she hadn't killed him in that hotel room when she'd had the chance.

He would be waiting.

Chapter 9

The senator from New York had been a mess. The memory of Gerry Jorgensen's face, downcast and overcome with lines of fear, worry and sorrow, sat heavily on Jesse. She'd seen her share of faces like his; people hanging on to threads of belief, whether that thread was religion or plain old personal willpower. But for herself, things were different. This case wasn't about extortion, terrorism or hefty return fees. This case was unique.

She hadn't been able to verbalize the words choking her. At the morning's meeting, she didn't mention the strange lead. Dealing with bloodsuckers wasn't anywhere near the realm of human comprehension. In her mind, thoughts of crazed vampires holding Elizabeth Jorgensen had coated the government offices with a slick layer of uncertainty that only she could see.

There had been no ransom note, no call in the three

days since Elizabeth had gone missing, and more than likely wouldn't be. It was possible, she supposed, that vampires needed money, but thought it highly unlikely they'd keep their fangs off a young woman long enough to organize. The officials sharing the room with the senator were clueless as to the possibilities, and her secret had made her heart ache, because it was a secret she had to keep, for now. The senator still maintained hope for his daughter's safe return.

The *r* in the word *risk* floated above her head, as did the question of whether or not the golden vampire had told the truth. If he had an agenda of his own for trying to lure her from the city, would it involve a trade? Herself for Elizabeth? A fresh blood donor?

Who the hell was he, anyway? Did vampires have names, first and last? There was no way she could have brought any of this up in such weighty government offices, insinuating that her informant might or might not be the kidnapper, and that he wasn't mortal. And if she had told them the truth, passing along the information the vampire had given her, what then? Likely, she would have been tossed out on her ear and labeled a crank in spite of her reputation and references. She would have been sent home.

Going home was not an option. She'd known this the minute the exquisite creature had stopped in that field. She'd been certain of it when his eyes had turned on her. His presence hung with her, right beside the Jorgensen girl, tearing her concentration into two equal parts.

She made all the typical moves, said the right things to the people helping the senator, without bothering to pay close attention to what the others in the room suggested. Yes, they started the usual rounds of searches. Feelers were already in place. Things were moving in manageable lines. But phone taps and security guards weren't going to help if Elizabeth had been taken out of the city by vampires.

The question of what a bunch of vampires wanted with a young girl, if not money, played over and over in her mind on a continual loop. The answer brought on a round of dry heaves. *Food*. They wanted to feed on the girl.

She'd barely made it out of the room after being shown a photograph of Elizabeth Jorgensen, a slim, pretty young brunette. Visions of Elizabeth had messed with her equilibrium as she'd rested her head against the bathroom sink, repeatedly dowsing her face with water, groping for composure and wondering how long vampires might last on the blood of one poor girl.

How long did it take for life to drain away, one drop at a time? Elizabeth might already be dead. Lord help them all if she became like *them*.

"Please, no. Not that," Jesse muttered, feeling faint from the sheer number of loose ends, and less than confident in her abilities at the moment. If the blond vampire proved credible, it would mean that a whole new world ran parallel to the known one, darker than anything anyone might imagine, and layered with its own rules. In order to confront the special circumstances of this case, and without knowing for certain what the rules governing the undead actually were, she'd have to add both knowledge and a few new skill sets to her repertoire, and wasn't sure how to go about it.

Well, actually, she did know where to start. *He* had warned her of this by telling her she'd need his help.

She'd walked in a fog to the car, and had remained silent on the ride to the airport. She glanced sideways at Stan now, having been motionless in her seat in the chopper for some time as they winged their way out of the city with no armed guards, not a single CIA agent in tow and none of the usual negotiations arsenal as they headed for the countryside.

She was on her own here. There was a good possibility she was the only hope standing between the missing girl and her death.

Mulling over her plan, Jesse peered out the window. She would send Stan off as soon as they landed, and Stan wouldn't like it. Men had a built-in protective gene that made them want to watch over the women. Even vampires, it seemed, were not exempt, if the chiseled one who had killed his cousin had truly done so for her sake.

She was putting her life on the line to explore that point, though accepting the vampire's invitation was very probably tantamount to its own death sentence. Still, it was the only thing she could think of to do.

In just minutes now, she'd know how it would turn out.

Her hands lay quietly in her lap. Her breathing was irregular as Stan darted the chopper in and out of the snowcapped mountain passes. Stan hadn't said more than twelve words to her since she'd hopped onto the seat. His face was set and his cap in place, without its usual jaunty angle—suggesting that he was waiting for the order he assumed might come any minute now.

Jesse replayed that order in her head, not wanting to be alone, scared. But being frightened wasn't anything new. Being frightened this far off the grid wasn't a new experience, either. She'd waited all these years for just such an occasion. The chance to face a vampire and reap revenge for her loss.

For my family.

There was no way she'd expose Stan to the leeches. He had been so happy with his four-hundred-count sheets. He'd looked comfy in his boxers and brown socks when surprised in the hotel doorway. If she never saw Stan again, she'd remember those things. If today was the day her time was up, it would be important to know that Stan had gotten safely away.

The air in the chopper was loaded with unspoken thoughts that made Jesse afraid to look down at the ground. If she saw the vampire there, would he be gloating? Smiling? Sharpening his teeth in preparation for a meal willingly self-delivered?

"Shit."

"You just said that," Stan remarked. "Not five seconds ago."

Glancing over at him, Jesse sensed his need for conversation.

"E.T.A.?" she asked in an attempt to keep Stan, and herself, on stable ground.

"Ten minutes, but I can always turn around," he replied.

Jesse watched Stan's frown deepen.

"Just saying," he muttered.

The plan, Jesse reiterated, was to wait until they landed before telling Stan to hit the road. She didn't have the strength to fight him and everybody else. She didn't know how to keep Stan away from the vampires. She wished she had brought the military with her, all of them loaded up with an endless supply of silver-bullet-spraying automatic weapons. Maybe even a few of Stan's tanks.

"Boss?"

"Yeah?"

"You aren't going in there alone. I won't let you."

It was a sentiment she didn't need; one that made her stomach clench. In silence, Jesse looked out over the fields. Recognizing the meadow at last, she experienced the now-familiar flicker of excitement deep down inside.

All cops had this strange love-hate relationship with anxiety, she reasoned in self-defense over that flicker of excitement, and she'd had her share of years on the beat. After a ton of stress overload piled up, the anxiety became more like excitement, fueling the need to get on with the task and see where it took her. Would she evade death this time? Facing a gun, gang, robbery, had never been like confronting an honest-to-God freak of nature. Normal reactions weren't going to get her far here. They would find the castle, tucked into the mountain like a canker, and *he* would be there.

"Boss?"

Jesse shook her head, refusing to engage Stan in conversation. She wanted Stan with her, and Stan probably felt that. She didn't want to face this alone, and had to. She had always been alone, preferring it that way. This was nothing new. Relationships hurt. Intimacy led to loss. It was the usual mantra.

However, if she had a real friend, she thought now with sadness, it would be someone exactly like Stan. Smiling grimly over that, Jesse took a stronger grip on herself. It was going to be Jesse Stewart, solo. All by her lonesome.

Drawn by a sudden chill, she looked up, saw the castle as they rounded a grove of trees. Her chest tightened.

"Who are you?" she whispered, alarmed by the scale of the vampire's lair.

His fortress was several stories high, white enough to be almost blue and topped by miles of dark slate roof.

In times gone by, this would have been the perfect spot to ward off intruders.

"Prince Charming's castle," Jesse muttered facetiously, chills covering every available inch of her body, and then some.

On this outing, she could clearly see that only a portion of the castle had fallen into ruin. A single turret. The rest of the building remained, a gigantic edifice that must contain a hundred or more rooms. Chances were good it housed at least one dungeon.

She was willing to bet it lacked a furnace.

"I didn't like it before, and like it even less now," Stan grumbled, heading for the building. "I don't suppose it needs a landing pad. You know, since vampires turn into bats. With wings."

Jesse locked her attention on the castle. She was at a huge disadvantage in a place that size, where its occupant knew all the twists and turns of his not-so-humble abode. Hell, she was at a disadvantage anyway, even if she didn't actually go inside.

"Land reasonably close," she directed, her voice registering her doubt. But this meeting was crucial. She had questions in need of answers. Maybe the vampire would give her those answers before he killed her, and she could get them to Stan. She had tracking devices in her coat pocket, her duffel bag, and taped to her underwear. She was wired to Stan through a freckle-size microphone duct-taped to her chest.

Maybe that was why her chest felt so tight.

He won't kill me for a while, Jesse told herself to soothe the gnawing pressure, and it was a good idea to hang on to that hope. He'd had two opportunities to kill her already, and had passed. He had placed his mouth on her, instead, and had whispered warnings about this case that now rang in her ears with the efficacy of a shout. Fact was, there was a good chance his warnings were only signs of greed, and that he wanted to keep the privilege of sinking his teeth into her for himself.

Well, here she was, about to knock on his front door. She'd find out soon enough which way this was to go down.

There were silver bullets in her gun and extra custom-made rounds in her bag. The sharpened stake lay in her parka pocket. She wore Gore-Tex boots with plenty of tread for adhering to slippery surfaces, and had brought a climbing rope she knew how to use. Short of burning incense in a chapel, along with a few muttered prayers, she was as ready as she'd ever be to face the devil in his own den.

"I see a flat spot," Stan announced. "Not exactly a landing pad. More like a missing driveway."

He banked, and leveled out the chopper. "Do you see anyone down there, Jesse?"

"Who in their right mind would be down there?" she snapped, then regretted it. Stan's jaw was tight. His hands were white-knuckling the controls.

"If," he said hoarsely, with a quick, meaningful glance in her direction, "you think I'm leaving you here, you are mistaken."

"You forgot the key word, Stan."

"What's that? *Please?*"

"Boss. The key word here is *boss,* and it applies to me, whether I like it or not."

Another glance from Stan that she felt, rather than saw. "Whether or not *you* like it?" he said.

She nodded. "That's no pleasure palace down there, but it's my plan to go in, and I'm sticking to it."

"I'm going with you."

"I'm going alone." There, she'd said it at last, point-blank. No taking the words back now. No misunderstandings.

"Then you'll have to fight me first," Stan argued.

"I have a gun," Jesse pointed out.

"I'm bigger and stronger than you are, and eat guns for breakfast."

Jesse would have laughed at that, any other time. She wished it was that time now.

"I'll need what strength I have for whatever I find in there," she said soberly. "Fighting with you is stupid and draining."

Stan fell silent.

"I'll have your back, then," he finally declared, turning the chopper so that its front windshield faced the castle, setting the bird down in a flurry of displaced snow. "Everybody needs someone at their back. Even you."

His statement brought an unexpected moistness to Jesse's eyes. She was, she thought, becoming a whimpering idiot, and turned her head to hide the gathering tears, refusing to let them fall. Her fear had escalated. She'd bitten her lip, and the cold made the puncture sting. Her hands, minutes ago quiet on her knees, were shaking noticeably. But she would follow her plan. Stan would get away, and she would face this. It would be step two in confronting her past, whatever the outcome.

"Stan," she began, her unspoken sentence fading with the idea of how absurd what she was about to say might sound to him. "I have to do this for reasons you know nothing about. I owe it to someone I loved."

Stan's big head swung toward her. "Whoever that is,

they'd be even happier to know I didn't listen to you or leave you here."

She did not have the energy to continue the argument. And she could not explain anything to the man sitting beside her. Any further show of friendship on Stan's part, and she was afraid she'd cave. Already the icy air flooding in when she pushed the door open made her want to scream. The skin surrounding her scar pounded, keeping time with her pulse.

In a hundred rooms, there were at least a thousand windows, she estimated. Was the glorious bastard with the golden hair observing her from one of them? Sharpening his canines?

Tearing off the headset, Jesse jumped out of the chopper, landing squarely on both feet in the slush. Stan was powering the bird down; she waved at him, pointed adamantly to the sky. "Go," she shouted above the whir of the blades. "Please," she added. "Please, Stan."

And Stan, processing the direct command, gave her a look of sad weariness, then finally nodded his head.

Standing rigidly against the wind and the debris the chopper kicked up, with her legs apart, her head lifted and her eyes blurring with frozen tears as Stan did what he was told, Jesse watched him lift off—against his better judgment, and against hers.

She thought about all the times she had successfully reunited missing children with their loved ones, and how often she had faced dangerous bastards and nutcases crazier than squirrels. Why not, she thought, go all the way by confronting the undead?

Taking in a big gulp of icy air, Jesse pressed a hand to her chest and whispered "testing" into the microphone to make sure her vocal cords were working.

* * *

She had come.

What had it cost her to do so?

Lance moved quickly through the castle's passages toward where the chopper had left his guest. Her presence was bright, like a night-light in the dark.

He had not called her to him. It had been her decision to seek him out. Did that make her extraordinarily brave, or foolish?

Tuning his ears to the fading sounds of the helicopter, far off now as it flew over the forest, Lance's interest began to simmer.

Jesse was alone.

Damn her, alone.

He could try to protect her from the creatures she sought, but who would protect him…from her?

Hesitating in his flight down a long stone stairway, feeling her through several layers of granite as if she stood before him, in person, Lance resolved that others in the distance were also sure to turn their attention this way. From the underground dens where his off-kilter relatives hid from the light, those vampires would soon realize that humans rode in helicopters. With hearing similar to radar, they'd be able to perceive the chopper's waves of displaced air in the quiet landscape surrounding their hiding places as being unusual. Even those knowledgeable about himself—his strength, age and power—might venture this way by nightfall, if hungry enough.

At the worst, he had until dark to speak with Jesse. At best, if he could quickly get her inside the castle's thick walls, he might have twenty-four hours with her before having to lock her up and toss the key, for her own safety.

That was, after all, why he had lured her here. To keep her safe.

Sighing over the image of Jesse being locked up anywhere without a fight, Lance hurried on. The little hybrid deserved to know the truth, and that she had built her life around a false premise. She hadn't lived, after her brutal attack, because of any miracle of therapy, but because of what she'd been given. A gift that had left her with a foot in both worlds. How was he to know that this gift would also insure that she'd never completely fit in with the rest of the human race? How was she to understand that, if he didn't enlighten her?

Yet telling her about his world, including her in it by confessing what he'd done to make her this way, meant he would have to break the ancient oath ruling his own existence. Explaining what had happened to her would mean telling her about himself. A risky concept.

Confessions had never before been a temptation. Not once since his creation, his rebirth, had he uttered words to define himself, and what he had become. Rather than tell his story to the other woman he had loved, so long ago, he had driven that woman away.

Maybe, he thought now with a powerful lunge in stride, he just hadn't loved the other one enough. He didn't recall ever feeling like this: anxious, energized, wary. Jesse had tugged at his heartstrings early on, and continued to do so.

So little, the young Jesse had been. So perfect, so frightened and brave. It was a shock to know that she still had a hold on him, and that he thought of nothing else but seeing her again, being near her, if only for a few more hours. True enough, by giving her a sampling of his blood, he had stretched the boundaries of his oath as a Guardian. Still, he had been careful not to truly harm Jesse either time.

He who had survived duels, tournaments, battles, plagues, wars and the sluggish passage of time, at last felt the residual beating of a heartbeat that had been dulled for centuries. He was drawn to the woman he'd shaped into something special, provoked by his own creation.

He'd been famous in some lifetimes, in his own way, he thought as he headed down the staircase, and anonymous in others. He had been both honored and despised, reviled and rejoiced. And always alone. Jesse wasn't going to change that. Nevertheless, his choices were to keep the vow of silence fully, or break it. His options were to help keep Jesse alive by locking her safely away, or else tell her everything and hope she'd leave the country before anything worse happened to her.

There was a third alternative he didn't want to contemplate. A terrible one. He could give her more of what she'd need in order to survive this fight. More blood. His blood. Shore her up, further the connection as the blood built up within her to the level of a new strength. If not actually bringing her over to his world, coming precariously close.

Either way, kept in the dark or dipped in the light of understanding, the hunt for Elizabeth Jorgensen would be Jesse's coming of age. As well as his own, perhaps.

"What will it be, Jesse?"

Hunger for her filled him as he strode on, that hunger reminiscent of raging need that was nearly all-consuming and an entity in and of itself. He had helped to create the very thing that attracted him now. He had done this.

And she was here, within reach.

* * *

His dark-haired, brown-eyed hybrid stood there, unmoving, as he threw open the great oaken door with a force that echoed through the castle's foundations. Never ready for the full effect she had on him, Lance stopped abruptly.

Out of her element, Jesse looked small, not much more than a child, as she stood a few paces away, bundled in a heavy orange coat, with a green canvas bag dotting the snow by her feet. A courageous, fierce child, who also looked cold, frightened and uncertain.

Although she held no weapon in her hand, it didn't take an immortal's keen senses to know she'd be prepared. He smelled the iron of the gun at her back, and more weapons were stored in the bag. Searching her face, noting her downcast eyes, he said, "You must be frozen. Won't you come inside?"

Must get you inside. You are way too conspicuous out here.

Her reply was terse. "You're going to play the part of host? Lord of this castle?"

"It is my home," he said.

"Really? Maybe you've just taken the place over from its former occupants."

"I'm afraid it actually is my home, lock, stock and barrel, as the saying goes. My refuge, if you will."

"Yet you told me about it."

"Actually, I didn't."

He watched Jesse process that, knew she delved back in memory to seeing him in the meadow. He also saw that she wasn't going to ease up. She shifted her weight from one foot to the other to gain better purchase on the icy ground.

"How many humans have you invited here? I wonder,"

she said, perhaps rhetorically, not voicing the rest of her thoughts on the subject.

"Two. Humans," he replied, using her delineation.

"You said to trust you, so I suppose you won't warn me if this is a mistake," she said.

With his gaze riveted to her chilled, expressionless face, Lance fought the desire to make her look up. *One little suggestion, and you will do as I ask. But then, what sort of host would I be?*

"Isn't it a bit late for this conversation?" he remarked. "I did mention that your quest for the missing girl, in this instance, is a mistake. You knew the danger in coming here, and yet here you are, alone. Unless you have reinforcements in the trees, awaiting your signal."

He didn't have to tear his attention from her to know that wasn't the case, and that no one waited in the distance. It was just Jesse and a tiny arsenal of weapons that he could flick away with a simple hand gesture if he chose.

He wondered again why she had dared this, and if her blood had dictated this meeting without her knowledge.

"Why don't the officials in the city know about you?" she asked, her discomfort obvious in her tone. "Does anyone around here know about you, and what you are?"

"Some of them do," he admitted. "However, it has been a long time since I had contact with any of my neighbors. It wasn't a pleasant sort of contact when I did."

Jesse appeared to be surprised by that. Her beautiful brown bloodshot eyes opened wider.

"So," she said, "if I had mentioned to the men at

the meeting this morning about the vampires holding Elizabeth, they would have understood? Believed?"

"They wouldn't be here, as you are, but yes, they may have understood. Some of them, anyway."

"Why wouldn't they have been here?"

"I seriously doubt you'd want to know the answer to that question."

"Oh, I'm pretty sure I would," she insisted.

"Then I'll tell you, if you'll come inside."

"I don't think I'm ready for that. How about if we talk out here?"

Lance understood her reason for being on his doorstep. He had anticipated this very thing. She had come to him prepared to barter for whatever information he had regarding the Jorgensen girl. Short of that, she planned to use the weapons she'd brought with her to gain the information.

She wasn't sure he was telling the truth, and trying to gauge which way this current confrontation was to go down. If it turned out he had something concrete to offer, she was, by her presence here, willing to offer up something to return the favor. That thing very possibly was herself.

Lance almost grinned at the absurdity of it all. In order to help her, he had to earn her trust. Not tossing her over the side of the hotel obviously hadn't done the trick.

This courageous beauty was, in essence, agreeing to sacrifice herself for Elizabeth Jorgensen's return. Make a trade. What drove her to this? Her own hopelessness coming to the fore? Joy of watching the happy family reunions of others?

Her willingness to sacrifice herself dazzled him. She had put her blood to good use, and for decent causes.

She would be a respectable adversary for anyone on the wrong side of the law. Yet her presence here also indicated that her wounds went deeper than he had at first seen, if her own life mattered so little to her.

There was a certain recklessness in her stance, he noted. Her face was pale, but her eyes, red-rimmed from lack of sleep, still shone. Jesse's vendetta against the monsters responsible for the death of her family had been temporarily shoved into the background, overtaken by her need to help another young girl fight an unknown fate.

Jesse was living vicariously through the victims she helped. In this case, Elizabeth Jorgensen. In the happy endings of others, if there were any, Jesse might imagine she gained closure on her own issues—though this was never really the case.

She knew what vampires did. She maintained no illusions about what would happen to her if she met with them, after her brief encounter with himself and the scavenger in the city's alley. She realized all too well that she couldn't stand up to a vampire, really, and that in a battle of wills and muscular strength, he would win.

Yet here she stood.

His admiration for her was no small thing. For the purity and strength of her convictions alone, he wanted to reach out to her, comfort her, as he would have done when he was mortal. But he wasn't that person now.

Lance's hands fisted, a subconscious tensing. Jesse didn't want consolation, and hadn't come here to get it. Nor would she accept any that he offered. In her eyes, he was the enemy. She was here for information, ready to barter whatever she could, her face as white as the snow at her feet, but undeterred.

How many successful cases and happy reunions will it take for you to find peace, Jesse?

With my blood inside you, helping to drive you, is peace possible? Alas, I've never found it.

"Very well," he said, feeling a surge of caution about telling her anything right then, drawn to Jesse with an intensity that set his teeth on edge. "I'll tell you something, a reward for being here."

The need to be close to her wouldn't benefit anyone in the long run, not her, not himself, he concluded. But he couldn't take his eyes from her. Although he was loath to hurt her further, hurt is what she had come here for. And there was always a chance the Jorgensen girl would still be alive when they found her.

For now, no matter what their agendas might be, he had to get her inside the castle walls, contain her scent and her presence here and keep those things from reaching others. He needed time with her in order to decide how to proceed.

"In the past, certain officials in this city made a deal with the creatures you call vampires," he explained, since it was clear Jesse wouldn't budge without some show of faith on his end.

He watched her features fall with just those few words.

"A deal with vampires? You're lying," she said.

Lance shook his head. "You asked for the truth, and came a long way to get it. At my invitation, and as my guest, I see no reason to lead you astray."

"Can't you?" she snapped. "When I can think of a few reasons without trying hard."

She'd bitten her lip. A drop of blood, now darkened with cold, beaded beneath her teeth like a ruby gemstone.

Lance took a step forward, catching himself before taking another.

"What deal?" Jesse demanded in a voice that had noticeably lowered in volume, either from cold or disbelief. "What kind of deal would anyone make with a vampire?"

"You are frozen. Your heart is sluggish," he complained.

"Screw that. Tell me what you know. Clarify."

All right, Jesse. Another hint.

"A deal was struck for the officials not to notice a few missing people each year," he said, then waited for her reaction, which came swiftly.

"No!" she shouted, horrified as the meaning of that disclosure settled in. "For what? What could possibly cause anyone to turn their backs or make a deal like that? Killing innocent people?"

"In return for not noticing the missing people, the vampires were to stay out of the city."

Against her bloodless face, Jesse's arteries stood out like veins of blue marble. The ruby droplet on her lip had turned as black as the night to come, and that speck called to him with a voice of its own.

Staring at her lip, feeling his own blood jump in response, Lance carefully held himself back from the quick rise of the forbidden thirst that gnawed at his insides.

"You told me they were all over the city," she said. "The vampires."

"Vampires, like everyone else, sometimes renege on a deal if it suits them. They weren't the only ones to change direction. The city officials did not always honor their own agreements. After many people went missing, complaints started coming in. The officials faced a public outcry."

Jesse's gaze rose further, seeking truth.

"Vampires were humans once," Lance continued. "Every one of them, at one time, walked and breathed and made choices, for better or worse."

Tearing his attention from her lip, Lance swept his gaze over the rest of Jesse's face. He said, "People are both good and bad, liars and saints. A vampire's personality changes when it dies and reawakens to its shocking new world with the ravages of hunger upon it. As in all worlds, there are decent creatures you call monsters, and real ones."

He waited for her to either say something or challenge his own place in that world he had so briefly described. She didn't do either.

"Vampires reanimate, creating more of their kind, whether by accident or on purpose," he went on. "Each time a vampire creates another vampire, the blood in their veins further dilutes, so that every new generation of vampires has better odds of veering off balance and forgetting former alliances. And so on. The original blood of an immortal is ancient. The form it has taken in the 'bloodsucker' population is what drove me here to this castle's remoteness in the first place, away from all of that, not toward it, as I had vowed."

It was the reason he and the others like him had been created—for overseeing those others stumbling accidentally upon immortal life. Culling the good from the bad. A divine executioner's task. Yet there were only seven blood brothers in the beginning, and only seven today if they had all survived. Their creator had died after giving birth to the Seven, drained of the blood she had willingly given to them—blood that was royal, beyond the limits of the history of civilization, and preserved in the vascular bundles of himself and the other six of his true brethren.

Some of that blood now swam in the capillaries of the woman across from him.

Has it brought you here, Jesse?

"There are hundreds of the creatures you call vampires in this part of the world alone," he said.

"Liar," Jesse repeated weakly, the light of defiance dimming in her eyes.

He needed to tell her more. Explain enough to get her moving. Tell her that guarding against such fanged hordes, worldwide, was a pathetic plight, and how his vow had enlarged over time into the necessity of helping the mortals those monsters came into contact with. But the thought of his blood mingling with hers, inside her, coupled with his own rising thirst, was a seduction, a thrill akin to puncturing a nerve. He wanted to make love to her, and merge their bodies. She alone was brave enough, strong enough, for a tryst with his soul. Maybe his loneliness would finally be abated with a woman who was no mere woman at all.

You would know the truth if you looked, Jesse. Don't you know you're special?

"Please," he said. "Come inside."

She didn't move.

Come, Jesse, he sent to her, tapping into the bond that had shown up on her lip as a crimson jewel. A bond she had not even begun to acknowledge, at least on the surface.

She took a step, holding back as best she could, uncertain as to why her foot had moved.

Come.

She took another rigid step, her expression stricken with understanding. She knew what he was doing.

With a sideways shift and a slight bow from the waist, Lance moved aside, leaving the doorway to his castle clear.

Chapter 10

A bombardment of sensory input rushed at Jesse as she stepped across the castle's threshold, best summed up in stunted, singular adjectives. Ancient. Cold. Freaky. Frightening.

Chilled to her marrow and beyond, she was too frozen to shake warmth back into her cramped muscles as she soaked in the details of her surroundings. Her nerves were on full alert.

She stood in a vaulted hall composed of bare stone walls and stone floors, all that rock probably whitewashed at one time and now aged to a gray patina. Funny color, she thought, for vampires who can't stand silver.

She had expected years' worth of dust and piles of rubble, and found neither. The place was empty. There wasn't a stick of furniture in sight. No paintings, rugs or drape of fabric warmed the place, providing an inkling of someone in residence. That's because some*one* wasn't.

Some*thing* was.

In testament to that, she saw no windows in the great hall—no big surprise—though light slanted downward in ribbonlike streams from somewhere high overhead. Candles hung from sconces attached to the walls around her, if not exactly mimicking hazy daylight, then producing a similar effect. The result of all this dim, drafty bareness seemed as imposing to Jesse as the castle's fortresslike facade. Neither of those things compared with the problem of facing the creature who reigned here.

As her unearthly host walked past her, Jesse rode out another chill. She remained just inside the hall with her back to the door, ready to run if the need arose. Working to quell her rising panic over being alone with this creature in his windowless lair, she studied more details of this vampire prince and his nightmarish palace.

As on the first time she'd laid eyes on him, he wore a white untucked shirt, this time over dark, loosely fitted pants. He wore the black knee boots. Once again, he seemed impervious to variations in temperature, and even more inhuman for it, up close.

The icy breath Jesse had been holding hurt her throat. A nerve-racking, sharp stab of anxiety dissected her emotions—no help at all in warding off her body's continuous quaking.

What would this creature do now? Would her life continue or not? Facing those possibilities, she had to admit, reluctantly, that the bastard across from her was nothing short of stunning.

The bleak gray surroundings made him stand out

even more than usual, and quite exotically, as if a set designer had created this scene for him to star in. The black pants, white shirt and unblemished ivory skin, when contrasted with the starkness of the silver-gray room, made him seem almost colorful, and definitely the center of attraction. His blond curls that she'd likened to a halo gleamed here just as unnaturally in the candlelight.

Jesse swallowed her fear, refusing to address the disturbing words gathering at the back of her mind. *If only he were human.*

"It has been a long time since I told a lie," he said, halting on a stone step, expecting her to follow as his bare, long-fingered hand reached for the carved banister of a stairway leading upward and out of sight. "At one time, I was heralded for my honesty."

"Then what happened?" Jesse parried, her gaze riveted to the swinging movement of his hair against his collar as if some hidden clue remained clouded by all those curls.

She allowed her attention to drop to the open neck of his shirt and the show of more taut skin, and fielded the urge to run her hands over him to prove to herself that he was what he was. More disturbing, a snap of heat accompanied the thought of having been up close and personal with him, twice.

Hypnotism? Mind control? *Pathetic. Dangerous.* Was she merely picking up on what she supposed his thoughts might be? The intensity of his stare brought up another word. *Devour.*

Keep it together. Don't give in to whatever he's doing to you. Fight.

The vamp above her on the stairs smiled wearily, as though he had indeed read her mind and was sorry getting close wasn't going to be a possibility. His expression seemed to hold more than a hint of sadness.

Jesse shook off the shiver of apprehension working its way through her body. The vamp's appearance had to be some sort of glamour. Nobody was this perfect. There was a better-than-decent chance this creature's looks had been artificially generated. He could, in fact, be a hundred years old and sleep in a coffin.

Jesse continued to avoid his eyes, knowing the possibilities awaiting her there, and fearing them. The loss of her will could not be condoned. She had to be careful.

She began to flip through her mantra.

Losing control is not an option. I've fought too hard to maintain, to lose it now. Stay on top. Don't give in.

Mid-mantra, her stomach turned over with the desire to chuck it all and look into his eyes. Stand up to him. Show him that someone would dare. All cops and law enforcers looked into the eyes of their adversaries to assess whether anybody was home. Avoiding this vampire's gaze was wearing on her. Her body, quite apart from her mind, wanted to address this—which meant that anxiety was chipping away at her reasoning powers. She needed to move, work, fight, get somewhere.

This is what they did. Lure with their looks. She knew this.

The cavernous room seemed to echo a whispered *Beware.*

"It's actually quite comfortable upstairs," her host said, breaking the silence Jesse only then realized had lengthened as he turned to take several more steps with his perfectly proportioned legs.

He moved as lightly as if his body were composed

of clouds instead of muscle, though she could see the muscle beneath his white shirt. He was a thing of grace and brooding angles, just as she'd first noted in the meadow. A brilliant, if toxic, collection of ingredients, so flagrantly like a man in shape and substance.

"What? No dungeon?" Jesse quipped.

"Oh, there are several dungeons. I doubt if you'd be comfortable there, though. And as I've said, you are my guest."

"I brought protection."

"I know," he said.

"How do you know, just to be clear?"

"I can smell what's in your bag and tucked at the small of your back, just as I can smell your fear."

"What does it smell like?" she asked.

"The metal?"

Jesse shook her head. "The fear."

The vampire turned toward her fully, his hair falling in silky curtains around his face. Jesse caught a breath, then chastised herself for it. The rawness of his energy reached out to her, just as if he had extended a hand. The room virtually expanded with his presence, pushing outward so that the air moved in and around her. If she closed her eyes, she thought, she'd imagine him beside her, breathing on her neck.

Her scar pulsed in reaction to the thought. At least that small bit of herself recognized him for what he was. Monster. The same kind of monster that had branded her in the first place.

Putting a hand up, Jesse stopped with her fingers halfway to her throat as a flash, like a hidden-camera lightbulb, lit her mind so suddenly, she winced in the dim gray hallway.

White shirt. Halo of fair hair. Energy.

Those concepts rode the fringes of her subconscious, telling her this creature was familiar. Not being able to place how she knew him was driving her insane. She'd felt this every time they'd met. But maybe that, too, was a false sense of security he'd planted in her mind so she would follow him up the staircase. So that she'd trust him, as he asked.

God. Extra caution was required to separate the threads he was weaving, lest she be caught in his web of deceit.

"Iron," he said, his smile slightly dissolved. "Fear smells like iron. Also like the ozone of an impending storm."

"You think I smell like that?"

"Yes, only better."

"You smell like this place," Jesse said.

"How so?" he prompted, surprise lifting his tone so that it echoed off the bare stone.

Tossing the flip reply that had been on her tongue, Jesse went for truth instead. "Yours is the smell of rocks and the lighted wick of candles."

Even those things didn't fit him precisely. She tried to be more specific. "Leather and pale skin…" Her description trailed as another flash went off in her mind, highlighting a memory that may or may not have been real this time; one that was, as always, partially hidden, elusive and dangling just beyond her grasp.

She couldn't be sure about what was real. She'd seen this creature in the alley that morning, so picturing him surrounded by darkness wasn't a stretch. What, then, about the red haze in this jagged bit of memory? The very deep crimson aura around him that triggered her anxiety alarms?

"I've encountered smells like those before," she concluded. "I can't place or describe them exactly."

"Do they bother you?" he asked.

"Shouldn't they? I suppose you're causing this? Instilling a false calm so I'll be caught off guard?"

"I'm doing nothing of the kind. Well, perhaps I am, in a way. I'd prefer, however, to think that anything I've done is to *prevent* you from being caught off guard."

"Why do you care about what happens to me?"

"Caring is what I was created to do. Although I may have forgotten about my task for a while, you've managed to bring it all back."

Caring? Was he serious? Beyond that, was he trying to make a point? If so, she didn't get it. Vampires took lives. Vampires didn't care about anything other than their next meal. Yet this vamp was suggesting that bloodsuckers had feelings, morals. What a crock! In no possible universe could a being with the ability to *care* have done to her parents what had been done to them. *No way in hell.*

Still…some part of herself, some chip that had detached from the more reasonable parts, wanted to understand what was going on, really. She wanted to make sense out of all of this. Was he going to help her find Elizabeth Jorgensen, or did he have another motive for getting her here?

Did the fact that she was still alive mean anything?

Concentration was important, and she was having a hard time keeping hold of hers. She was slowly losing the ability to focus, aware of self-control inching away. She wanted to explore the familiarity angle. She needed the time to think and gather herself together, and didn't have that luxury. Darkness was a couple of hours away. She'd planned on being in and out of here before then.

"You're willing me to be at ease?" Her hand finally covered the scar on her neck, though holding it didn't do much good in keeping the ache to a minimum.

"Are you at ease?" her host asked.

Her silence lay heavily between them.

"Then I'd be incompetent, if that's what I was going for, don't you think?" he concluded.

"Why am I here, since you're going for honesty?"

"You want to know about Elizabeth Jorgensen. I've found out where she is, and you've come to ask for my help in getting her back."

"Have I asked for your help?"

"You're here, aren't you?"

Jesse's anger rekindled. "Yes. That's why I've come. Not to be your guest, your dinner, or to waste time. Finding Elizabeth is what *I* was created for."

"I know that, too," her host conceded in the same gentle voice he'd used that morning to try to soothe her. "We'll get to that. My housekeeper makes a good cup of tea," he said, turning from her, heading upward. "Unless you'd prefer something stronger? My housekeeper is not like me, in case you're wondering. I don't, nor have I ever fed from her. I have not made her my minion. You can ask her if you like. Her name is Nadia."

"How will I know she's not…"

"You will know, I promise. I can also assure you that we're not in the habit of drugging anyone by way of a teacup or wine goblet. The dungeons are completely out of the question, being that they are in disgusting need of repair."

The vampire actually grinned over his shoulder at her after saying that. It would have been a heart-stopping grin, too, Jesse noted, coming from a full mouth like his—an intriguing mouth that not only hid the wrong kind of teeth, but a mouth that had recently rested on her mouth. Except for the fact that her heart had stalled one too many times lately. Heart-stall twice in two days was unacceptable, unnatural and taking things too far. This time, she had hoped to be prepared. It was too late if she wasn't.

"You seem unconcerned about time being of the essence," she said.

He stopped and turned back. "No one is more aware of that fact than myself. However, a plan is needed, don't you think? Details? I promise we'll get to it as soon as you've gotten to know me a little better."

"Is Elizabeth Jorgensen resting?"

"No. I am certain that she is not."

The vampire was not going to give in and she couldn't make him. If Elizabeth was dead when they got to her, Jesse was going to take it out on this creature. That was a promise she made to herself.

Rolling her tense shoulders, she hoisted her duffel bag and put one foot in front of the other, walking warily toward the staircase, heading toward *him*. If she didn't look up, maybe she'd be all right, at least for a while longer.

One step up, and Jesse hesitated with her hand above the banister his hand had skimmed, afraid to touch anything having to do with her host. The place was probably booby-trapped. Although her fingers were trembling, she gripped the railing anyway, and hauled herself onto the next step.

He was watching. His attention was like heat; the hot and creamy kind that accompanied passion and slipped between your legs. The kind that made women come unglued if they weren't careful…and the sort of intimacy she'd avoided so far. Which made this particular show of the vampire's power to lure all the more sinister, and stopped her from reaching for her parka's zipper. There was nothing remotely normal about her attraction to him. It was disconcerting that she'd tuned in to his sexuality. It had to be true that vampires exuded special pheromones that could dial right through an unwilling victim's defenses. The Dark Seduction that lead to total surrender.

She glanced up accusingly. Her brutally handsome host shook his head.

"You are merely opening up to the possibilities," he said.

"What possibilities would that be?"

He was a master of the "concerned" expression. In fact, if it were possible for him to look paler, at that moment, he did. Was his wary demeanor insinuating that he didn't know about the oddly erotic sensations he caused in her? That he wasn't toying with her on purpose, or causing these unwanted feelings of arousal?

Maybe...

Looking up at the vampire—at the set of his features and the way he stood there, Jesse knew suddenly that he really didn't want to kill her, and that he actually expected to help her with this case.

It was as if she had tasted light—that same light she'd sampled that morning when his lips brushed hers. If truth had a texture, this was it, soft, and not too bitter—though this new awareness wasn't altogether free of the need for concern, because the light was rimmed in scarlet.

"I don't think I like you having such an advantage," she said. If this creature wasn't planning on biting her, drugging her or tossing her into a dungeon, there was something else he wanted from her in return for his help. He expected something. And it would be a whole lot better if he looked more like the gaunt freak she'd tussled with that morning, instead of himself.

"If you're so expert at mind games and in tweaking other people's perceptions of you, what do you need me for?" she added. "Why not just go and get Elizabeth Jorgensen, yourself?"

"Is that what you want?"

No, she wanted to shout. She didn't want the Jorgensen girl taken from vampires by another vampire. The thought of how Elizabeth might react to such a thing made her shudder. But she would have accepted it, all the same, if this vampire proved to be as good as his word. The end result was the prize here. The Jorgensen girl's safe return.

"You said I'd need to learn a few things in order to get Elizabeth back. Why don't you just tell me what I need, so I can get on with that?"

The vampire's hint of a grin, whether sad, amused or condescending in origin, showed very white teeth, two of those teeth slightly longer and obviously sharper than the rest. *Fangs.*

Jesse rode out a wave of shock. She had wanted the truth, had asked for it, and the truth is what she was getting, from between lips that had rested on hers. Possibly she'd find out what other secrets he held if she looked into his eyes. She just wasn't stupid enough to try it again.

But she wanted to.

He was doing something to her, all right. Fangs. Pheromones. Remote castles. It was scary stuff, and no matter what he had to offer that he hadn't yet mentioned, she was in trouble by remaining to find out. The heat of his nearness hadn't gone, despite the evidence of his species. He was affecting her, big-time, and looked like a god up there on the stairs. A god with a bite.

Her fingers tightened on the banister. She didn't so much as turn her head to look at the door. Because of Elizabeth Jorgensen? Because she had her own point to make—of being able to handle this, of standing up against forces of nature so far beyond human reckoning as to be completely alien? Because she did not fear death, and every moment of the last twenty-odd years had been borrowed?

"There is a fire upstairs," he said. "I will explain everything to you there. Come," the lord of the castle urged, and Jesse imagined she felt his gaze slip through her wavering veneer, again.

Her gaze rose a few centimeters. Not to his eyes. If the creature's pheromones could get to her from several feet away, his eyes would possibly seal the deal.

Or those fangs.

When he turned, Jesse followed, drawn upward as if drafting in his wake, hating every step she took and dreading what she'd find in the upper reaches of his domain. If he had information, she needed him, even though each step she took distanced her from the exit, and escape.

She had finally gone insane. Around the bend. Setting one foot inside this place had pretty much confirmed this. As she eyed the vampire's wide back and the way his shirt fluttered so softly over it, and as she watched the silent sway of his gleaming curls, she found herself hoping with all her might that Elizabeth Jorgensen was alive. She hoped to God that all this wasn't for nothing.

Rubbing the uneven ridges of her scar with nervous fingers, trying to ease her growing fear, Jesse realized that she should have brought the army. She really should have.

"Stan," she whispered, without tapping on her chest to make sure her pilot was listening, wondering how much he had already heard. "Are you there?"

There was just no energy left to regret the fact that no reply from Stan was possible through a one-way transmitter.

Death. Lance remembered dying, sometimes relived his final breath of fragrant springtime air. He would never be free of the memory of the moment he had ceased being human and had been reborn to the Blood. Vivid were the associations of leaving the known plane of existence, and the pain accompanying the event. The excruciating trauma of exchanging one kind of existence for another.

He wanted to tell Jesse he was not the undead, as people tended to think of his half-crazed, distant relations, but no longer living on the human plane of existence, either. He was unable to die again, except by the most extreme means, while he also had all but lost the will to continue.

He could mention that he was no longer privy to the variances of the seasons, illness, dark, light and love, having long ago surpassed all but the latter of those things. What kind of female would understand the turns his life had taken, and where it had led?

There had been only one female of his breed that he'd ever known. His creator. Yet look what she had done, and what had been taken from him.

Not long after his change, and the demise of his maker, he had adored the fair Gwen. Though in the end, Gwen represented nothing more than a wisp of life he had no right to grasp on to when he had become so very much more than that.

Now, here he was, contemplating removing Jesse from her world and everything she knew, when other lives were at stake. Vibrant Jesse, serious Jesse, hell-bent on setting the world to rights, had a mysterious hold on him. The woman who looked at him with the little girl's eyes.

"Help them!" little Jesse had pleaded in that alley so long ago, her face a bloody mess as she screamed for him to aid her parents. She had not wanted help for herself. She'd had no thought for her own safety.

"Help them!"

Those memories drifted in the stairwell as he climbed, with Jesse behind him. It seemed that Jesse would still give up her safety for the benefit of others, which made his own current needs selfish by comparison. Nevertheless, he knew something of the woman behind him now. He'd seen how desperately she wanted to be saved. She knew it would take someone so much stronger than herself to rescue her. Someone able to cope with the issues coiling through her.

She was wired to her pilot through a microphone she'd just whispered through, as if Jesse believed Stan might actually be able to help her here. Stan, against an impenetrable fortress that had withstood armies of angry invaders for more years than Stan could probably count in decades on his fingers and toes. One swarthy pilot against a Guardian of the Blood?

It was inconceivable that Stan could help her, though Lance envied the pilot Jesse's trust. Stan was able to get close to Jesse. He had probably touched her, watched her eat, heard her laugh.

Did she laugh? She who presented such a solemn

exterior? He'd seen no lightness in her, though he had looked deep. A great swirling emptiness lay where hints of light should have shone. Sarcasm had replaced humor. Drive had replaced some of her fear.

What would the pilot do if he knew everything about his boss? Lance wondered. If Stan found out what was inside her, would he turn away and sprint for the hills?

If he told Jesse the truth, she might wonder if she'd be worth saving. If she realized that she was, in essence, closer to the monsters than she'd ever dare to imagine, and only had to bleed to see this…that knowledge might hasten her self-destruction.

Sacrifice. He nearly said the word aloud. Jesse was offering herself up without knowing all the rules of the game. The rules attached to life itself.

Jesse, the fighter.

I was once like you.

She would see it all, know the worst, if she went after Jorgensen. Pitting her against the vampires she despised might send Jesse spiraling further into herself. He had to help her. He owed her that much.

He was either going to be her guide, her lover, destroyer or executioner. Decisions were just minutes away.

Those minutes seemed like centuries.

Chapter 11

The place her host had chosen for her to see was a shocking contrast to the hall beneath. High up in the castle, at least a hundred stairs above the hall, the room he led her into was a sumptuous cavern of scrolled paneling and pastel-hued fabrics, reminiscent of what she might have expected from Louis XIV.

The elegant, if slightly worn, richness, was too much to take in and process after the stark hallway. Too much of a surprise. Jesse felt terribly out of place and way too current in her bright orange coat. Especially when confronted with the next past-life throwback standing in the middle of the room.

A woman stood there, seemingly carved of the same marble as the vampire, until she lifted a hand in greeting. Dressed in an amber-colored floor-length dress reminiscent of some other age, the woman's steel-gray hair was worn pulled back from her face, ending in a thick braid that fell to her waist. Small-boned and fragile-featured, she bore the lines and creases of being well past fifty. Big eyes of an unknown color trained on Jesse. She was smiling.

After a first rush of relief over actually finding another person in the castle, Jesse's wariness doubled. This could be a trick, after all. The woman might not be human.

"Sit," her host invited, gesturing to a chair placed beside the largest fireplace Jesse had ever seen, one that took up a good portion of an entire wall. Inside the hearth, a red-orange fire roared with the mesmerizing lull of wood smoke and physical warmth.

"So," Jesse said to her host, ignoring the woman and the fire for the time being, although she badly wanted to know who the woman was, and also desperately needed to thaw. "You do feel the cold."

"I remember the cold. The fire is for Nadia, and for you."

So, this was Nadia, the housekeeper. Not a vampire, her host had said, and yet she also had an unworldly air of otherness.

Jesse nodded to Nadia, carried her duffel bag to the chair and dropped it on the floor. Then she turned her backside to the flames. Next to Nadia, on an end table, sat a tray with a teapot and three cups—which meant that both Nadia and her vampire employer had anticipated they'd be a trio for a while.

"Refreshment?" her host asked, as if they were at an afternoon tea party. And truthfully, at any other time, Jesse thought, she'd have killed for some steaming tea to take the edge from a standoff like this one.

Moving with wiry grace, Nadia poured tea into all three cups, and handed one to Jesse. After taking a cup from the tray for herself, Nadia sat down on a blue settee in a swirl of amber fabric.

"You don't drink tea?" Jesse asked her host, without touching hers.

"It's not my drink of choice," he replied.

Because he was partially hidden in the shadows of a corner, Jesse dared to look straight at him while considering his reply.

"Especially not when I'm uncomfortable," he added.

"I'm making you uncomfortable?"

"You are," he conceded, surprising her again. She hadn't expected any hint of weakness on his part, nor the tables being reversed on the discomfort factor.

A damn vampire enigma.

"The only woman I've been around for some time is Nadia," he explained.

"Woman, or mortal?"

"Female, we'll say."

"Yes, I can see where that might be a problem for you," Jesse agreed calmly enough, though the china cup in her hand was rattling against its saucer, a dead giveaway of the quakes going on inside herself.

"Can we get on with it?" she said. "Let's start with who you are. I know what you are, so you can skip that part."

Her host bowed his head in acknowledgment of her parry. "My name is Lance Van Baaren."

"Van Baaren, like the coat of arms on the front door?" She recalled the carved artwork, scratched and weather-beaten.

"The same."

"Just so you know, I've known of the existence of your kind for a long time, and also that I'd bump up against one of you someday," Jesse said.

"None of this negates the fact that you can't save Elizabeth Jorgensen on your own. It's completely foolish to think so."

"And if you're going help me, please explain why we're still standing here."

"Elizabeth Jorgensen is three leagues from my door. She is being held in a village that has death attached to it, and where people no longer care to live."

"By *live,* do you mean literally or figuratively?"

"Only the undead trespass there now. The sort of undead you despise."

Jesse suppressed another spike of apprehension that threatened to tip the cup and saucer in her hand. Elizabeth was close. Three leagues was hardly any distance at all. What were they waiting for?

She tried to cool her reactions. She had to be extra careful now. Her unusual host would soon tell her what he expected in exchange for this round of information.

"How are those undead different from you?" she asked, feeling antsy, holding back.

Her question drew another rustle of fabric from Nadia. Jesse's sideways glance found the attractive woman's lips upturned in what looked to be a private smile—suggesting she found Jesse's question amusing. But Nadia, like her employer, didn't care to enlighten. Van Baaren's housekeeper took a delicate sip of her tea without looking up. *Her* hands weren't shaking.

Jesse pondered how she quickly might reach the gun in the holster tucked into the waist of her pants without drawing more attention to herself, and whether the vampire might be persuaded to hurry things up if threatened. She bet he wasn't intimidated by much, nor too often.

"I swear to you," her enigmatic host said, "that you can drink the tea."

The rich, strong smell of steeped leaves floated up from her cup enticingly. *Rich and strong*—the same description she'd apply to this vampire. Noting those similarities, a flush of warmth crept up Jesse's neck, more untimely embarrassment than anxiety related.

When she looked up from the cup, Lance, the vampire with a name, was three feet away with his hands resting on the back of Nadia's couch. Althought Nadia did not flinch or otherwise appear worried, Jesse worried for her.

"Why would a vampire go against his own, in order to help me?" Jesse asked.

"Ah, we're back to that. You thinking we're the same."

In an addition to his statement, Jesse thought she heard him whisper, *"I helped you once before, remember?"*

But had she imagined those words? Did she imagine the flush that she knew tinted her cheeks? Or the heat of his nearness? These things should have been warnings. Red flags. Stern reminders that vampires were not to be compared to mortals, and never to be trusted. Vampires might have been people once upon a time, as this one had told her, but they were as far removed from the human state now as was possible.

Lance. She didn't like that he had a name. Thinking of him as Lance, instead of *the vampire,* made it harder for her to see him as a monster. Seeing him here, in this beautiful room, was confusing.

No longer caring if the tea spilled, Jesse placed the cup on the seat of the chair beside her. She slid her hand up under her jacket to brush the handle of her gun, feeling better when she found it. The stake was in her pocket, the gun loaded and handy, but she had already witnessed the extraordinary speed this creature possessed. One wrong move, and by the time she'd have a weapon in the open, he might be on her.

"I told you," he said, reading her unspoken thoughts. "I do not feed on mortals."

"No? What do you feed on?" Her hands continued to shake. Her knees felt incredibly weak for all the show of bravado she was attempting to put forth. No negotiations in the past had prepared her for this.

"Do you want to quiz me? Waste more time?" he asked. "If I wanted to hurt you, I'd have done so by now."

"With Nadia as a witness?"

"Nadia has been here a long time, of her own free will, and has never witnessed anything of the kind."

"Is that true?" Jesse asked the woman. Demanded, actually.

"Yes," Nadia said. "This is true."

"Why are you here?" Jesse asked her.

"Lord Van Baaren took me in when I had nowhere else to go, and offered kindness. At first, I stayed to repay his kindness to me. Then I stayed because he needed my help and my company."

Jesse's stomach knotted. Lord Van Baaren! The vampire was a nobleman?

Leaning back against the stone of the hearth for the support her legs no longer provided, she said to Nadia, whose neck was visible above her gown and showed no puncture marks, old or otherwise, "You know what he is?"

Nadia said, "Of course I know."

"You're not afraid?"

"I have been here a very long time and have been

treated like family when my own family was killed in the same village of which you speak."

Jesse frowned. "The village where the missing girl is? What happened to your family?"

"Thank you, Nadia," Lance said, before the woman answered, and Nadia again got to her feet, as if his thanks held some secret, coded command for her departure. She smiled at Jesse sadly before heading for the door.

Jesse watched her go without being able to do anything about it. What was she supposed to say? Run, you idiot? The same command she should be heeding, herself?

Nadia said that Lance had helped her after her family had been killed. If that was true, she and Nadia had something in common. So, where had Lance, or someone like him, been when she'd been in need? She could have used some kindness back then, as her parents lay dying. Maybe help would have saved her from the fires of hell.

Maybe. Still, help from a vampire was a laughable thought. She'd digressed into believing him capable of kindness. The truth was that she'd have tried to cut off his limbs if they'd met before, for being one of the creatures that had taken her family from her. It would have been guilt by species.

And she had crawled up from that pit all by herself, in the end.

"We're alone," she observed, nervously angling her body toward her host. "Isn't that a surprise?"

"It's best not to dwell on the past. Nadia has been through enough already. And she is busy with other things tonight."

"Fine. Then let's get to it, shall we?" Jesse pulled

herself straighter, feeling the cool butt of the gun in her fingers, as she thought…

Showtime.

The hybrid's next statement kept Lance's boots nailed to the floor.

"You can't make me believe you have a soul," she said. "Yours has been surrendered. No soul, no conscience. Therefore, saying you want to help me is a crock."

After absorbing the shock of the vehemence in her tone, Lance rounded the couch, stopping just short of touching distance from her. "Are we to discuss theology?"

"No," she replied. "I'm sure you've had a long time to perfect the explanation."

"I have a soul," he said.

"You aren't alive. You're broken. Corroded."

Jesse's face drained of the becoming pink flush after the several seconds it took for her to realize he was holding her hand. She tried to pull away. Gripping her wrist tightly, waiting until she stopped struggling, Lance opened her fingers, uncurling them slowly with his own. His body reacted as if this were indeed the first time he had ever touched a woman. The current in the air around them pulsed with wayward electricity. Lightning again, searching for ground.

He pressed her flat palm to his chest, above and to the left of his rib cage. "Do you not feel it beating?"

She didn't answer, overcome with the surprise of finding the unexpected. In those silent seconds, as each stroke of his heart transferred to her palm, she lost more color, went whiter.

"Broken, perhaps," he conceded, keeping her there, forcing her to confront her fears. "But not soulless. Nor heartless." He leaned down to look into her face. "Not without conscience."

Her attention was on his hand, on top of hers, pressed to his chest, and she was the breathless one now.

"I am not like the others," he repeated. "Similar only in that I once drank the blood of my maker in order to become what I am."

"Vampire," she whispered.

"Guardian. A being apart. Destined to remain outside the whole because of those differences in my blood."

"All that Guardian business aside, you admit that you drink blood." Her voice was quieter, and riddled with panic that tasted to him like rusted iron.

"Only once have I drunk from another being, and then only to fulfill a vow," he said.

"And now?"

"I exist on the flesh of the animals Nadia also needs to eat. I do not require blood. Rarely do I crave it."

"Require. Rarely." Only he could have heard her. "The craving exists."

"Thirst is always present," he admitted, realizing he'd just told this woman more than he'd ever dared to tell anyone. Not even to Nadia had he exposed what was left of his soul. He hadn't been positive he had a soul until… Jesse. He wasn't completely sure that acknowledgment of its existence was a good thing.

"I have," he said, "long ago learned to exist without the things I cannot have."

Exist. He had not said "live" because Jesse would have argued that point and been right. The differences were subtle to an outsider. However, this outsider needed to see the light if she hoped to survive. She needed the ability to adapt, and had to start by overcoming her prejudices.

Her pallor was already a concern. Jesse was thinking back to the night she'd encountered the others and had witnessed death, firsthand. He could see the wheels of her mind turning.

It was understandable that she didn't believe or trust him. He'd seen the carnage that had once been her family. But in this instance, he had to convince her to pay attention. The problem was getting her to believe him without telling her about herself—a thing he couldn't yet do, since speaking those words would alter her life forever.

"My heart aches for Elizabeth Jorgensen, as yours does. My heart aches for you," he confessed.

"How does your ache feel?"

Her arm was taut to the point of strain, her fingers again beginning to curl against his shirt, recoiling from her discovery.

"Why does a vampire care anything for Elizabeth? What would you know of loss and longing?" she demanded.

"More than you might imagine," he said. "I've been walking this earth longer than you have, and have seen my share of loved ones come and go."

She stopped tugging at her hand, recognizing the truth in his remark. Her latest blood gift, paired with this closeness, was indeed opening up her senses. He knew something else through this touch. Jesse was attracted to him, and had been from her first sighting. She hated that realization as much as he was titillated by it.

Blood to blood, Jesse. No escape.

As he watched, she took in and held a troubled breath, trying to assimilate, draw lines, put the puzzle together without having the right pieces at her disposal. Lance saw by her expression that she was coming up empty-handed.

"I was mortal once," he said. "As were the rest of your monsters. I am removed from some of that humanness, but not from all. Not nearly as much as the others. I breathe, but not to survive. My heart beats only as a frank reminder of the parts of my past life that remain. I did not leave my emotions behind when I—"

"Died?" she finished for him. "You did die?"

He nodded. "I died to this world and was reborn to another."

"Just like the others have died and then stuck around."

He was trying to make her see, when all Jesse knew was pain. She used the darkness at her core to fuel the anger and strength needed to get her through life day by day. She focused on challenge, needed challenge. She trusted no one.

But she saw herself as one thing, when she was another. It was a flaw she remained ignorant of.

"Not like them," he said. "My transition was peaceful, willful, invited, accepted. I was chosen to fulfill my new role. I knew what I was to become."

His hybrid almost looked up again. Lance withheld the silent command for her to complete that gaze, though his heart thundered for want of it, as did hers. She was fighting the attraction. Fighting the truth.

She yanked her fingers from beneath his. "I've seen what you can do," she said.

Her voice was a rasping exhalation that moved the hair near his temple, as warm and as fragrant as he had remembered. It took that one thing for him to acknowledge how close he'd gotten to her as he allowed her scent to wash over him, knowing the exact second he truly was lost…

Lost to the plight of the wounded dove. His dove. She might never be fully healed or whole again, he knew. You couldn't take the loss of innocence back, but you could try to offer consolation.

He was going to help her, knowing full well his attachment to Jesse went beyond being her partner. His blood demanded more. His thirst for her was a gnawing nightmare. The throb in Jesse's neck, mirroring each erratic beat of her heart, sang to him, inviting him closer, filling his own hollow chest with a hope that felt curiously close to redemption.

Guardian. Lance silently repeated the word that defined his existence. His task wasn't to guard the mortals, but to guard the blood. Protecting humans had been a side effect of his task. Protecting the blood, keeping it, preserving it, ensuring its survival, had been the original objective he had modified for his own purposes.

He was a vessel. No longer a man as the living humans defined it. He was a walking, talking, receptacle for the purest form of vampirism. He had agreed to this, swearing to protect what he carried. The only way for him to turn from his task would be to empty his veins completely. Slit his wrists, let the crimson fire flow out, and fade away.

He had once considered doing just such a thing. Some time ago, he had begun to wonder why the ancient blood had to be preserved, and for what purpose. The sheer number of creatures with diluted fluid in their bodies struck him as a slap in the face to his cause. Hidden away, as he had been for a while, he had become useless, directionless.

But he was needed now. Jesse's presence reminded him of this.

Sensing her scrutiny, Lance shook off the plaguing thoughts. Of importance here was that he had passed some of that ancient blood to her. He had contributed to the darkness she harbored, albeit unknowingly. Therefore, he was guilty of the same sort of road toward dilution that he loathed in others—though he'd had the sense not to turn Jesse. She still functioned as a human being, if a messed-up one. It was too late to turn back time in order to reshuffle the options.

What was done, was done. If Jesse's darkness went away, if the will to fight was taken from her, the void might be filled with something else. Something better, or worse. Revealing the truth about the particles in her blood would spiral her toward a new future.

As God was his witness, he didn't understand why he had feelings for the woman, but had no idea how to let her go. It wasn't possible for him to ignore his own reawakening. Giving Jesse more of himself could very well help her to get the missing American girl back, and it might be the only way she'd survive the task. But telling Jesse everything would ensure her departure, for good.

Selfish. The word taunted him. Jesse deserved to be allowed to live or die as she chose. He should not interfere more than he already had. But in all truth, it was doubtful he'd survive another hundred years of solitude after seeing her again.

You have to be given the option to decide your fate, as I did, Jesse. I must allow this.

Stepping closer to her was automatic, a defiant act over thoughts of sending her away. In actuality, Jesse had nowhere to go at the moment. Her back was to the wall. He stood in the way of her escape.

Mere inches separated their bodies. If he stepped aside, she'd run. But which way? Toward America? Obstinately toward the senator's daughter? There was only one way to find out. In either case, he felt as if he had already doomed her. He had only seconds more with Jesse Stewart, when for once in his long-endured existence, he needed so much more time.

Tilting her chin up with his fingers, Lance spoke softly to make his words all the clearer. "You are right, Jesse," he said. "We have met before. And I've never forgotten you."

Chapter 12

His statement made no sense to Jesse. Of course they'd met before, three times now on proper footing and once from the air. This third time was definitely the charm. She felt the rug being yanked out from under her. Lance...this creature...was again too damn close for her health.

"Do you think I've lost it completely? That I'm not prepared to shoot your elegant hide if you don't hurry up and give me what I've come here for?" she warned.

Her fingers were glued to the handle of her gun. Everywhere else, her muscles were seizing. She didn't like this, saw no other choice but to threaten, if he had information she needed.

Is that the only reason I haven't budged?

The question nudged at her awareness as his scent curled into her with each new breath she took. He smelled inexplicably of light. His scent was smoky on her tongue, and in her mouth. But beneath those things lay the tinny taste of aluminum, and she knew what that was, having been around it frequently as a cop. *Blood.*

Light and blood. Opposite ends of the spectrum in an unpolluted world. But this world seemed to have room for it all.

Light and blood.

Fear raked across her soul. Her gaze drifted upward. "Help me," she said, searching the pale features surrounded by all those perfect yellow curls, refusing to acknowledge the look of sadness of his face. Did he feel sympathy? Could he relate to her situation?

Lance Van Baaren was a loner, like herself. If an empty fortress was any indication, he had one friend, Nadia, while she, herself, had only recently begun to consider Stan a comrade. He lived in old-world opulence, a nod to his past. Her apartment in L.A. was tiny, and hardly livable, but she'd never moved, liking the tight familiarity of the space, needing the safety of sameness and routine. Give or take the definition of the word *species,* she and this vampire were uncannily alike. They were damaged souls, and knew it.

"There are twelve vampires in that village," he said. "How many have you fought, personally? How many battles have you won? I'm trying to help you. I've always wanted to help you."

"Always?" Her throat constricted. He was speaking in layers she had to peel back, though she sensed he was again offering truth. Yes, she tasted his truth, and also that it wasn't quite complete. She had so many secrets of her own, she was sick of rooting them out of others.

"Twelve," she whispered. There were twelve fang-bearing predators surrounding Elizabeth Jorgensen. The thought made her sick.

"How can I get to her?" she asked, her heart hammering, when she didn't see how it could beat any faster. Small licks of fire nipped at her skin beneath her sweater and coat, adding to her unease. Lance's smoky scent was a part of that. She was taking deep breaths as if addicted. She was listening to him as if she believed what he'd said.

"Lance?" Nadia's voice interrupted from the doorway, urgent in tone.

He looked to the doorway.

"Wolves," Nadia said.

The beautiful creature holding her didn't move, but spoke over his shoulder. "We must prepare the traps, Nadia."

"Yes," Nadia agreed, turning, closing the door behind her.

"What's going on?" Jesse demanded.

"It seems that we will soon have company."

"Stan!" Both horror and relief flowed through her at the thought. She'd forgotten about the microphone.

"Sorry. Nothing so innocuous as your pilot, I'm afraid," Lance Van Baaren said.

"Then who?" Fear gripped Jesse. Someone was coming and Nadia had mentioned wolves. Lance mentioned traps. This had nothing to do with her or Elizabeth Jorgensen, surely?

Although she squirmed, the vampire showed no mercy. He kept her pinned to the wall with his lithe, so undead-like body, telegraphing to Jesse the fact that there was something unfinished between them that couldn't be postponed much longer. Jesse needed to know what he wasn't telling her. Her gun hand was crushed behind her.

"Close your eyes," he directed.

"No."

"Indulge me, please, Jesse. Close your eyes. I promise I won't bite."

"Sorry. I'm no one's afternoon snack, and I don't owe you anything. Your information about Elizabeth Jorgensen isn't complete and time is wasting. Whatever you know about her should be freely given in the name of justice, decency and all that's holy."

The vampire pressed a wayward curl from her forehead, the tips of his fingers cool against her overheated skin. Her lips were quivering, Jesse knew. An unusual weakness had overtaken her limbs. She absorbed the effects of his closeness through every pore and each breath she took, managing to bring up one strangled gasp, conceding that she'd be unable to stand much more of this. She had to get away from those eyes of his…

She closed hers. A new agenda formed in her mind. *Get away at all costs.*

When he spoke, his voice was tender, and all the more alarming because of it. "Listen," he directed.

Cries of foul play streaked through Jesse's mind like incessant chatter. Differentiating one sound from another seemed an impossible task.

"Listen, Jesse."

Purposefully, she slowed the chatter, rising above it, as she'd learned early on to do. Not exactly tuning things out completely, but pushing things to the background. With the chaos managed, her heartbeat filled her ears.

What did he expect her to hear?

The fire snapped as a log broke into pieces. Otherwise, the room was quiet. Suddenly, though, another heartbeat echoed her own. His heartbeat—the one she had felt with her hand on his chest, while refusing to believe a vampire possessed anything remotely as human as a heart.

"Listen," his voice demanded.

Besides her heartbeat and his, the snapping fire and the surrounding quiet, she heard a cry—a high-pitched, piercing sound.

Not a cry. More like a howl. The howl of an animal.

But how improbable was hearing that, when she was several floors up in a castle with granite walls ten feet thick?

She thought she heard the rustle of branches made brittle by a cold wind, and what sounded like footsteps in the snow. She thought she heard *him* whispering to her in a hazy litany of partial phrases.

Confused, Jesse opened her eyes…to find herself staring into the unending blue pools of the vampire's gaze.

Being close to Jesse again was foolish. While it was true he didn't require blood, the impulse was strong to have a taste of hers, hot from her veins.

"Tell me what you want." Her demand was rife with hints of inner agitation. Perhaps she sensed an answering need rising in herself as well. Lance saw this in her eyes, and he refused to let her go, holding to the connection that had snapped into place through this intimate meeting of their gazes. What passed between them was intimate, no mistake. The brightness in her eyes, the thrumming blood in her veins, the touch of her body against his…intensified his hunger.

Terror struck deep into the marrow of his ageless bones with the thought of what he could make her do, if he chose. If he made Jesse do anything against her will, he'd be just like her other monsters. No chance would remain for the sweet bliss of a mutual surrender. Hatred would emerge the victor.

Anxiousness jerked him back to Jesse's question, and her thoughts surrounding it. *"Tell me what you want."*

The truth, he knew, would shock them both.

Jesse sagged a little. Her eyelids fluttered. Now was not the time to tell her everything. She'd need whatever strength she possessed. If he took her defiance away, she'd be rendered so much weaker.

Nevertheless, her eyes pleaded with him for the knowledge he possessed, for answers to the questions she had temporarily misplaced. He easily saw down into her soul, and wanted to touch her there, in the spot where she hurt the most.

"Your presence is a temptation," he said, and watched his confession ripple through her.

"We have met before," he continued, loath to go deeper into it, and at the same time needing to see her connect with her fading strength. "You know this. Your soul knows this."

He heard Jesse's thoughts clashing, sensed the blackness within her moving in agitation. She didn't want to think back, he concluded. She didn't really wish to remember the circumstances surrounding the tragedy that had shaped her. The black spot she harbored was likely nothing more than a cloud of forbidden memory tucked away in a safe place.

He wasn't sure what to do about this theory. He didn't know how much a part of her the blackness had become.

"I can't explain things to you now. Time makes no exceptions for dire necessities," he said. "I had hoped to tell you more about yourself, but they know you're here."

"They?" Her voice was throaty.

"The monsters," he said.

"How do they know? What do they want?"

"Blood," he replied, his expression as grave as hers, he supposed. "They want blood."

Jesse's eyes were wide, the skin around them ashen. She had taken on the pallor of those she despised.

"You told them about me? Nadia did?"

"They have nothing to do with me, nor I, them. The helicopter alerted them to your presence. Your scent is a further lure."

She shook so hard that he leaned closer to her, his hips against hers. This gesture of protection gave him pleasure. She was again in his arms, and vulnerable. The blood within her was hot and eager. Her body both reviled and wanted what he had to offer. Her mind reached out to him, pleading for answers.

"What they want is you," he said, his face level with hers. "We all want you, Jesse. I'm sorry."

The vampire had her pinned to the wall with his arms on either side of her shoulders. His chest crushed hers. His thighs overlaid hers.

He had just apologized for this closeness and the approach of more monsters. The strangeness of the moment stunned Jesse. If she let her guard down, she'd be dead. If she abandoned her hard-won principles, nothing was left.

"Why me?" she asked after several seconds had passed, rephrasing the question she'd posed to him already, sensing a shift in his bearing and hearing whispers she couldn't decipher that hadn't come from inside her own skull.

"You're a female. A potent one. We can scent you from a distance. Tonight, after dark, it will be easier."

"It's not dark." Jesse didn't glance toward the curtained windows to make sure the statement was correct because she sensed the sun going down. Darkness was falling inside of her as well as in the periphery, beyond these walls.

"Soon the light will be gone," he said.

"And things that go bump in the night will what, take over? Scurry out from their hiding places? That's disgusting."

"It's life."

"Or the utter lack of it. The exact opposite of life, in fact."

"Maybe you're right," Lance conceded. "Yet here we are. Things other than the known ones exist. For good or ill, we share the space."

Jesse winced. "What about Elizabeth?"

"I will try to get to her. You can remain with Nadia. They can't get in here."

"Bite your—" Her retort broke off abruptly.

"You would provoke a vampire?" he asked, his muscles corded with the tension she remembered from their balcony duet.

"What else is there to do with one?" she countered with an absurd defiance.

Fearing how he might answer that question, Jesse tugged her hand free from behind her, without the gun. There was no room to get the weapon out of her waistband, and at the moment, Lance's weight against hers was both dreadful and comforting.

Calling up her disintegrating anger, she shoved at his

shoulders. The more she fought him, the more of his scent she took in. His treacherous pheromones were the reason her legs felt watery and her blood pressure had skyrocketed. He was doing this. If he wanted to play house, she either had to get to her gun or go for the stake in her pocket. She had to do something.

"Any female?" she said. "They can scent any female? You said *potent*. What does that mean? Is it my anger that ticks them off? Can they smell emotion? Anxiety?"

"Yes," he said, his tone low.

"Which one of those?"

"All of them."

"So, they heard the helicopter, put two and two together, knowing someone was dropped off, and now they can smell fresh meat up here? That's how you found me in the city? That's not ridiculous?"

"It's unusual, and the truth."

Her voice dropped an octave. "Elizabeth wasn't enough for them? What does that say about her condition?"

"You assume that greed is a vice that belongs only to the living," he whispered in her ear.

Twelve. He'd said twelve vampires had Elizabeth Jorgensen. *God*.

"You told me there are hundreds of them. In the world, how many?"

"Thousands."

Jesse's mind twisted against the possibility that she could indeed have brushed up against them in a crowd, on a street. Not just in an alley, but anywhere and everywhere.

"Different," she said. "How are you different from them?"

"I was put here to watch the others."

"To protect them?"

"I was to keep *them* from happening. Things got out of control. The populations exploded across all lines. My strength alone wasn't sufficient."

"Are there others like you?"

The features of the face beside hers furrowed, showing that the answer to her question troubled him deeply. "Six others," he said.

"Six, total, to keep watch on all the rest? How many of those six are nearby?"

"None."

Jesse's legs finally gave way. She felt them go, as if her bones suddenly just dissolved.

Chapter 13

She didn't fall.

Falling would have been infinitely preferable to being held in Lance's arms like the weakling she had never been.

She was being cradled against his chest like a damsel in distress. He was looking at her as though waiting for her to come up swinging. But her mutinous body sank into the curve of his arms as though she belonged there. For one second, an infinitesimal, useless amount of time, she wanted to give up, give in and see where this moment took her. She'd fought for so long. She was tired.

"I didn't drink the tea," she choked out through a dry throat. "But I can't stand up."

"You're not poisoned," Lance said. "Neither is this any indication of weakness. It's a system overload. A rewiring that's finally amounting to something."

"I don't know what you're talking about. Put me down."

"All right."

He didn't put her down. He closed his arms tighter around her, almost a reflexive move, Jesse thought, feeling him tighten in surprise.

Panic struck again. She had to get free, get out of this situation. She'd stake this vampire, put herself and him out of their misery—as soon as her wits returned.

But the panic she was experiencing, her mind warned, wasn't about devising a way to kill this magnificent creature who might have been around since the Middle Ages, for all she knew. The panic, she realized, came from being held in his arms, being near him, where some part of her felt as if she belonged.

Jesse snapped her head back so that she could see Lance's face. Her skin flushed hot, then hotter when she found him staring. There was no way to reach the weapon in her pocket, although he was looking at her as though she was about to become dinner.

"Not happening!" Her protest was vehement. She didn't move one single limb in a struggle to break his hold. Her chest rose and fell, heaving for breaths she didn't find, as the last remnant of a meeting with a vampire continued to burn a pathway along her neck. Putting both hands up to soothe the fire, Jesse swore she heard the whoosh of blood moving through her arteries. She thought she heard the same thing in his.

Afraid of losing her grasp on reality, Jesse fought to call up her anger. Anger overshadowed fear, and was the most important discovery she'd come across in that institution some people called a hospital.

Stay angry. Control the fear, the uncertainty, the anxiety, by wanting to fight the cause of those things.

She parted her lips to shout at the creature holding her. No shout emerged. A mouth, his mouth—equally as blistering as the flames covering her throat—kept her from making a sound by covering her lips and soaking up the cry.

Another memory hit Jesse as their bodies connected in this way. A white memory, appearing out of the dark, brought up a face—vague, blurry, unidentifiable— surrounded by light. In her mind, and with the maddeningly exquisite slickness of the vampire's kiss, she again heard the murmur of spoken syllables, seemingly tender whispered words of comfort, or something close to that.

Once again, she tasted copper, gagged, shut her eyes against the intrusion. Bits of phrases repeated in *his* voice. *"Opening up to possibilities... A rewiring..."*

He was trying to tell her something she was too confused to get, purposefully making cryptic explanations that were difficult to comprehend.

What the hell was going on?

His mouth...his taste...was familiar!

It was the third time in twenty-four hours he had kissed her.

She tasted sinfully good. So good that his original purpose for kissing her began to fade. If Jesse screamed, the wolves would hear. Their attention would turn from where it belonged.

That was why he'd prevented her protest by placing his mouth on hers, when he hadn't meant to invade her privacy in this way. But…he found her lips parted by that unspoken protest, and as electrifying as the weight of her body in his arms.

He slipped his tongue between her teeth, and his own fangs extended. His body stiffened. His craving intensified. It wasn't only the bloodlust twisting him. He wanted Jesse in the way a man wanted a female— stretched out across cool sheets, with his naked body pressed to hers, on top of hers, inside of hers. He desired to meet her, skin to skin.

He envisioned writhing, and uttered oaths of pleasure. Hot sweat, and hours, days, months, to explore her depths, over and over, time after time, with an immortal's unending stamina.

Keeping Jesse here was a necessity. His thirst became a sharp, insistent demand, crowding his insides, rising to the surface of the dark pool of control because the cravings hot-wired into him were primal enough to overwhelm the rest.

Stay, Jesse.

She tasted of fear, blood and repressed memories. His nerves jangled in recognition of the first two items on that list. Young vampires fed on fear, counting on it to drive any semblance of rationality from their minds. Fear was a turn-on to those who drank the blood of others. The excitement accompanying the confrontation of fear was an adrenaline rush that fueled the vampires' show of supernatural strength.

His fangs accidentally raked Jesse's bottom lip. The drop of blood she had exhibited from an earlier hour joined the one his slipup created, sending the texture of Jesse's lushness careening through him.

Below his waist, he swelled, as if there had been no hiatus in the lusting of the flesh. The pressure inside his chest flagged all sorts of reasons why he had to either put her down or get on with it…whatever *it* was to be. Bite her? Take her to those sheets and make love to her, with time being of the essence to someone else in need of saving? With trust on the line?

The wolves had come, preceding the monsters, announcing the monsters' deadly intentions toward what he held so dearly to his breast. His thirsty brethren would soon be on their way. *God help us, we are greedy bastards.*

The wolves were already baying at the rising moon. A blood moon, round, full, requiring sacrifice. The second full moon of a winter month. A rare occurrence. Here, where so many vampires walked freely, it was a night of undue greed and rampant terror.

Who will that sacrifice be?

Jesse gasped for a breath she wasn't able to reach. Lance kept his lips pressed to hers, absorbing her struggle, sensing that one small speck of her spirit wanted to give in to him.

Love and hate—extremes that were on Jesse's list of unacceptable emotions.

He ran his tongue over the tiny scratch his incisors had made, and swallowed. Small internal explosions made him groan. It took a lot of blood to turn a human into something else. Then again, Jesse Stewart hadn't been a normal human being for quite a while.

No conscience. That's what Jesse charged. In the heat of passion, he had to concede, conscience was sometimes overruled. If a vampire killed too many times, its conscience withered and died, unused, forgotten, left behind. But what about sins of the flesh?

Purposefully inciting negative emotion in humans was a tool he'd never used to further his own agenda, though he considered it now. He could show Jesse what they were, and what awaited her by his side. If he did such a thing, though—took away her will—he'd be one of the monsters, and as selfish as most others in the twenty-first century.

Jesse wanted to kill him, take him out, in honor of what others, loosely related to him, had once done to harm her. At the same time, she was drawn to him with a palpable hunger of her own. Her blood, mingled with his, predicted the attraction, sealing it in place.

Conscience?

In order for Jesse to remain as she was now, a hybrid missing any true link to immortality, she must not be allowed one more drop of the ancient blood. Already, she'd become unsteady, and also more aware. She heard the wolves.

*One slip of my teeth against your fine neck, and you would never be hurt again...*he thought. Therefore, the urge to speak to her came as a complete surprise. The fact that he could remove his mouth from hers, in spite of his body's objections, was another.

"Yes." Lance spoke carefully. "You know me."

Jesse's face went ghostly. Dark circles, like shadowed half-moons, underscored her eyes, those shadows echoed in the sound of distress she made.

"You are strong," he continued. "But that strength is sapped by the holes in your past, the things you refuse to see."

He rocked her in his arms. "Do you understand?"
How can you understand?

"Think," he said. "Think back, Jesse. Find me, so that you can trust me."

He wanted to meet her willingly, wholly, rather than in sectioned-off pieces. She'd been hurt badly, but hadn't he been through all the trials of life and punishment, as well?

The body he held quivered while his heart pounded out her heart's crazy, staccato beats. Her eyes remained closed. Clearly, she didn't want to remember any of the details that might help her face her own demons. She wasn't ready to relive the pain.

Did he want to make her?

Outside the castle walls, a wolf howled again—a harrowing sound that echoed through the trees and down the mountainside. The wolves weren't his enemies, but his watchdogs, warning of the night about to fall. Darkness would soon wipe out the starlight. A blood moon would light his doorstep.

"Nadia manages the four-legged beasts that roam the darkness in packs," he explained. "They look to her to supplement what winter kept from them. Their presence allows my attention to focus elsewhere. Their reward for such an unusual fellowship is as simple as a regular meal."

The wolf howled again. It, too, scented Jesse, from her footsteps in the snow.

She was listening for something else. Who did Jesse assume would come to her rescue? Were their conversations, transmitted through the tiny speaker taped to her chest, enough to bring help from her camp? What form would that help take? Did they mark him as the enemy?

"Nadia's family was killed by vampires," he said. "She came to me for protection, knowing what I am."

He was telling her these things to justify his character, so she'd not believe him a threat, when he was one.

"Tonight is special," he said. "A blood moon is thirsty, and requires fresh blood to round out its fullness. It's an old legend with some basis in truth."

His remarks seemed to stir Jesse's uncertainty. Her anger began to root, its taste that of burnt acorns, grainy and slightly acidic. The anger rose through her like a cyclone, whipping up a new strength she had yet to recognize.

Lance's need to possess her multiplied. Having Jesse in his arms made him seem, for a small span of time, the savior she'd once believed him to be. A far cry from her more recent evaluation of his character.

Thirst. Hunger. Outrageous cravings. I'm composed of those things, too.

He had wanted either to prepare Jesse or spare her that side of himself. He assumed she'd be safe if locked away. He'd planned on giving her to Nadia, then going after Elizabeth Jorgensen alone. He would get the girl, or what was left of her, back.

Then…Jesse. The hybrid who had turned his world upside down, compromised his retirement, and brought back his hunger for lust and love, long-dormant emotions. She had accomplished all of that in so short a time, gotten under his skin, when it was, in actuality, the other way around.

If he were to prove his trust, too much time had been wasted already.

Help me, Jesse. Don't fight, just this once. Let me be your protector.

When Lance glanced down, Jesse's brown eyes were open, and trained on him.

"Think back, Jesse, Find me."

The suggestion repeated in her mind with a stifling accompanying heat. Jesse's skin felt damp in a way reminiscent of having broken through a long-running fever. Her body ached. Her head ached. Beyond the sound of Lance's outlandish directive and the strange information about Nadia and the wolves, and something called a blood moon, Jesse again heard the cry of a wild animal in the distance. An unsettling sound. Gothic.

She was in a castle, in a foreign country, in a room belonging to the past. Unsure of how she had ended up in a vampire's arms, she stared at the ceiling, searching for a way to gather what was left of herself.

The silky blues of the elegant decor were like a backdrop of clouds, hovering. The fire's wave of heat escalated when she found her right shoulder tight up against Lance's thinly clothed chest.

"You know me... Go back, Jesse... Find me."

"Hell with Nadia," she managed to say. "Tell me who you are. Really."

She got that they were tenuously connected by a bond she hadn't figured out. He'd left enough hints about this, all of them cryptic and uninspiring, without actually telling her anything useful. Part of his game in keeping her from Elizabeth Jorgensen? No bite, no bloodletting, just a bit of hand-holding, a few heart palpitations and a show of decreased mental acuity on her part, while Elizabeth might be dying, dead already or worse.

This vamp's mission seemed to be a purposeful attempt to keep her from her goal. She swore she heard time ticking down toward the warning: *too late.*

"How am I supposed to know you?" she demanded, straining against his arms, the spell finally broken.

He set her down carefully, seeming to consider a reply.

"I brought you here to protect you," he finally admitted. "In the city, as I said, the others would easily have found you."

"Like they found someone else before me, I suppose. Someone named Elizabeth."

"Yes, though not quite the same."

"Stop with the runaround! Explain, so I can get on with what I should be doing right now. You must see how important this is!"

"Very well." He was looking at her so strangely, and in a fashion that turned her insides. Meeting his eyes again, right then, would be a slow form of suicide. But again, she wanted to look up. Cold was settling in now that he'd set her on her own two feet.

"Then point the way, and I'll go get her," Jesse said. "Please. You have no idea…" Her sentence failed, as explanations about her own past always did.

"You can't go," Lance said. "I can't let you go."

Jesse frowned, then turned for the door. "Now you sound like Stan." Before she reached the exit, Lance was there, in front of her.

"Either kill me, or get out of my way," Jesse said.

"You can't go where Elizabeth Jorgensen is," he repeated adamantly.

"Why? Is it a private club? Fangs necessary to get in? For all I know, you might be the king of the monsters."

His hands were raised to slow her down. "Night has fallen. You'll get nowhere on your own."

"The blood moon thing? Nonsense. As if that should mean anything to me."

"It will mean something as soon as you set one foot out the front door."

"Why?"

"Because you are not who you think you are, Jesse. You are not like anyone else, in fact."

"Compliment accepted. Now get out of my way."

"Shall I help you remember?" he said. "I've held off, knowing you don't want to go back there."

"Back where?" she couldn't help asking, anger keeping her tone level.

"To the balcony."

Unconsciously, Jesse reached for her shoulder.

"I fixed the arm," he said, "knowing you'd need it if you persisted in this fight."

As if his suggestion brought some of the pain back, Jesse rubbed her upper arm. "You made me imagine I'd been hurt."

His silence, minus any argument about her remark, forced the one question she'd been avoiding past her lips. "How? How did you fix my arm?"

"Our mouths touched—"

Jesse jumped in, drily. "You're saying vamps have

Novocain in their fangs, and that you numbed the pain?"

"Not Novocain, Jesse. Blood. It always comes back to blood."

The room went deathly silent and winter-cold, all former warmth a mirage. Jesse forgot to breathe until her lungs heaved, pleading for oxygen.

She went back in memory to that balcony, felt the prick of his teeth, gagged on the influx of an aluminum scent, and tasted copper. The rush of an icy wind assailed her as she hung over the side of the building, dangling from a damaged arm separated from its shoulder socket. The vampire had pulled her up, placed his arms around her and his mouth against hers…

And she'd awakened as good as new.

No. Oh, no. Jesse blinked, raised her eyes, her anger transforming into pure disbelief.

"It all comes back to my blood," he said, the expression of empathy way too lovely on his unearthly beautiful face.

Chapter 14

Lance watched Jesse's pink lips quiver, wanting to kiss those lips to stillness, as he might have been able to do as a man. The rest of her face was frozen in shock.

"My blood has made you stronger," he explained. "At the same time, that small transfusion has rendered you irresistible to others whose existence is ruled by thirst. Giving you that gift was an action I didn't take lightly."

Jesse didn't speak, looked faint, Lance thought, as she backed up a step, blown there by what she'd heard. Shocked to her very soul.

"If you go out there, the others will be waiting. If you return to the city, they will find you eventually. Your only recourse is to leave Slovenia. Soon."

He had driven a metaphorical stake into her with this confession, as he'd known he would. Her eyes had taken on a cast of wildness.

"A gift," she said. Just that, her breath insufficient for her to continue.

"I gave you blood," he said. "Now, you must stay here until I get Elizabeth back. If she is—"

"Alive," Jesse whispered.

Lance nodded. "When this is over, and with or without the Jorgensen girl, you'll have to go back to the States."

"Or what?"

The comment was so like her, Lance thought. Stubborn to the end.

"Or," he said, "you will have to decide what you want to be."

"Haven't you already taken that choice from me?"

"I've enhanced your perceptions, offered you a chance to survive this mess. Only that, and only a chance."

She backed up another step to lean against a chair.

"You have not been turned, Jesse. You're not one of—"

"I'm not one of you? What does swallowing the blood of the undead make me, then?"

"Better able to do what you want to do, on the path you've elected to follow."

"Oh, God. I'm going to be sick," Jesse said. "It wasn't a dream."

Suddenly, her head came up. She staggered sideways a step before yanking her spine straight. Maintaining a tight hold on herself, she asked, "What do you mean about deciding what I will be?"

"You can't go back, Jesse. I can't take the blood back, and it doesn't go away. Once inside you it disperses, interacting with the other cells it comes into contact with. You can deal with this and move on. You can—"

"Never!" she whispered. "I will never become like you! Not if I have any kind of choice!"

Anticipating this, Lance said, "I did what I did to protect you."

"You just said you've made it easier for vampires to find me, and that if there are monsters around, I'm toast. You told me there are hundreds, if not thousands, of the walking dead, including yourself. If you found me so easily in the city, after one, what—glimpse?—what's to say they won't find me anywhere I go, and that I'd be safe anywhere at all? And you found me before we'd met on that balcony. Before you had..." She blanched, hesitated. "Before..."

Both hands went to her stomach, then immediately to her throat. Lance knew what was coming, what had occurred to her for the first time.

"How did you find me?" she gasped. "In the first place?"

"I made inquiries about a helicopter, and the people in it."

He watched her think about that, knowing she'd soon find the flaw. She'd taste it. She was precariously close to the edge of reason. He had to slow her down.

"The blood works both ways," he explained. "It will be easier for you to find them as well."

"What if I don't want to find them?" she shouted.

"If that's the case, why do you carry a wooden stake in your bag or pocket? Why do you even know about silver bullets and not looking into a vampire's eyes? How were you able to recognize me? These things have *hunter* written all over them. You have *hunter* stamped on your heart."

"I..." It was obvious she couldn't make the thought work right. She started over. "I don't want to find them," she whispered. "I didn't really want to find any of you."

It was a confession, earnest, truthful, surprising, telling. Lance's heart slowed, as if it had received a direct blow from which it couldn't quite recover. This was the part of Jesse she had refused to face, the aftermath of those memories she had repressed. And it wasn't what he had expected.

The anger in her tone had fled, replaced by a hint of utter hopelessness, for which he alone was the cause. A curious sensation of heaviness came over him. Allowing the silence to lengthen, not sure how to proceed, Lance waited out the questions she didn't ask, and the one specific charge she hadn't yet made. Over that silence, he heard the whir of a helicopter, and his heart died a second death.

If she hadn't wanted to find the vampires at all… then his last gift had been for nothing. Could he have misread her so completely?

"Stay," he said to Jesse. "You're safe here. I can—"

"Keep me from doing my job?" she interrupted, her voice strained thin. "Stop me from doing what I can to help other people? Make me even more special?"

Lance tried one last time to make her understand. "I am a Guardian. My task is to protect the Blood, and in doing so, watch over those you call monsters. I can get Elizabeth back tonight, when you are safe. At least I can try."

"Go to hell," she said as she passed him, heading out of the room, toward the sound of the chopper's blades she shouldn't have been able to hear, but had. Toward the ride she knew would be waiting for her outside, and a blood moon that might end everything.

"I'd rather die for a cause," she declared in a throaty voice, "than be anything like you."

Jesse ran, expecting Lance to appear around every curve, but no one stopped her.

She ran as much from herself as from the creature who had manipulated her. He said she had swallowed his blood. If so, she'd done so unknowingly, unwillingly. Still, what did this make her? Not a vampire, she supposed, if she hadn't died, but no longer completely herself, either. No longer completely human.

What was the name for a human carrying around a sampling of vampire blood?

Halfling?

Hybrid?

Something else nagged, barely able to get past the importance of the other stuff. It was the idea of having known Lance Van Baaren prior to seeing him in that field. She'd been bothered by a feeling of recognition after first laying eyes on him—an almost bone-deep feeling of familiarity. Lance himself had hinted at a former meeting several times in their brief acquaintance. He'd made a point of it, in fact.

He hadn't told the truth about his inquiry of the chopper. Not the whole truth, anyway. This creature messed with her for a reason only known to himself, yet he insinuated his cousins were greedy?

She couldn't think, needed air, as she continued to grope for meaning. Sick, wanting to retch, Jesse hit the stone railing hard in her downward flight from the opulent room, and bounded on, too stunned by her thoughts to register the interruption. Painlessness had become a drag on her soul, possibly another freaky remnant of what Lance Van Baaren had done to her.

Maybe she didn't feel anything for the same reason her arm had miraculously healed. *Ingesting the blood of a demon.*

Reaching the cavernous entryway out of breath, facing the gigantic oak door that led to her escape and was carved with his family crest, Jesse leaned a shoulder against the chilled wood, daring to stop there.

The helicopter hovered above with a steady hum. She also heard the piercing cry of another wolf, out there in the night. But those things paled in comparison to the intimacy of her name being whispered passionately from the lips of the creature on the stairs behind her. An evocative whisper that went straight through her with a piercing flare of heat.

"Jesse."

No. Don't call me.

The heat was a charade, had to be, and as false as his world. A dead man couldn't give off or offer warmth, even though this one seemed to be wrapped in fire.

Without meaning to, Jesse turned to square off with her tormentor—golden, haunting in all his vampiric glory. Not only lord of the castle, but the keeper of secrets.

With her internal alarm switches tripping violently, Jesse said, "I'll bring them all. The whole freaking city's worth of law enforcement, if I have to. They will know where that village is. Someone will know."

"And you will lead them."

"Damn straight."

"Then you've learned nothing here."

"I've learned more than enough."

"Control it, Jesse," Lance advised gently, softly, though Jesse felt every word from where she stood as though he'd breathed his warning into her hair.

"Stay in control," he said.

Funny, Jesse thought. He assumed he knew so much about her, yet didn't know that control was exactly what she'd been attempting for years to maintain. He wasn't aware of how horrifying it was for her and every last fiber of her being, to be joined in any way to one of the creatures she despised.

Not only had she lost her self-control and her wits by coming here, and by daring to hope he'd help her, she'd now lost another portion of her soul as well. There might not be anything left. She was sinking, breaking up, losing her form. Something dark slithered around inside her.

Just one more thing. Have to know.

"What will it do to me? Who will I be?" she asked, daring Lance Van Baaren to answer truthfully, testing him as much as herself.

"You," he replied. "Only more so."

A terrible understatement, Jesse realized, while knowing that she'd found the truth she sought.

"It's why I heard the wolves and the chopper through all this stone?"

He nodded.

"And why I came here? Your blood in my veins gives you an advantage over what I do?"

"I did not call you. You came for reasons of your own."

"Answer my question, damn you!"

He nodded again, and she found his presence as electrifying as always, even knowing what he was and what he had done.

"I can call you, if I choose," he admitted.

"I'll have to comply?"

"You now have a choice, and the means with which to resist."

"Truly a two-sided gift, then," Jesse said, wondering if such a *gift* worked both ways. If she'd be able to call him if she chose to.

"Can *they* call me? The others?"

"No."

"Then your blood truly is special in some way?"

"Older, undiluted and unique in that it's now a part of you as well."

"Why me?" was what slipped out of her next, and again the most important question of all. It wasn't that he'd found a kindred spirit, as he had told her in the city. Either he had chosen her for another reason, or everything that had happened was merely an example of how sick random coincidences worked.

There had been no real explanation as to why the monsters had chosen her parents to maul, leaving little Jesse for dead. And now, she just happened to get this job in Slovenia, on the other side of the planet from Los Angeles, and had found Lance running in a meadow. Had being dealt a near-death blow by the bloodsuckers in an L.A. made her recognizable to them somehow?

Another thought came. Had she ever really recovered? Did she carry the scent of death in each breath she continued to take?

More flashes of light filled her mind, like the turning patterns of a kaleidoscope. Images shuffled by quickly, appearing, then distorting, sucking the life out of her muscles.

Widening her stance for balance, Jesse threw up her hands to ward off what was coming her way.

Bloodred alley. Panic. Ugly smells of thrashed, torn flesh.

A descent into darkness, interrupted by light.
Not the beam from a cop's flashlight, but from...
The presence of an angel.

The suddenness of this image was peppered by a sentence of remembered words. *You know me.*

You...know...me.

We have met before. Go back. Find me.

More images came from the tunnel of time.

Hands peeling her from the grimy pavement, and brushing away the tangle of hair and wetness from her face.

Strong male arms holding her.

Light eyes seeking hers.

Her own mouth opening, shouting, *"Help them! Please!"*

Warmth closing over her when she was so very cold.

A whispered command she wanted to obey. *"Live, Jesse."*

More lips on her neck.

Brutal pain. Oncoming darkness.

Then the insistent, startled voices of police officers on the scene, stunned by the sight and unable to move.

Those pictures faded abruptly, leaving a stain in their wake. A red stain, outlined in gold. And there, among the gold, was a pale face, bathed in light.

"God, no! God help me!" Jesse exclaimed, looking up at Lance Van Baaren, using every ounce of willpower she possessed to remain standing at the foot of his staircase.

"I was dosed with cursed blood long before arriving here!" she exclaimed.

Knowing she was right, and with a last, horrified glance at Lance Van Baaren, Jesse spun, yanked on the door and stumbled outside.

Chapter 15

Sprinting outside into the night, Jesse felt her heartbeat swerve way off-line, felt her mind go numb.

Immediately captured in the brilliance of a spotlight, she stumbled to a stop and looked up, her ears filling with the sounds of the noisy helicopter—sounds that were, for the moment, as confusing as all the rest.

Don't go into shock.

Hold on.

She wasn't cold, didn't feel the brisk bite of the wind or anything else, other than the vampire's gaze on her back.

She refused to acknowledge what stood behind her. The mere thought of him upped her internal heat levels, saturating her chest, her stomach, her legs with lingering flames. This wasn't an attraction born of anything natural. His hold on her arose from the actual physical phenomenon of hosting his blood.

How far back did their relationship go? All the way to that alley, and the event that had kicked off every round of action since then? He had been there, with the other vampires? She had believed him to be an angel?

Go back. Find me, Jesse.

She'd found him, all right, and wished she hadn't.

The urge to retch returned as the chopper landed twenty feet from where she stood. The spotlight remained on her, nearly blinding in its intensity.

She didn't walk forward. Her legs weren't behaving. She felt the particles of Lance's blood inside her, now that she'd been made aware of them, although that, too, seemed impossible.

"Jesse."

Her skin rippled in response to the way he said her name, in spite of her brain knowing the score. He followed her, hoping what, to convince her to stay? Give her more bad news?

To apologize for her parents?

He actually wanted her to believe he'd saved her life. And maybe he had, either by accident or on purpose. Saved her for what, though? Her parents had died gruesomely at the hands of his kin. She would have welcomed death every minute since then, in return for their lives being saved instead of her own.

"I will get Elizabeth," Lance said.

Jesse glanced over her shoulder, and said vehemently, "Over my dead body."

Haven't you done enough? what was left of her soul admonished.

"No favors," she added, her voice breaking up. "No more favors."

Someone stood beside her, smelling faintly of aftershave and engine oil. A big hand gripped hers, pushed her torso over double and pulled. Seconds later she was in the helicopter, with Stan, who was bundled up in a hooded jacket that covered his head, jumping in beside her. Before her second choked breath, they were lifting off.

She saw Lance standing there; a lone figure not even remotely dwarfed by the size of his fortress. A creature without a need for an impenetrable castle at all, given what he was, except perhaps for the reason he'd offered. A respite from the chaos of the world.

Lance Van Baaren. Vampire. Guardian.

Guardian angel.

Hers?

Then where were his wings?

The world on the ground, with Lance at its epicenter, spun as the chopper banked. Smaller shadows emerged from the forest, racing toward Lance as if he was also the center of their universe. Unable to make those shapes out, Jesse thought *wolves*.

She'd bitten her lip again, and tasted blood. Not sure she'd be able to utter one more word to anybody, including her pilot, Jesse leaned back against the seat. She wanted to be down there, facing this, and also wanted to put as much distance between herself and the vampire as possible.

Like distance mattered anymore.

Lance Van Baaren had been *there,* with her. In that dark alley. Amid the carnage. He'd bitten her torn and bleeding neck, topping off the pain with more than a little of his own. Saving her? Hell, he was now a part of her, as a tangible explanation for all those rumors about psychic abilities, her uncanny reputation for tracking the bad guys and smelling the wrongness of a site. God! Were those the gifts he'd referred to?

Is this how they had recognized each other?

"Blood to blood," she muttered, understanding the meaning of this, at last. It was a fatal attraction. She carried him around with her.

A groan bubbled up from her throat as she wiped the blood from her lip with the back of her hand. Static came through her earphones when Stan placed them on her head. The world continued to spin, taking her with it, because she wasn't Jesse Stewart, and had never been.

Stan was saying something in a worried tone that broke through her internal chatter. She had to say something. This is what she lived for, she reminded herself. Helping others. If she gave in now, another innocent soul would be lost.

Gritting her teeth to get a grip on the dizziness, Jesse tuned in to the man beside her.

"I take it that didn't go so well," Stan said.

And Jesse almost laughed.

Lance stared at the helicopter as it disappeared over the trees, taking Jesse from him, unenlightened and running.

Not completely unenlightened, he amended. Still, in this case, half an explanation was worse than none.

Jesse knew she wasn't quite human. She was registering how long she'd been this way, skirting the edge of the darkness she harbored. She may already have plucked a fragment or two from those balled-up, suppressed memories. Her reactions were easy to imagine.

The rational part of his mind warned that it was inexcusable her pilot had overheard much of what had passed between Jesse and himself. Personal things. Intimate things. Having Stan know about him, and where he called home, made for one person too many in the loop. Lance considered this as his heart rate continued to accelerate…alongside Jesse's.

She was an explosion waiting to happen. Her inner darkness had risen to extremes, and there was nothing he could do about it. She would mistakenly imagine him a part of that darkness, when his objective had been the opposite.

There wasn't much time before Jesse's return with the militia, if her pilot had already called them. If Jesse dared to use outsiders at all, that is, being aware of the deals this government made with vampires in the past. Given Jesse's abhorrence at hearing that news, and with what she might be thinking about him and his part in her past, she might go after Elizabeth Jorgensen alone.

Lance felt real anxiety at the thought of Jesse finding that village. He scented fanged demons on the wind that very moment, heading his way. Not all of them. Not all twelve. A few of Jesse's monsters would remain in that village to welcome her when she arrived.

There was something else on the wind. Something nasty that he couldn't quite identify. He stood there, searching the sky, consumed by extraordinary feelings of loss, as the rounded edge of the unholy moon rose above the mountains.

"Blood moon."

The night truly was cursed. He should have known better than to tell Jesse anything tonight, but she'd been so blasted hungry for the truth kept hidden from her. She needed to be made aware of the danger to herself.

Lance dropped his gaze, scenting damp fur and animal saliva. The wolves were coming in, heeling to the beast wielding the greater power. Himself. Such hadn't always been the case. Immortals and Weres had once been enemies, vying for blood and meat, until he'd helped them in the mists of the past by protecting one of their own from slaughter.

Twenty wolves charged toward him, snarling for more of the flesh Nadia fed them. Vampire flesh, snared in the traps set out for the crazed ones who crossed his land.

The traps and the wolves would take care of a few of Jesse's enemies tonight; the fanged foes scenting her helicopter, her footprints in the snow and on his own clothes. Beneath this particular moon, the outcome seemed dim for anyone ignorant of the real ways of the world.

Nadia would seal the doors, but Jesse was no longer behind them. Jesse was out there somewhere, hurting, angry and despising him. He'd seen in her soul her willingness to sacrifice herself for the Jorgensen girl. He had witnessed the twisted sort of strength she possessed, one she now knew to be based solely on a gift coming from outside herself.

Jesse was tied to those demons she hated, and there had been no time to explain to her the differences. In point of fact, he was a demon. A vampire. Immortal. Lance Van Baaren was, as Jesse had so aptly put it, one of the walking dead.

"But it is the differences in emotion and intention that set me apart, just as those things set one human being apart from another," he whispered to Jesse. "The only thing left is for me to prove this to you, and in return make you hate yourself less."

And hate him less.

If he wasn't to have her, intimately, helping her was the least he could do.

"I would change everything if I could," he went on, as if she could hear his confession. "I would toss it all, give everything up, for the chance to be with you. As a man."

Chances were, however, and in the meandering ways of fate, that by taking it all back, by never having given her the blood strong enough to overcome her wounds, Jesse wouldn't be here at all. She'd have died in that Los Angeles alley.

The wolves, their shiny pelts as black as the night, their huge muscled bodies wired by oncoming moonlight, nipped at his legs, hungry for action. Lance heard Nadia behind him, speaking to the pack as only she was able to do, with a chilling howl that echoed across the valley.

He heard the distinct sounds of Nadia's imminent transformation from her humanlike form—the pulling flesh, the snap of bones—and again glanced up at a moon that was as much his housekeeper's as it was his.

"There are more things on this earth than you realize," he said to Jesse. "Nadia, for instance."

Turning back to his sanctuary in time to see Nadia finalizing her alternate shape in the doorway to emerge with brilliant gray fur covering her glossy muscled hide, Lance knew that though he would have help from unimaginable places, he'd have to act fast or lose Jesse to the darkness, for good.

Jesse glanced over at Stan's hands, visibly shaking on the controls as much as hers were in her lap. From beneath this hood, he said, "You are okay, Jesse? He didn't hurt you?"

The question should have been: How had he not? By giving her the blood enabling her to survive a savage mauling…by making her endure the death of her parents as well as the stint in an institution…by frightening the daylights out of her and then giving her blood again on that hotel balcony…Lance Van Baaren had played God with a mortal soul in crisis.

He had been present at the worst moment of her life. He had heard her plaintive call for help. What were the odds of that, and of finding him here? How did things like this happen at all?

And then what? The vampire who'd bitten her when she was a child had now found her alive and kicking, and felt guilty for being the source of her specialness?

She was sick, shaking and on the verge of tears. Angry didn't begin to describe her feelings. As the vampire had explained it, she'd been enhanced, supersized, upgraded, for her own good. Not by any interference or workings of an angel, but by those of a predator who just happened to look like an angel.

A fanged angel.

And there was no taking a blood donation back.

Although she wanted to shout for Stan to get her on the ground where she could be sick in private, she didn't ask. No one would benefit if she curled into a ball and cried. Stan had heard too much already. His posture was haggard, jumpy. She was obligated to answer his questions, with a vampire's blood in her veins.

"Not hurt. Shaken," she managed to say.

Take control.

Think.

Remembering everything said in that meeting was beyond her. The microphone taped to her chest was a good one. Even through the thickness of her coat, voices would emerge clearly enough. Some of that information should have been kept secret for the sake of Stan's sanity. Look what it was doing to hers.

Stan said, "Well, that's a relief. Jeez, Jesse. And FYI, I don't get it. If that creep says he can get Elizabeth, why hasn't he done so already? I heard some of what he said to you."

Without waiting for a reply, he barged on. "I've spotted that village, three leagues from here. That's what he said, three leagues. There's only one like that, and you're not going to like the looks of it. So, who do we get to charge in there? Who do we call, if it isn't already too late?"

Stan brought up a valid point, proof positive of two heads sometimes being better than one. If Lance Van Baaren was a Guardian, and a sort of benevolent immortal, as he'd said, why hadn't he already picked up the girl? Why make her seek him out, holding that promise over her head? He hadn't mentioned a trade, and he had let her go, just as he had done twice before.

Make that three times before.

"We can go back to the city and get help, or we can radio this in, have reinforcements on the way and fly over there now, ourselves," Stan persisted. "What's it going to be?"

The honest truth was that she didn't know how to answer Stan's questions. She'd been wallowing in self-pity-coated fright.

There was no one to talk about this with, except Stan. If she didn't get her act together and move ahead, she'd be the cause of another girl's downfall.

"Sheer numbers of law enforcement might do the trick," she said with wishful thinking. "Overwhelming numbers."

Then again, each individual brought in to witness this peculiar set of circumstances was never going to forget it or sleep soundly again. She was the poster girl for that fact.

And the big, bad, ugly news turned out to be that she wasn't quite human, after all. She was composed of bits of both worlds, thanks to an early rendezvous with a wicked, wingless angel.

Just how unique am I?

Do I possess the skills necessary to get us out of this?

There was no doubt about her connection to Lance Van Baaren, or about believing him. Up in the air, as far as she and Stan had already traveled, vibrations of the provocative immortal reached out to her as if his arms were actually that long. Deep within her veins and arteries, fueling her muscles and her thought processes, *he* lurked. His blood moved inside her like a caress, luring her back to him, calling her, if not with his voice, then with his very existence.

A hospital can drain me, then provide another trans-fusion of cleaner blood, assuming I'm not saturated to the cells.

More wishful thinking, since there was no time to even consider such a thing.

So, how much to tell Stan? She didn't know how to confide in anyone, had never trusted another person. Yet keeping it together meant she had to do both now.

"Something happened to me back there," she began, her thoughts halted when the spectacular brilliance of the biggest moon she had ever seen hit her eyes. A terrible light, irreverent, unholy, if Lance had spoken the truth about that, too.

"Blood moon," she muttered.

When Stan nodded, Jesse swung her attention to him. "You've heard the term?"

"Sure. I'm from Kansas, where it's called a blue moon. Used to have something to do with the harvest, but it's really just a nickname for the second full moon in one month. Doesn't happen too often."

"Why call it a blood moon?"

"Supposedly, in science fiction anyway, the theory goes like this—if you're a werewolf who shape-shifts during the full-moon phases, having two full moons in one month makes the second shift a pain in the ass. Literally. The second moon brings up anger, pain and all sorts of other corrosive shit, making even a nice easygoing werewolf jump off the deep end. Too many of those happenings, and the moon takes on the color of the blood shed in her name."

Looking sideways at her, Stan added, "So the stories go. And not that I read a lot of science fiction."

Jesse steadied her voice with a hand on her throat. They were speaking about supernatural fantasies here, things right out of fiction and nightmares. "What about vampires? How would a moon like that affect them?" she said.

Stan shrugged. "I imagine it might be the same if the moon rules their thirst in some way."

"You know about the thirst?"

"Our puffy-shirted pal explained it pretty damn decently, don't you think?"

Right. Stan had heard that. He'd been privy to her own comments in that castle as well, whatever the hell she'd said.

"So, a blood moon is like lunar catnip," Stan added, "for werewolves and vampires."

Jesse grimaced.

"Van Baaren is a vampire," she said. "A real one."

"I get that."

"Do you believe it?"

"You convinced me."

"No qualms? You just believe what you've heard on that receiver, simple as that?"

"It was right in your face, boss, and on that microphone. Not to mention that I just saw a pack of wolves running toward that place. Why would this happen, if not for some kind of supernatural reason?"

"Nadia feeds them." Lance had told her that.

"Or else they may have been trying to get away from that big moon," Stan proposed.

"That's absurd." Jesse resisted the urge to look behind her, over the trees, experiencing an honest-to-goodness desire to go back to Lance that, she reminded herself, was comprised of nothing intelligent, and was only due to the foreign blood in her body.

His blood.

Blood was intimate. She and the vampire had been as intimate as two beings could be without a sexual exchange. His teeth had thrust into her…breaking skin, sharing fluids. Was biting a human the equivalent of an orgasm for a vampire?

Jesse stared at her hand, dropped from her throat to her lap. He was there—in her fingertips, her palm, her wrist. She felt him as surely as if he held her hand. She felt him in her stomach, her hips and her thighs. There, a part of her. *Inside* her. Like a lover.

"Yeah," Stan agreed. "Just about as absurd as believing a bunch of vampires are holding Elizabeth Jorgensen in a remote village where no one lives anymore, except for them."

"Shit," Jesse whispered, not daring to think about the other body parts feeling Lance's presence, like the untouched recesses of a messed-up virgin cop's womb.

"Shit? You got that right," Stan said. "And we seem to be stuck knee-deep in it."

Jesse swiped at her lip as if the speck of blood still clung there. The accompanying scent of aluminum resisted removal. The chopper seemed to be filled with blood-laced air. She easily smelled Stan's excitement, too. Beneath his hooded parka, he had started to perspire. Moonlight, smelling like clouds and storms and stardust, reflected off her portion of the windshield.

"Theoretically, if there were vampires in that village, how many soldiers do you think we'd need to get Elizabeth out?" she asked, resting her head against her window to cool her cheeks.

"Your hundred ought to do it."

"I doubt if there are a hundred cops in the city."

"And not that many silver bullets on the planet," Stan said. "So, how else can you get the drop on a vampire?"

"Expose them to sunlight," Jesse said, wondering if that was true. Lance had walked into an alley in the daylight. He had stood in his front yard that afternoon, facing her, and hadn't been burned.

Again, she was unsettled to note how she'd registered the differences between Lance and the term *freak*.

Not a lover, damn it! More like a parasite!

"Cut off their heads," she added to the list. "But who'd actually be able to do such a thing?"

"Stake through the heart," Stan contributed, then sighed. "Like sharp wooden stakes are available at every hardware store in Slovenia in the middle of the night."

Jesse entertained the same notion Stan had been about to add to his comment. *Beneath a blood moon, were all bets off?* With those unspoken words, and the light bouncing off her window, her head took on an uncomfortable fuzziness. Luckily, some reasoning made it through.

"All of those things, including dousing them with holy water, may be fiction," she said. "Yet there has to be a trip switch. Some way to turn them off. Why are vampires allowed to exist when they're so difficult to get rid of, and mortals are so easily taken down?"

"Vampires were taken down once," Stan reminded her. "They were born people, right? Maybe a second life is charmed by tougher skin."

"Except they are no longer alive, so the word *life* doesn't apply. Still, they move around and talk, how? What animates them? It isn't right."

Neither was it plausible for a human to sustain vampire blood in their veins and live to find out about it.

"No one said life was fair, or even easy, did they?" Stan suggested, going philosophical.

Indeed, Jesse wanted to agree, no one had ever said that, because everyone knew better once they got into the rhythm of it. Cops especially had this figured out.

"We're talking about vampires, Stan."

Stan nodded. "I didn't get to see the fangs. I'm assuming you did. And you aren't prone to lying."

Not until now, by making you think you're sitting next to a regular human being. Someone like yourself.

"So, we're confronted with a fresh ball game here. A new slate. The world has gone mysterious, and we have to adapt," Stan concluded. "Like in an *X-Files* script."

Jesse wasn't so out of it that she didn't notice he'd said *we*. She wanted to hug Stan for that, and planned to do so if they made it out of this alive. Even if the odds of that happening weren't astronomical.

"Boss?"

She turned her pounding head.

"You said you were doing this for someone you loved. What exactly did you mean by that, if you don't mind me asking? I mean, we've drifted way beyond anything being too bad to talk about, haven't we?"

Maybe Stan was right, but was it possible to speak of the unspeakable? Already she tasted the residue of darkness on her tongue that was connected to her secrets.

Test the waters.

Try.

"Vampires killed my family," Jesse heard herself say, "then almost killed me. I've met these monsters before, Stan. I've seen what they can do."

Although Stan didn't immediately respond to her confidence, his hands threatened to break the controls in his grip.

Chapter 16

Stan dropped the helicopter lower. The moonlight disappeared behind a grove of trees.

"This is it," he announced, buzzing in a wide arc around the edges of that grove. "I told you it was odder than hell."

The first thing Jesse saw was what looked like an outline of thick white paint surrounding the buildings beneath them.

"That's not paint," Stan said. "Here's the crazy part. The entire place is surrounded by crosses, graveyard-style. Except that this village isn't big enough to house all those bodies, if people are buried under those things."

Jesse refocused her eyes, though she didn't actually have to. The crosses stood out brightly against the dimmer landscape. Row after row of them lined the road in and out of the village. Seen from above, they resembled a strangely assembled fence of prison bars, sealing off the village's buildings from the forest. Sealing off its occupants.

There were too many crosses to count. Jesse smelled the wood they were composed of, as if the chopper's windows were open. She tasted their purpose. If the crosses didn't actually succeed in holding back the occupants of this place, they'd been placed here as a hindrance.

"No one is coming out to greet us," Stan observed. "Maybe those crosses work a little. Shall we make that call?"

"Wait a second. Let's take a closer look, do a little recon. I can smell them down there."

"I'll pretend you didn't say that," Stan said, following her orders. "And hope they can't actually fly. Or jump."

"Twelve," Jesse said. "He told me there were twelve vampires, and that some of them would be en route to his castle, hearing the chopper, scenting me."

Stan gave her a sideways look she didn't have to see. "I'm changing my original assessment to two hundred cops or soldiers," he said. "Maybe five hundred. This place gives me the creeps."

What he didn't say, Jesse knew, was: You didn't really just say you smelled those things down there. As in, with your nose.

"No one visible before you came back to get me, either?" she asked.

"The only things moving between here and Dracula's castle that I saw were the wolves."

"Hungry wolves, I hope."

"As a matter of fact, they looked hungry to me."

Jesse stared down, not too sure any of this was real. She should have been screaming, and darting off to the city where she'd have a modicum of protection from things like this. Here she was, eyeing a village of immortal mutants, scenting their presence as effortlessly as she smelled Stan.

Was this new strength part of Lance's *gift* to her? He'd said she would be able to sense them, just as they did her. If so, these creatures knew who, and more importantly what, floated above them.

Come and get it, freaks!

She was the lure for calling vampires out of their hiding places. If they left the village, she and Stan might possibly find the missing girl.

It takes one to know one? Blood to blood?

"He said something about traps," she told Stan, shivers replacing the erotic intimacy of Lance Van Baaren's invisible caress.

"Maybe your vampire put those crosses here," Stan suggested. "Oh, wait. If he's one of them, he can't touch those things either, right?"

Stan was a quick convert to the paranormal world, thankfully. And Lance had touched the crosses. Jesse knew this.

"I'd be willing to bet he can touch a cross." She had been out of breath one too many times lately when dealing with this immortal, and sounded winded now. Lance Van Baaren was like a magnet to an affection-starved loner like herself. His warmth was unexpected. She wasn't free of the influence of those pheromones he exuded. There was no way to shake herself loose from his touch while she remained this close.

Is that why you told me to go back to the States, vampire?

Why then would he want to send her away, if he was

as evil as the rest? When he could twitch a finger and watch her run back to him? He'd copped to that sort of power, admitted it earnestly, then told her to run away.

Are you a good guy?

The final picture of this puzzle remained maddeningly elusive.

"There's nothing in the books about someone like him, Stan. I'd bet everything I own on that."

Stan nodded warily. "So, is this guy like the head vampire? A master vamp? Jeez, I can't believe I just asked you that."

"Different, yes. He is different." And he was thinking of her right then. Haunting her. The muscles around her scar contracted with the attention, as if wanting his mouth close to the old wound. Her mind rebelled firmly against such a thing.

"Then maybe he'll get here and get the girl, like he said," Stan concluded. "Fight fire with fire."

Jesse averted her face so that Stan wouldn't see the blood drain from it while she focused on the next set of questions. Did a vampire have to honor a promise? Was honor a part of their makeup, at all?

The crosses were here, all lined up. For reasons unknown to her, they preserved the suggestion of his tampering, and had captured some of his light. If Lance Van Baaren hadn't put the crosses here, he'd at least touched them, as surely as he had touched her.

"Can we take that chance?" she asked. "That he will help?"

"I just don't know. This is…" Stan faltered.

"Then let's make that call," Jesse said, stopping her pilot from straining for the unreachable. "Even if my conscience kills me for bringing others here."

* * *

The village had been closed off years ago, having become synonymous with death and suffering. All mention of it had been removed from maps of the area. Because no one in their right mind traveled through this part of Slovenia these days, it had become a no-man's-land. A dead man's haven for holed-up vampires.

Lance sprinted through the trees, toward that evil place, seeing new malice ahead, needing to exert himself and desiring time to think. A cold wind pressed against his face. An ill wind, bringing to mind the times of the black plague in England. This was another plague, just as deadly.

The moon reddened his path, infecting his pale flesh with a dull red sheen. An omen? Bad things would happen if Jesse's helicopter landed anywhere near that accursed town.

He had chased the monsters out of there long ago, after their initial killing spree. He'd then tried to seal them off. With Nadia's help, he had built and placed the crosses enclosing the evil, and for a while the crosses had done the trick. Although vampires could exist for a long time without blood, it seemed they weren't exempt from rustling up some creativity when the thirst finally overwhelmed.

Unless someone or something else had helped them.

He had recognized the gaunt drifter in the city that morning as it emerged from the shadows, sick and starving. Tonight, just moments ago, more familiar faces had slipped their cage, heading for his home, breaking free of this village he'd been keeping an eye on.

Nadia and her kin would be waiting for them. She and her wolves—riled up with the full moon and a hunger of their own, born of the night the vampires arrived in their village forty years ago to destroy a peaceful human-Were population.

"Jesse? Do you hear me?" Lance covered ground with his hair streaming out behind him. "Do not go there. Do not touch down. Some new thing has taken up residence in that village. I'd been near there when I first saw you up in the sky. I've been distracted from seeking it."

More than a thirsty vampire, Jesse.

The scent is of blood, with intellect behind it.

Different.

If he called Jesse back, she'd be hurt one way or another. But between the two things—himself, and what roamed that village—he was by far the safer bet.

"Jesse! Listen to me. I know you hear. Stop!"

Jolted in her seat, Jesse reacted with a swift "No!" that caused Stan to shift uncomfortably beside her.

"No, what, Jesse? Don't make the call?"

She put a hand to her head, wondering if a good slap to her temple might chase away Lance's voice. "I can feel him calling to me. I'm not crazy. Not...crazy."

"Never thought you were," Stan said. "No matter what the other guys we know might have said." He glanced sideways. "Sorry. Bad time for a joke."

"You do believe me, Stan?"

"I do," he grumbled.

"Then you won't argue when I ask you to set this chopper down?"

"Okay, maybe just a little crazy," Stan amended, eyeing her cautiously.

"I want to go down there."

"My two cents would go something like this: No way."

"He's coming, Stan. I have to meet him."

"Like hell you do. How do you know he is coming?"

"I told you. He calls me. His voice is in my mind right now."

"Telling you to go down there?"

"Asking me not to."

"So, you're ignoring that advice because...?"

"He's a vampire." *And so am I, partly.*

"Maybe more than a little crazy, then, for going to that castle in the first place, alone," Stan mumbled. "He didn't bite you or anything while you were there?"

Another joke? A real question this time? Jesse moved her fingers over her forehead to find a light layer of perspiration gathering on her brow. It was becoming more difficult to ignore *him.* She wanted to tear off her jacket to get rid of the lingering hint of their closeness.

"He didn't bite me there." The truth, if flawed. He had bitten her long ago, seemingly in another lifetime. His little blood donation, appropriate or not and under such dire circumstances, and quite possibly saving her life, had brought her to this very moment in time. To a place teeming with bloodsuckers.

"Where?" Stan asked.

Jesse looked to Stan for clarification. Was he asking where she'd been bitten when she was a kid? Did Stan know about that? Her fingers dropped to her neck, to the continually throbbing scar.

"Where do I set this tin can down?" he said.

The wolves were all around, some of them on Lance's heels. Their menacing growls were the only sounds in the meadow, other than the crush of grass and snow beneath their paws. Nine black coats glistened like polished alabaster.

The scent of the new intruder, stronger as he neared the village, filled him with foreboding. It was red, dangerous and female.

Was he perceiving Jesse's anger? No, something else. And damn it five ways to Sunday, Jesse had already touched down.

He felt the halting effect of the planted crosses as he rounded the northern edge of the forest. Their holy presence pounded at him like a web of invisible warriors. Nevertheless, holy relics were a hindrance to those with dark intentions.

He had already passed this particular test, once wearing a crucifix to remind himself of how far he'd come. He had endured years of monastic life in order to master the wretched torture of no longer being one of God's living children who were chosen to live and die peacefully, with an invitation to heaven.

But he wasn't sure about that conclusion by the time he'd parted from the monks. His existence had been honorable, nearly always, since his creation. Just maybe, he decided, he was a force for good. One of God's legion

Like Jesse's angel.

In the most distant of his lifetimes, in the beginning, he had protected the Holy Grail as one of its champions, he remembered as he ran. He had been one of seven brothers-in-arms set up to keep safe the mother of all holy relics that was rumored to restore peace and tranquillity to a ravaged, war-torn land. It was a task that he and the six others who had taken the blood oath of immortality had pledged to accomplish. A shining quest. A task at which they ultimately failed, leaving the

Seven to fend for themselves as time passed everyone else by, in a world that had forgotten about them and their secrets.

He had persevered for centuries in the shadows until strong enough to take some of the lost sunlight back. He had lived long enough to outdistance most threats, and no longer cared about them.

Except for one very real threat. A female with amber-flecked brown eyes and a scarred neck, who hosted the purest blood of the Seven in her delicate veins. A female, after all this time, reminding him of the things he had given up in favor of higher pursuits.

Jesse.

His last chance at what? Normality? Setting things straight? Making things right? There was no going back. He'd explained this to Jesse. Had they met centuries too late?

The anguish of possibly losing her was brutal. Fate, the mysterious phenomenon that was ongoing, ever present and not to be overlooked or underestimated, had him by the throat.

A vampire's ultimate irony.

The presence of the vampires hit Jesse in wave after wave of goose bumps that erupted from her insides, out. The whir and steady hum of the blades overhead was the only sound amid the darkness of this gigantic sinkhole of hell on earth. Jesse held her breath for as long as she could, so she wouldn't say something stupid, or scream.

"Use the spotlight?" Stan asked. "It's too frigging dark out there. I can't see anything beyond the paint on those crosses. Closer up, those crosses are downright eerie."

"They're here for a reason."

"Maybe nobody bothered to tell *them* that, if they've gotten out long enough to snatch the senator's daughter."

Stan, Jesse noted, appeared to be waiting for something. He'd been glancing over his shoulder repeatedly. Jesse studied him closely.

"How long before the others get here?" she finally asked.

"Twenty minutes, max."

Jesse raised an eyebrow.

"Okay. You got me. I confess," he said. "I called them earlier, while waiting for you. I only told them I thought I knew where the girl was being held. Nothing about vampires and…things like that."

"All right," Jesse said. There was nothing to be done about it now. If she was to face what came down here, and on her own terms, she would have to hurry.

"He was winning," Stan added. "You have to be one of the bravest people I know, and one of the strongest in spirit, but Jesse, we both know from what came through that microphone that he almost got the better of you in there."

Jesse stared through the windshield without bothering to argue because Stan was right. Stan, this last bit of confidence revealed, had heard every last thing, maybe even her heavy breathing.

With shaky fingers, Jesse pulled back the neck of her sweater, then the collar of her coat. "This is what they did to me when I was a kid." She pointed to her neck and the remnants of the old wound on it. "The rest of it—the things they said about me in the precinct about being psychic, along with some other, less favorable names—are because of this. And because of him. The man in that castle saw to it I would live a while longer by sealing this wound with his own kiss of death. He was there when my parents died, Stan, and I... I believed all this time that he was an angel."

Stan sat like stone. Not one muscle moved when he said, "Vampire, Jesse. He's a vampire. You said *man,* insinuating that there's a human being in that castle."

"Self-preservation," she whispered, without missing a beat. "With his blood in my veins, what does that make me?"

"You," Stan said. "It makes you the you I'm sitting here with right now. It also makes you responsible for my safety." Though partially fake, his grin radiated plenty of warmth. "So, if you can smell these suckers, and with whatever voodoo you're known for, boss, tell me where they are, and what we do about it."

Well, Jesse thought irrationally in a circumstance when rationality stood between life and probable death...this had to be some kind of record. Two males liking her, for reasons beyond her ability to explain the phenomenon. She actually might rest in peace at last, she supposed, knowing she had friends in all the wrong places.

Chapter 17

The helicopter's twirling blades glinted silver, spinning fast, reflecting the red moonlight.

Shutting the engine down wouldn't have occurred to Jesse's pilot, Lance reasoned, since a wingless chopper was a dead end in terms of an exit. Like a grounded dragonfly, the metallic silver beast sat in a field beside the village road pockmarked with crosses, with its doors open. Abandoned.

"Bloody hell!" An oath from his past. "It's too late."

He saw her, then, and his heart burst with short-lived relief. Jesse was walking up the lane with her pilot, who waved a flashlight in front of them that would have been insufficient in the best of cases. Both Jesse and Stan held guns, but they may as well have been holding water pistols if they weren't able to see anything coming at them.

Jesse.

She stopped abruptly. He felt the shudder that racked her thin, wiry frame. He sensed how the fine, silky hairs at the nape of her beautiful neck curled with the latent blast of his wish for her to halt.

He heard her say, "He's here."

Her pilot halted. "Is he friendly, or do we have to also watch our backs?"

"Which is it to be, then?" she asked, speaking over her shoulder. "Friend or foe?"

And then he was beside her, standing in the meager beam of Stan's flashlight. He watched Stan stumble sideways, and wondered if this was the pilot's first sighting of a vampire, up close or otherwise. Stan smelled of nerves, pumped-up muscle and anxious perspiration. Ringing those things was the oddly familiar odor of animal. A surprise. But Lance couldn't address that now and turned his attention to Jesse. She stood her ground, her weapon steady in a two-handed grip, her face as wan as his own.

"Elizabeth is nearby," she said. "I can feel her."

"She's in the church." Lance turned his face to the wind.

"Strange place for a dining room," she said.

Jesse's pilot looked back and forth between them, hoping, Lance knew, that Jesse didn't mean what he thought she'd meant. That a feast was taking place up ahead, in a holy place. The ultimate blasphemy.

"Manners don't always take precedence in the dark," Lance remarked.

"She is alive." Jesse cocked her head the same way he had.

"Barely," he conceded.

"Why is she alive?"

"I don't know."

"Yet you knew it. You've known all along."

"Yes."

"What else don't I know?" Her question was voiced in a calm outward tone that hid as many unspoken horrors as the dark, silent buildings around Jesse. "Is she really there?"

"She is, yes."

"How many days, hours, meals does it take to change that?"

"It only takes one bite from a scavenger who knows no better and needs above all to feed the thirst. An experienced vampire can spread that out for days."

"So," Jesse said, wincing over the image of such a possibility, "we can extrapolate that there are experienced monsters here."

Lance nodded. "At least one. The one I tried to warn you about."

"I can't feel the difference," she admitted.

"I can."

"Why don't they come out?" Stan asked gruffly, his flashlight beam moving into the distance. "How many are there?"

"Six," Jesse answered. "There are six here." To Lance, she said, "Who's the star?"

Lance quieted the riot of emotions that were tied to Jesse's. No easy task. She had become a large part of his renewed vigor since that first unbelievable sighting. Thoughts of nothing else, other than being near her, had strengthened the bond between them, leaving him a prisoner of sorts. No doubt she felt the same.

Jesse's precarious hold on her prejudices was slipping, as he watched her. She still hated her monsters. She thought she hated him for what he was, what he had done in the past and what he was doing to her now.

Which meant that he was doing something, affecting her. Her soul was in turmoil over this.

"There are monsters in all of us," he reminded her. "In varying degrees."

"So, what's the pronouncement on the one in there?" Stan asked. "The one who found a way to let the others out, and is waiting for us? What degree is that one?"

"Cold," Lance replied. "Coldhearted and cruel. Not for helping her kind escape, but due to the worst motive of all."

"What's that?" Stan asked.

"Her?" The vehemence in Jesse's voice trumped Stan's. But Lance said to her pilot, for Jesse's benefit, "The motives are greed, power and jealousy. The pleasure of draining a living being a few precious drops at a time, just because it can be done. The feeling of absorbing those few drops. Jealousy of a heart able to keep its own rhythm, when a vampire's no longer follows the deep tracks of time. The power an immortal wields over a mortal's failing hold on his own life. The taste of a soul as it slides down the biter's throat."

"Jeez," Stan muttered.

Jesse's heartbeat had picked up with his earnest explanation, as had her pilot's. Unlike Stan's, however, which came across as a loud, regular boom, Jesse's pulse skidded all over the place, searching for a groove.

Jesse tasted the truth in his words, knowing now, and for certain, that she was changed forever. Not because of any physical alteration discernible on the surface, but for knowing what was inside her. Her inner blackness was bubbling up. He had uncorked the bottle.

Hiding what she was would be impossible, she was thinking. Among L.A.'s huge population, she'd have to keep to the shadows, where other fringe populations existed. Not belonging to any one place. Never belonging. Although no one would know the truth about her, she would distance herself on her own, without really needing to, out of self-loathing.

"I'm sorry," Lance said to her again, needing to say it, willing her to believe him by pushing his earnestness toward her from the outer reaches of his own soul. "My intent was to help you survive. I was sure, seeing you here, so far from Los Angeles, that you had come for me, whether you knew it or not. I still want to believe this. You see, as it turns out, I'm as greedy as all the rest."

Jesse's gun wavered. Observing this, her pilot spoke.

"So, maybe, if we get out of this alive—those of us who actually *are* alive—you two can have a chat," Stan said. "Right now may not be the best time. I have no special skills, but I can feel those suckers coming. The hair on my arms is standing straight up!"

They were coming, all right, silent as a pod of stealth submarines. Night was their time, darkness their mode of transportation. The undead flowed through the shadows like tattered, streaming bits of it. The blood moon had opened her arms to the creatures of the night.

"Must…get Elizabeth," Jesse stuttered, looking up at him suddenly, as if he'd spoken aloud.

Lance felt a streak of electricity zing through her with an intensity that left her breathless.

Yes, we are connected. Bonded. In telling you so, I have sealed your fate.

"If you are sorry, if you care, if you are what you say you are, help us get Elizabeth Jorgensen back," she said, the defiance in her voice challenging him, pleading with him to take up this task.

"Alive," Stan added, moving closer to Jesse in

a guarded stance, turning his head to search the moonlight-dappled darkness beyond his flashlight.

The night smelled rancid, Jesse thought. Standing on the outskirts of the deserted village with her gun raised and her senses wide open, she was afraid to rely too heavily on those senses, with Lance planted firmly in front of her.

Although the moon, whatever kind it was, shone fiercely enough to lend shape to the buildings closest to her, Stan's flashlight illuminated Lance Van Baaren's anxious features as the beam of weaker light made a pass.

Jesse sucked in a stale breath. She heard Stan grunt as his beam quickly lowered to the ground. The vampire's face had glistened in the light.

The metal of her gun felt foreign in her damp palms, but her fingers were glued to it, one of them resting lightly on the trigger. "I'll never be like you, even if I'm halfway there," she said.

Her blood, however much of it she possessed, pounded in her head, as if opposing this bond caused her more pain. She still found Lance a thing of incredible beauty. She wanted to reach out and touch his perfect physique. She wanted him to open his exotic lips and tell her everything—who she'd become, and what would happen if they made it out of here.

Lance Van Baaren glowed in the red-dyed darkness, a being not belonging to either world, wholly. Not dead, not alive, he rode the currents between worlds, creating his own place, his own race. And he was trying to take her there with him.

She could shoot him and be done with it. If she squeezed the trigger, part of this would be over. And if she succeeded in putting him in the ground for good, how would she learn to live like this? There would be no one to light the way. Worse yet, she'd never view his perfection again, or feel his heart next to hers.

The last thought didn't come as a shock. But the moment was disrupted. One of the freaks was watching her. She felt its eyes on her back.

The horror of where she was again washed over her.

"Get away!" she said, as much a command for herself as for the pair of vampires, one of which, even now, had the power to steal her breath away.

"Jesse?" Stan's voice drew her. "Something's over there, by the door."

Jesse heard growling and more fierce noises. Saw movement too fast to nail down. Stan's flashlight beam swept to the east, catching a glint of glossy black pelt passing through the light. An animal, on all fours.

Jesse took aim. A pale hand came up to block her. "Wolf," Lance said, as if that should make any difference in a potential target.

Stan said to him, "Are they with you?"

Lance nodded. "They will warn us."

"How will they do that?" Jesse snapped. "Open their muzzles and whistle?"

She felt Stan's eyes on her this time, and heard his unspoken question. *Are you losing it, boss?*

That's exactly what she was doing. Losing her mind.

"I'm fine," she said. "There are wolves now, on our side. God. Where's that church?"

"Stan," Lance said without taking his eyes from her. "Take her back to the helicopter before it's too late."

"And I'd listen to you, why?" Stan said.

Lance's voice added to the chill of the night. "Do you want her to find out about you, whether or not she finds the girl?"

Jesse looked to her pilot, confused by that statement, unable to see Stan's face beneath his hooded parka. Lance stepped closer to her, filling her vision. He pressed a lock of her hair behind her ear, ignoring the gun biting into his chest. "Go," he said. "Do this for me, Jesse, if not for yourself."

His voice was an instantaneous lull, a singsong demand that flowed through her head, her body, her obstinacy, transporting her somewhere…else.

Darkness overlapped darkness, and she was again in someone's arms, limp, weak, numb. The impulse came to argue, to protest and break away from the invisible bonds Lance wove, until that impulse dissipated.

She was in someone's arms, being carted away from the buildings, and perhaps out of danger. Helpless, unable to move, Jesse gave one last look over the wide shoulder of the vampire carrying her, to see a wolf, black as the night, eyes gleaming darkly, its dangerous mouth open, standing complacently by Stan's side. As if they were friends.

Chapter 18

She came to her senses slowly. The sharp tang of metal and plastic hit her like an old-fashioned dose of smelling salts, forcing her eyes open…to more darkness.

She was confined in a tight space. Panic set in when she couldn't move her arms. For a horrifying second, Jesse thought she might be trapped in a coffin, and issued a bloodcurdling scream. Then she saw the light sheering off the windshield, and knew it was a windshield. Her panic ebbed. She was in the chopper.

Where was Stan?

Her eyes adjusted to her surroundings. Jesse lifted her head from the seat back. Her confinement was the harness. She moved her fingers across familiar straps, and found the buckles and the release.

The events leading up to this untimely little blackout came hurtling back to her in a cold head rush. Lance had done this to her. With his voice.

Also, there had been a wolf. And an unusual moon. She held up her hand. No gun.

Turning her head, she took in the eerie glow of the rows of crosses, which all of a sudden seemed twice as ominous as before.

Swallowing the bitter aftertaste of temporary defeat, Jesse pulled at her restraints.

She ran on legs the consistency of lead, with her spare revolver in her hand. Stan had been left with the vampires, out there. She'd never forgive herself if anything happened to her friend.

As she raced on, the dank village smells morphed into an odor of decay so intense, it acted as its own barrier. Mold and mildew odors joined in. Lance had told her these vamps could smell her from a distance, so how did they stand a place that stank of charred wood, the decomposing bodies of former occupants and spores floating in the silent, stagnant air?

Poor Elizabeth. She might be alive, but would she recover from this? Be locked away for years, in a straitjacket, every time she tried to remember?

Jesse's uncanny radar stopped her in time to keep her from tripping over a lump in the road. Was it a body? *Oh, please! Not Stan!*

Not…Stan.

But she realized without looking that what lay by her feet wasn't human. The scent drifting up was of damp fur. The body still gave off heat. This had to be the wolf, dead no more than a few minutes, which meant she couldn't have been blacked out and in that helicopter for long.

Sidestepping the animal corpse, Jesse hurtled on— between the crosses, into the nest of buildings, with only the moon to light her progress. A faraway part of herself noticed how well she moved in the dark, though the thought was fleeting. She opened her mouth to shout for Stan, then thought better of it.

Rounding a cottage that lay in ruins, its roof sagging and its door hinged open, she paused. The back of her neck prickled. Spinning on her heels, she said to no one immediately visible, "I've come to take Elizabeth Jorgensen home."

Did these walking cadavers know the name of the girl they'd been feasting on?

"Have you, now? Come here for that reason?" someone asked. A female voice, with a noticeable British accent. And another surprise. Jesse hadn't ever contemplated the possibility of female vampires. A big mistake, she realized, since she also had that kind of blood in her veins.

Jesse aimed her gun at the shadows beside her. "Where is she?"

"You have come to make ridiculous demands? Offer a trade?" the female returned with a calm that reminded Jesse of just how far up the creek she actually was among conscienceless bloodsuckers.

The word *soul* floated in the air around her. Lance had told her he had a soul, and she desperately wanted to believe him. What were the odds of finding another misplaced soul among these shadows?

"I'll trade a round of silver bullets," she said.

"I'd be there before you squeezed the trigger," the female threatened.

A cold shiver passed through Jesse's body, in one side and out the other, in an east-to-west pathway. A directional cue. She leveled the gun toward those distasteful eastern shadows and pulled in a breath of fetid air.

"Try," she warned.

The darkness blurred, warped. A hand grabbed her by the throat, but not before Jesse squeezed off a round. The explosion was deafening. The fingers on her throat fell away. Whoever the hand belonged to issued a shocked, slow wail, and then came the rain of ashes—the dirty remnants of the vampire.

More hands reached for her. Too many at once. Whipping the gun around, Jesse fired again, at random. Another wail went up. More filthy ash hit her in the face.

She fired a third time, swinging the weapon as she was knocked off her feet. A puff of stinking air arrived. More ash.

"That makes three!" she yelled, thrashing on her back in the dirt, smelling not only the presence of the two monsters holding her, but a third vampire as well. This third one was a more powerful bloodsucker, instinct told her. Its feel was weightier, more painful, like metal spikes jammed to her bones. It stank of dank, wet earth.

"Get…off…me!" Jesse barked.

A shoe came down heavily on her chest and pressed in. All Jesse managed to see was a long stretch of fabric; yellow, tinted with a red film from the moon bouncing off the ruined roof over their heads.

This was the female who had addressed her a minute ago. She…*it*…was the master monster here, the one Lance had tried to warn her about. The creature who had set free the other vampires from their holy, cross-filled prison, and who was behind the kidnapping and torture of a young girl.

"No soul," Jesse whispered as a gleaming set of razor-sharp teeth came lethally close to her face, and as she feared the end might be near.

Silently, and with all her might, she issued a call to Lance. Perhaps a last message, born of fear and acceptance of the fate at hand. *Save the girl. You promised.*

She acknowledged the drumming in her neck and the awful ache of her scar coming to life. Felt the prick of teeth scraping across her throat in search of an artery. The predator's teeth rested momentarily on her scar, as if surprised to find the ridged tissue. Then they moved in a slow drag across her skin that stung like the rake of a primed cutting knife.

The female spoke, her tone vehement, acidic.

"He gave it to you," she hissed. "That selfish, arrogant bastard."

And then Jesse's windpipe took a blow that turned her world pitch-black.

Lance's head came up. A voice, like a shockwave of dispersed night air, slammed into him. He turned. Jesse's pilot pivoted alongside.

"No," Lance said.

"Jesse?" Fear was etched on Stan's hooded face.

"The church," Lance directed. "Go there. Only one of them holds Elizabeth at present. She's very near death, hanging on by a thread."

"I have to get to Jesse," Stan growled. "The girl is important. But Jesse…"

"You can't help Jesse here. Not in this instance. I have to face this. It's partially my fault."

Stan shook his head adamantly, rocking onto his toes. "Jesse first."

"No!" Lance said with a restraining hand on Stan's arm. "It's for me, because of me."

Stan had the sense to believe him, as well as the instinct to give in to the powerful alpha immortal, like the rest of the Were clan. Stan had been holding on to his shape longer than he had the strength for. He was shaking all over, his face as gray as the ash on the ground as he fought his true nature.

"Go to it," Lance urged. "Let the moon take you."

Without wasting any more time, Lance ran like mad back toward the village center, where the very beat of his heart lay.

He knew her. The village center was wrapped in her smell, and reeked of her immortal presence. The master here was as familiar as his own feet. Although he'd known this villain was female, the slap of familiarity was a surprise.

"Hello, Gwen," he said through clenched teeth, yanking her upright, pressing the length of his body tightly against hers from behind before she could react.

The fragrance of flowers, twisted and modified by the centuries of blood she'd ingested and the loss of sunlight to enhance its glow, permeated her waist-length hair—still as fair in color as his own. His old love was skeletal, hardly more than stretched skin over bone, where once she'd had the lush, vital curves of a pampered queen. Her tresses, much envied in the past, were matted, falling over her shoulders like strips of unwashed, tangled rags.

Lance kept her from moving by wrapping his arms around her arms. He whispered, "It would seem you got your wish, after all."

"No thanks to you," she said. But the woman he had

pushed away for her own sake centuries ago listened without a struggle, her body as cold as the patch of frost at their feet.

"To what do I owe this honor?" Lance asked quietly, eyeing Jesse on the ground, unconscious, but breathing fitfully. Jesse was alive. The scraggly creature he held in his arms had not killed her.

"I heard she was here," Gwen said, "and that you'd gifted her. I came all this way to meet the woman who had tamed you into submission. Yet she isn't one of us, after all. Look at her, my love. How pathetic she lies there. White and pathetic and sickeningly human to some degree."

"I did not bring her over," he said.

"Nor did you change me," Gwen snapped dangerously.

"I do not hand out immortality, as well you know. That was not my purpose."

"Nevertheless, here I am," Gwen taunted. "Tainted, of course. I could not find the Six, though I searched long and far for your brothers. My immortality is not pure. Not a match for yours. Still, I exist."

"You've let the vampires out," he said.

"To bring you here."

"The crosses were for the protection of the mortals."

"I'm old enough that tricks don't matter. Neither do your precious mortals."

Lance took a tighter hold on her. "You did this for me, Gwen? Brought the American girl here for me? Hoping to lure me?"

"A gift from an old flame. Though there's not much of the girl left. The others in this village, weakened by your restraints, couldn't be made to wait. You starved them, my love. Your own kind."

Lance ran a hand along her shoulder, feeling every jagged bone. "You know better," he admonished. "They are not my kind."

"Nevertheless, the trick worked."

"It did," he agreed, noting the damage Jesse's gun had dealt, smelling the ash all around that meant she'd taken out more than a few of her monsters before falling prey to this one.

"And now?" he said to the creature he held.

"You will love me again," Gwen said.

The flavor of her lie was muddied earth. Lance felt the hatred emanating from her that had simmered for centuries. Gwen was a killer now. Psychopathic. An instrument of death whose diluted blood had no doubt sired numerous others, and who had loosed the potential for a reign of terror upon the Slavs in this part of his country. Gwen, once so beautiful and golden in his memory, was an abomination, just as he had feared she might be.

Heat rushed through his veins. Blood pounded in his ears. Gwen couldn't be allowed to exist. What were the chances she'd go away or repent her sins? After finding Jesse and realizing what existed in Jesse's veins, Gwen would never allow her a moment's peace. Jesse would never be safe. She'd have nowhere in the world to hide from this shunned vampire's grudge.

Still, he'd find killing Gwen difficult. She was the only other woman he had loved, or thought he loved, until the real thing came along to prove the difference. Jesse.

He listened to the sounds of fighting in the distance.

Nadia had arrived—a familiar touch of wolf on his sensitive skin.

A half-starved vampire was no match for two werewolves bent on revenge, let alone a wolf pack. Perhaps Stan and Nadia were working together to free the American girl. He sensed Elizabeth Jorgensen, too. Alive. Gwen had at the very least seen to that, whether or not she meant to. A last mistake? A final triumph? Who knew, since truth had no part in Gwen's existence these days.

Moonlight dripped over him, over his captive and over Jesse's body on the ground. Tonight, the moon was thirsty. Sacrifices had to be made. The village would be cleaned up, Gwen among its casualties. That ought to satisfy a blood moon. But the ultimate sacrifice? His own sacrifice? He'd let Jesse go. Make her pilot whisk her away to safety, without so much as a last agonizing pressure of his lips on hers.

"A parting gift, Jesse. Your life back," he whispered.

"No!" Gwen twisted in his grasp. "You cannot have her."

"I won't have her," he said, meaning it.

"Then you will have me." Gwen's remark belied the severity of her need for revenge. The odor of that need seeped from every pore of her emaciated body.

A cry went up from the wolves, closer this time; yips and howls of triumph from Nadia's creatures. Animals trained to trap and rip apart ripe vampire flesh before the monsters dissipated completely.

He heard the padding of running paws and the heavier footsteps of the two werewolves leading them. Dried blood laced through the foul air in the village center as a stocky figure appeared beneath the roof cover, carrying a girl in his arms and trailed by a pack of wolves as black and as feral as the overlapping shadows.

Jesse groaned, slowly regaining consciousness. Lance's heart went out to her.

"For the sake of what we had," Gwen pleaded, eyeing the gnashing jaws of the oncoming wolves.

"Yes, for the sake of that," Lance said. Then he let Gwen go.

He didn't truly believe she'd run away, predicting how this would play itself out, knowing how it would end.

With the speed of a malicious Reaper, Gwen dropped on top of Jesse, her fangs bared. Before Lance reached for her, the wolves, in a heated wave and with the force of a hurricane, swept Gwen away.

It only took one good bite to the jugular from a well-trained enemy for the woman Lance had left in a long-faded past to become dust.

And he was on his knees, beside Jesse.

Chapter 19

Jesse was deathly cold, but maybe not dead, because her head hurt like a tractor had rolled over it.

Moving a leg, she encountered the chill of crisp sheets. A little voice in her mind whispered: *Four-hundred-count.*

She opened her eyes, cringed at the light streaming over her and over the bed. Sunlight squeezing between the slats of a shuttered window.

Daylight.

She shot upward, and was pushed back down. Finding the nerve to look around, Jesse found herself buried beneath a fluffy beige comforter with the consistency of a cloud. An elaborate footboard rose up just past her feet. She wasn't on the ground in a cursed village. It was no longer night.

The gravelly voice of a man broke the silence. He exuded an aroma of damp hair and muffins, and was trying his hardest to remain calm when he was anything but.

"You awake, boss?"

She turned her head, her pulse tapping out her wariness, her body ready to leap.

"It's morning," Stan said.

Jesse let that news settle, took a breath, calmed herself. "Hotel?"

"Bingo," Stan said.

"You okay?" she asked.

"Fine. Elizabeth will be too, in a month or so. She's in the hospital with the senator by her side."

How the hell had she missed that part? Oh, yeah. A vampire in a yellow dress had her teeth on her throat.

Her hand went to her scar. "Status?"

"The girl's had several transfusions already. She lost a lot of blood, but she'll make it."

Jesse already knew that, somehow. How had she known it?

"The senator and this government are waiting to shake your hand," Stan went on. "I think they might throw a parade in your honor. Not to mention the quite remarkable bonus they'll be adding to your usual fee."

She knew this, too. Maybe she'd overheard people talking.

"I told them no parade," Stan said teasingly, though his tone came across as thoughtful. "No fuss."

"Thanks," she managed to say. "Appreciate the help."

"Hey, no problem."

"No, I mean *thanks*." Jesse looked closely at the man who had faced down death with her, by her side, way above and beyond the call of duty. Beyond even the realms of the believable.

He nodded solemnly. "You all right, Jesse? Really?"

"I think so. No new holes, anyway. How do I look?"

"Like—"

"Death warmed over?"

She was sorry the second that came out, and turned her head. "I guess I can't say that anymore, right?"

"You can say whatever the hell you like. To me, anyway," Stan said.

Stan, she saw, was a little ragged around the edges. A bandage, smelling of plastic and antibiotics, hid a cut over his right eye. Some sort of iodine tincture painted the scratch across his nose, highlighting a palm-size bruise.

"It wasn't a dream," she said.

He shook his head, probably wondering what she'd remember, while knowing in his gut that she knew it all, and maybe even about the secrets he kept. She saw this as clearly as if he'd spoken out loud.

Dear, dear Stan. What secrets was he hiding?

"You brought both of us back here? Heck, Stan, the parade should be for you."

Stan shook his shaggy head again. "He brought you here."

Those words twisted through her, tasting of smoke, stone and leather. Exotic, sensual, golden fare.

Fingers on her scar, she found another memory. Lance's mouth on hers, pressing the life back into her, seeing that she called up what she needed to make it this time…as always.

Lance Van Baaren. In the blood-washed alley, looking like an angel. In the hotel. In the castle, the village, picking up the pieces of the puzzle she'd lost, helping to get Elizabeth Jorgensen back.

Everything, even this room, revolved around the golden vampire and his choice of actions.

He had given her back the blood she'd lost so long ago—its consistency thick, and tasting of copper. His blood, sliding down her throat and into her bloodstream, united them in a supernatural way that had carried her all the way to the here and now.

To him.

The vampire had done all this, and had brought her here to heal. Not to his castle, where he'd have the advantage, but to the hotel, and Stan. To sunlight on a beige comforter, surrounded by the sounds of civilization.

All the things Lance Van Baaren would never have.

For your own good, he had said. But what did he know of that, or about her needs? She was restless, and knew why. She was hungry for…him. And he had gone.

Voices were buzzing beyond the window. Stan's heart beat loudly in her ears. The sheets, whatever count they were, felt rough against her sensitive skin. She found the light, though welcome this morning, too bright to stare into…

And *he* was thinking about her. The vampire with a soul. The being who called himself a Guardian, and whose blood flowed through her.

The old enemy? No. Not at all like them. Different. Honorable, in the end.

"We can leave tomorrow," Stan suggested. "You're under a doctor's orders to stay in bed until then."

"Okay," she acquiesced.

"Like hell," Stan said, reading her easily enough.

"I have one more trip to make," she confessed, only then realizing this was true. She had to thank Lance for, if not herself, Elizabeth Jorgensen. She had to see him one more time.

"I won't condone it, Jesse," Stan grumbled. "Because this big doofus, sitting here next to you, is going to admit, verbally, right this second, that I don't want to lose you."

After a short span of silence, he added, "There, I've said my piece."

Jesse's heart nearly broke. It actually shuddered. So, she thought, this was what friendship felt like. Nothing at all like pain. This was joyous, heartwarming, new.

"We won't lose each other." She laid a hand on Stan's rugged face. "Not ever. Friends?"

Stan nodded soberly. "Friends."

"Partners?"

After taking a second to take that offer in, Stan showed the beginnings of a surprised grin.

"Good. I'd like to rest now," Jesse said. "I need to think."

"Like hell," Stan repeated, but he got to his feet. "I'll be cleaning up the bird, in case you need to find me."

When their eyes met, he smiled.

The chopper touched down. Jesse hopped out. The whir of the blades filled the quiet, echoing the hum going through her mind.

"Vampire," she whispered, staring up at the castle.

Turning, she looked to Stan. He nodded. They hadn't discussed this visit. On some internal level, Stan had known where she wanted to go. Why she was here remained the question at hand. Which reminded her… they'd need to talk about Stan's secrets if they were to be partners. Fair was fair.

"Lance," she said, slightly louder this time and with the weight of her presence behind the use of his name.

She felt him acknowledge her from a distance—a sudden flare of heat in her limbs and a sensual vibration—knowing he didn't move from wherever he was. His touch seemed to hail from a far place, as if he wasn't tucked behind those granite walls at all. Had he left the privacy of his retreat, moved on, because too many people knew about it? Because she did?

The heat he caused gathered into a central ball of fire in her abdomen, where it revolved for several slow turns before beginning to dissipate. Jesse folded her arms across herself automatically, hugging the warmth to her torso and feeling so very cold everywhere else. But this heat wasn't to be trapped. It remained elusive, as did its cause.

Lance had gone from this place, taking with him some of the color, intensity and spark that had flared between them. He wasn't coming out to meet her. He didn't want to see her. That much was clear. Not even to say goodbye.

A great sense of loss descended upon her as his front door, with its carved Van Baaren crest, remained closed. This need to see him was stupid, really, Jesse told herself, since despising vampires had been her lifelong mission.

From now on she'd be able to find vampires everywhere. Thanks to what this one had done, nothing in her future would look the same, be the same. It wouldn't even smell the same. Lance had seen to it, and virtually guaranteed, that her life would be altered.

Hating him was the more appropriate response, in spite of owing him for Elizabeth. In the girl's case, he'd done a good, decent thing. A soulful deed. Just, she supposed, as he'd tried to do in the past by saving her own life, while pretending to have the gifts of an angel.

Now, as she stared at the closed door, a gaping emptiness yawned inside her, in the place once warmed by the vampire's fire. She wasn't powerful enough to find him if he didn't want to be found. She carried the blood of an immortal in her veins, but was not immortal, herself. She had one foot in this world and one in another. Different, in a new way. A being apart. Like him.

"What will it do to me? Who will I be?" she had asked him.

"You. Only more so."

She hoped to God he was right.

At least, she thought as she headed back to the chopper, one question had been answered; the one that had plagued her since she found herself alive, so long ago. She knew the reason behind feeling like an outsider.

Unable to talk about her feelings, she pointed over the trees. "Ready to go home, Stan?"

"Not to mention relieved, a million times over," her pilot confessed.

She should have agreed. Wanted to agree. But the farther they traveled—past the meadow that had kicked this all off, and the village, as empty now as a ghost town—the more unsettled Jesse felt. The more restless and empty she became.

Did she know the reasons for these feelings, as well? Yes.

Looking down at the ground, Jesse nodded.

I will see you again, vampire.

Chapter 20

Los Angeles seemed like its own planet of chaos after the wide expanses of underpopulated Slovenia. There were people everywhere, lights everywhere. Tonight, the glittering City of Angels seemed like one big freaking lightbulb.

Yet it also took on the haunted cast of loneliness, as only a city its size can seem to a tired traveler.

Jesse exited the car, thanked the driver and hoisted her bag over one shoulder. After giving her apartment building a cursory once-over, she headed up the walkway toward her cottage at the back. A few residents, coming and going at this time of night, waved, but she didn't know their names, and only that they were people. Mortals. Not a bloodsucker in the bunch.

Removing the key from her pocket, she stopped before reaching her doorstep and turned back to the street, seeing nothing, feeling something.

Tossing her bag on the front step, she dropped the key in her pocket, waited out a few pounding heartbeats and whispered, "Something." Then she strode back down the walkway.

The alley's nearness hit her before covering the four blocks to get to it. The place called to her with its dark whisper. She'd never returned to where she and her parents had been waylaid, but she remained conscious of it with the certainty of a homing pigeon.

"Time to face you," she said aloud, then jerked to a stop as the old superstitions returned. There was a good possibility that with her energy drained from the last few days, she wasn't strong enough to face this place yet, and might never be.

With one leather jacket-clad shoulder to the wall of the brick building on the alley's south side, and several deep breaths, she finally stepped forward, away from the yellow glow of the streetlight and into the pool of darkness.

"Yes." The word escaped with a soft hiss as her fingernails scraped the old brick. "I've dreamed of you for years."

In the unwholesome blackness, dimly lit from somewhere above, she saw the dark stains on the walls. Faded crimson smears. Remnants of what had once happened here, still visible enough to taunt her.

Voices reached her. Sounds of tearing flesh.

Next thing she knew, she was on her knees in the filth, with her hands covering her mouth and her eyes closed. She was swaying back and forth with the same mindless motion she'd once used to comfort herself with in the hospital. Broken glass particles cut through her jeans, biting into her knees—a distant pain. Her hair, fallen across her face, hid the rest of the view.

The damn place was alive. Its dark heart rammed against her like a fierce, freezing wind, and stank of death and destruction. She'd lost so very much here. Everything.

Something else nagged at her. A shiver raced up her spine. On her knees, she was vulnerable. Jesse opened her eyes and got up. Adrenaline spiked, white-hot.

A disturbance surfed the air where nothing should have been worse than what she was already feeling. Reaching for the disturbance, she focused hard, and looked around.

Fragrance. The faint odor of worn leather, and wool.

A rush of anticipation filled her. Recognition stirred, blocking out the stench of blood-trapped memories and the aftershocks of a secret remembered pain. Something had entered the alley, and that thing had a name.

"Look," he counseled, his voice deep and filled with the rustling softness of velvet. "See it for what it is, Jesse. Not for what it was."

He spoke again. "It's just a street to nowhere. Nothing more than that."

As dizzy as she was, and as sick as she felt, Jesse listened to the voice. Really, *he* couldn't be here. Another dream? Imagination working overtime? Her subconscious speaking?

He had become a part of this terrible space, woven into it like threads of light. His presence was as strong as the alley's, when by all rights it should have registered as another black hole. Maybe she was crazy to believe this vampire had followed her here, all this way. But Lance Van Baaren was here, no mistake. Her newly honed radar told her this.

I'm listening.

I feel you beside me.

She tested speech, found it possible. "It's—" she began.

"Over," he said firmly. "It was over long ago. Somebody just forgot to tell you."

He had been right about most things so far, but how could he know about this? How personal it was. How the events here had shaped her.

Jesse searched for the flashes that had manipulated her past, found them.

Blood. Red. Dripping. Familiar screams. Sounds of teeth tearing into flesh. Demonish shapes coming for her. The world going black, fading to white...

The images stalled, due to the vampire's closeness. For a moment, their time together overcame the memories of the distant past. Lance, in the meadow. Lance, holding her near the fire. His mouth on hers. Her failure to fight him off. She hadn't even tried.

Shaking off those memories, she again called up the ones related to where she stood.

Blood. Voices. The world fading into...gold. A vampire's whisper. "You know me."

The flood of images ceased abruptly, as if someone had stuck their finger in the dyke. "No," she muttered. "That's not right."

"Sometimes," the vampire beside her said, "you have to put the past behind you, where it belongs."

"So, you're a psychologist now?" she said, groping for a retort. He may have—make that definitely had—seen to it her life would be altered. Without permission. Without gauging the consequences of his actions.

"Sage advice from one creature to another?" she added with less force, since the persistent vision was of Lance holding her, kissing her, all the while willing her to understand why he had done what he had done. She had blocked this out…until now.

"A creature who might honestly know about the past," he corrected. "Give some credit where it's due."

She said nothing. Couldn't.

"What is it you want, Jesse?" he asked, moving closer to her, appearing finally, taking her breath away, as he always had.

"Peace." She didn't have to consider that answer. It's what she had always wanted.

"You think returning here will offer that?" he asked.

"I'd hoped so. But then I found you here, instead."

She shook her head, and added, "What have you done with my memories?"

"Helped to put them in their place. That's what you wanted, isn't it? That's the peace you spoke of?"

"It isn't that easy."

"The pain never fully goes," he agreed. "Though it's invariably easier to manage if you share it. If you're not alone."

Jesse's heart inexplicably turned over. The alley became quiet. She waited for the nasty visions to return, picking up where they left off. None did. It seemed as if they were…gone. Wiped clean. As though they had never really existed.

As if *he* had chased them away.

The red smears on the brick had dulled to a weather-worn pink. The dripping blood of her nightmares began to take on the shape of scrolled graffiti—the tagging of a neighborhood gang.

Paint. Not blood.

The stink of her surroundings became that of rotting garbage overflowing from nearby cans.

What the hell just happened? All of a sudden, this alley seemed less like a doorway to hell, and more like a really dirty, pathetically underilluminated dead end.

Time had moved on, bypassing this place and what had happened here, while she had been stuck. Her parents wouldn't have wanted her life ruined by pain. They wouldn't have wanted her to be alone.

There were monsters, yes, but they didn't rule this place now, tonight. She had seen the creatures up close and had lived to tell about it because of the creature beside her. The plan to rescue Elizabeth Jorgensen would have failed if it hadn't been for him. She wasn't quite strong enough to fight the bloodsuckers. And she was dangerously, hopelessly attracted to Lance.

Although her body had hosted tainted blood all along, she'd made it her life's objective to help others. This immortal's blood gift had not negatively influenced her choices or options. She'd done a lot of good things.

So had he. Things like saving her life, and helping to rescue another lost girl. Maybe other examples she knew nothing about. This vampire, immortal, Guardian or whatever he really was, no longer fit with her profile of his species. He didn't fit anywhere at all, really, except here, in this alley, beside her right now.

They were two strangers who weren't really strangers at all. Two beings, fully human once upon a time, whose lives had taken a different turn.

Was she cursed by what swam in her veins? Damned?

"No. Not cursed. Nor damned," Lance said, seeming to understand, as he always did, what she was thinking and feeling. Maybe he was the only one who ever would.

For all the sudden enlightenment, Jesse couldn't stop

shaking. Because there was a new fear to face. Lance Van Baaren, himself. And the depths of her feelings for him.

"You were here," she said. "In this place."

"Yes. Too late."

"You couldn't save them," she said.

"Only your heart beat faintly, yet enough."

"They got away? The monsters who killed my parents?"

"They did not leave this place," he said.

He speaks the truth. Jesse closed her eyes.

"Come, Jesse," he said. Lance—the golden angel who had offered light in this place once before, and who now, strangely enough, offered hope where it never had been possible.

She accepted his hand. The charge of her fingers meeting his made her insides tighten. It was useless asking how he had arrived or how he knew she would come here. They were indelibly tied together, not only through blood, seemingly, but by fate.

Unless he actually was her guardian angel…

If so, what might an angel require as payment for helping her out of a jam?

His bare fingers closed over hers firmly, and Jesse felt the sensation all the way to her bones. His fire burned everything in its path, leaving a trail of private, intimate pleasure. He seemed as stunned as she was by the magnitude of the effect of this personal touch. She heard his heartbeat above the thudding of her own.

There was something else he wanted from her. He wanted to make her like him, since he couldn't go backward, since the blood couldn't be taken back or removed. The only way for them to be together was to bring her over, fully. Finish what he had started.

They had come full circle, alley to alley.

And she no longer wanted to fight the hunger she felt for him.

"I won't be like *them*," she said, looking up at the tall, stately creature…captured now, as she always had been, by his golden aura of otherness, and by his gaze, so evocative and filled with emotion. She sensed a hunger in him that matched her own; a wariness that matched her own. But the uniqueness of his feelings for her, combined with the power and energy of his ancient bloodline, offered her a lifeline out of the pit of despair.

"You would never be like them," he agreed. "It isn't possible."

Jesse's eyes drifted upward, seeking more than compliments. Tiny licks of fire ricocheted across the scar on her neck.

"You can live your life in any way you choose," he said. "Your future is up to you."

The rich timbre of his voice was like a stroke of his hand across nakedness. A melting promise. His inferno was inviting, and extremely sexual. The adjective she'd left out this time was "vile." She knew now that she'd never been completely immune to his allure. Was this the meaning of the phrase *blood to blood?* Either the fluid in her veins caused the attraction, or else she'd been more like him than she cared to admit, from the start.

"What about your future?" she asked, her tone throaty. "How will you live yours?"

"In the world I've shunned. No longer shut away," he replied.

"Because of—"

"You."

It was the truth. Lance Van Baaren, as still as marble,

his beautiful, chiseled features taut with a tension she wanted to wipe away, was letting her know that she had influenced his life for the better. A last confession? The reasoning behind what he was about to do?

"You'll kill me now," she said.

"Will I? I don't think so. Not today."

Liar! He'd been killing her bit by bit, messing with her chemistry and her equilibrium since the first night in this alley. He'd been a part of her all this time, in the background like a vague idea, unformed. Like an unresolved craving. Like a waiting lover.

All it took to realize this was for her to find him.

Truth...

Finding him hadn't been his fault, she saw in hindsight. She had been the aggressor. She had accepted the Jorgensen case. It had been her order to bring the chopper down in his meadow, an action that just happened to cause the strengthening of their bond. Lance hadn't sought her out. As far as she knew, he might never have returned to L.A., remaining a recluse in another country, in his castle fortress, on the other side of the world.

Fate...

Their lives had become entangled because of more than a few decisions they had made. She had wanted to kill the vampires. As one of them, and with her own soul intact, she might still have that chance. A better chance.

"Why not today?" she asked, chancing another look around her, thinking that this alley was as fitting a place as any for a date with destiny, and that death couldn't have arrived in a more elegant package.

"I'm ready," she said, feeling curiously calm without the pain of the past. The space inside of her, left by the disappearing blackness, begged to be filled. She awaited oblivion, in whatever form it might take.

"Ready?" Lance Van Baaren said, his body leaning toward hers. "Then perhaps you've come to the wrong vampire."

Chapter 21

Lance looked her over in wonderment. Jesse assumed he'd take her over the edge of that abyss now, and she didn't care?

Be careful what you wish for...

The fighter in Jesse just didn't see. He'd never brought anyone still living across that line separating life from death. Everything he stood for went against such a thing.

She awaited his answer. Her lush lips were parted. Her heart was beating rapidly, sending its message to him as surely as a lover sent a love letter. In this place where her loved ones had died, she was ready to join them. Or else what? Join him? Become like him?

Her motive was all too clear. She would give up the preciousness of life to become a hunter. She had grown weary of living her life the way she'd lived it. In her eyes, she'd been helpless against the complexities of the world and its shadow realms. So, two birds with one stone—pay off a debt she assumed she owed him, and continue with her quest.

Again, a temptation, no matter her motive. A win-win situation. Except that he wouldn't really have her, nor would he be able to predict how she'd turn out, if she wasn't willing to give up life as she knew it for the right reasons.

It all came back to intentions. He could not *take* her life. Jesse had to offer it, not from a position of hate or injustice, but because she wanted something more from such an event. What would that be?

Are you as lonely as I am, Jesse?

Through their bond, assessing his state of arousal would be easy for her. His hunger was wrapping around them like an extra pair of arms. His thirst, so carefully kept hidden in the depths of what he was, showed itself now with the extension of his fangs. She was so close…a bite away, and smelling of passion, emotion and her own otherness. Not one bit of her hinted at confusion or withdrawal.

But it wasn't enough. She needed to offer more.

It was she who had him oh so delicately by the throat. Not the other way around. A situation to which she seemed blind. He could barely control himself, yet couldn't walk away without knowing for sure what that light in her eyes meant.

He took her by the shoulders, hoping she'd look into his eyes, without willing her to do so. If she had lied about her motives, without knowing this herself, she wouldn't make this connection. It was a final test. He'd tasted this need in her, but she had to acknowledge the truth.

His body jerked when she obliged. When her big

brown eyes met his, all of his former lives collapsed into the distance as they stood, connected, for seconds, minutes, maybe even years. Jesse's eyes were bright and seeing, and reflected her deepest needs.

Jesse wasn't offering herself up due to payment of a debt. He saw the flare of her hunger, exposed. He heard her soul cry out against it, but once in the open, there was no turning back.

She wanted…him.

Him, no matter what he was.

On some level, she'd begun to trust, and dared to believe.

Fires raged as Lance drew her closer with the snap of his arm, as his senses filled with the perfume of her clothes, her hair and her desire for him. Her blood pounded out a new rhythm against his chest, matched by his own. She was as afraid…as he was.

It was a dangerous slow dance. Every one of her curves, as well as each angle, molded to him. He ran his hands over her arms, waiting for her to stop him. Maybe even waiting for divine intervention. Instead, her body strained closer. Her splayed hands moved slowly across his back. All the while, as the world faded away behind them, her eyes held his.

"Is it painful?" she asked, her lips moist, her question demanding.

"Yes," he replied.

"For someone used to pain?"

"Yes."

"Do you know if you're damned?"

"Not knowing which side we're closer to, be it heaven or hell, is the risk we take, if given the option to take it."

She whispered, "What about the flight of your soul? Did you feel it go?"

"It doesn't have to go," Lance said. "I spoke the truth about that."

"Then you are still *you,* only more so?" She tossed his own explanation back at him. "You were a good man?"

"I tried to be."

"Why do you want me, Lance?" she asked, although she already knew the answer. "Blood to blood?" she whispered.

Those words, torn from her parted lips, burned a channel directly to the male parts of him, remembering all too well what might happen next if she kept looking at him that way, while smelling so good. But he was also aware of something else. Something new was happening inside him—a vague pull he didn't recognize.

"We'll revisit this later, and see if your decision sticks," he said.

It was a lie. He knew it. She knew it. His hunger was nearly out of control, and this moment was pivotal, important for reasons neither of them fully understood, except for the part about filling the emptiness, easing the loneliness and being lost in each other's closeness. Craving that closeness.

Sweet God, Lance thought as her gaze continued to electrify him, and as the answer to the dilemma slammed into him. The missing part of the equation was...*love.*

He loved Jesse with the force of every life he'd lived, all rolled into one. There was no other, would never be another. The feeling washing over him was of having that love brought into focus, into the light, in this place, this minute.

Love had blasted away the evil of this place. Yet it could so easily be lost with one misstep.

She had to love him back. That was the signal he awaited so impatiently.

When her eyes finally withdrew, he mourned the disconnect. When she tilted her head, as he'd envisioned so many times in his daydreams, baring the naked, glistening skin of her neck…he brushed the length of her old wound with his fingertips.

Is it me you want, Jesse? Or power to hunt the monsters? You must show me which need rules your decision.

Her life-pulse beat strongly against his fingers. He lowered his head, angled his face toward that pulse. Hesitating a breath away from her, he closed his eyes, and dared to touch that spot with his lips.

Anxiety shot through her, and a bit of fear. Yet anticipation was the buzz Jesse gave off. Anticipation of meeting him on his own ground. She wanted to be a crusader, yes, but she also wanted him, no matter what he was. He alone, in all the world, could understand her, she was thinking. He alone could touch her depths.

He heard her whisper his name as the final piece of the puzzle snapped tight. His fangs grazed her neck, and she stood there, open to this, open to him.

You have to offer, he sent to her. *You have to be willing.*

Just one more chance to change your mind, Jesse.

He took her soft skin between his teeth, touched his tongue to the old wound and absorbed her shiver. She did not move, or run away.

He bit down lightly, only a nip, not enough to draw blood. That action, so minor compared to what lay ahead, opened the gates, and brought the words he needed from her.

"Not alone." It was the voice of her soul calling to his. "Never alone again. It's the only way to save us both. Try, Lance. Save me. Love me. Please take me where you are."

There. He had his answer.

He had her trust.

Her mouth opened when he found it. He kissed the breath out of her, enfolding her in his arms, crushing her close. She answered his ardor with a willingness he had not imagined.

The kiss was a drowning kiss, deep, endless. She ran her tongue across his fangs, pricked her lip. The taste of her blood, mixed with a single teardrop, fallen from her eye, filled them both.

She grew hotter, her pulse wilder, but didn't struggle against it. For seconds more, Lance reveled in the poignant sweetness. Jesse had relinquished the control that had reined her in. For a few minutes, she had surrendered herself to the union.

She had given up a lot.

Now, he had to do the same.

Reluctantly removing his lips from hers, taking hold of her hand, Lance turned from Jesse's alley. With his love beside him, he felt the wind of change on his face.

Jesse was on her back, on her own bed, in her apartment. How she got there was a blur. Whether or not she was still clothed didn't cross her mind. Her attention was riveted on the immortal who left her breathless.

Her world had become one of pure sensation. A touch

of his fingertips here…the taunt of a warm exhalation there…on her bare skin.

The fangs were in evidence—an iridescent gleam in the partially darkened room. He could have used them twice over, and had not. The vampire had torn himself from her in that hole of an alley, and brought her home.

He braced himself over her, on the bed, his weight on his arms. Patiently holding himself back, he scored several small bites to her right shoulder in an upward sweep of his teeth. Lean thighs, as taut as the rest of him, pressed against hers. The sheer enormity of his hunger for her caused him to shake.

And he had turned on a light, knowing how much she feared the dark.

Jesse wanted to see the entire length of Lance Van Baaren. The glorious whiteness of a creature unused to the sun. But she didn't take her attention from his face.

Each move he made caused her to curl toward him. Her body vibrated as his silky curtain of hair brushed across her breasts.

Surrender. The unspoken word floated between them. She knew what it was supposed to mean. If she joined with him willingly, body, mind and soul, offering up herself, her mortality, her life…the union might catapult her into another realm. One where intentions were everything, and time ceased to exist.

A new existence, free of old fears. A long-overdue love. A new start.

Did she dare hope for all that?

Already his ministrations were life-altering, the pleasure he offered extreme. For the first time in her life, something pleasurable, if completely insane and dangerous, had overtaken her past. Golden light extinguished the darkness. This was no lie, no falsehood. The truth she now knew, the one hidden in the darkness she harbored, was that she hungered for this immortal as much as he hungered for her.

It was useless to deny how much she wanted him.

And his blood.

Her thirst lay coiled inside, an integral part of this. Perhaps he had given her too much of himself already? Did he know?

His eyes came to meet hers, so vividly blue as to be human. She took his face in her hands, and felt the weight of his body shift, until he was stretched out on top of her, with no space between them and no air to be breathed that didn't involve his breath. The pressure in her chest was not conceived of darkness this time, nor was it the pain of withheld memories. It was the weightiness of true connection with another being. The very definition of love. This was a mutual merging, equally surprising to them both. No one person desiring this more than the other. In this, they were already one.

She wrapped her fingers in his hair and tugged, wanting to feel his masculinity, and at the same time mar his incredible beauty with her nails. Wanting him inside her in an altogether new way. Impatiently desiring it all.

"Some think I am the dark," he said, withholding that thing she wanted most at the moment, though Jesse felt him hard against her.

"They would be right," she said.

"You no longer fear me, my love."

"I'm different."

A wicked smile played on his lips. She tugged again on his hair, said, "How long?"

His pale eyebrows arched in question.

"How long will my eyes be closed?" she asked, hearing the rumble in her voice, feeling the tip of his erection slide into the folds of the place no one had ever dared to touch.

"Seconds. I'll be here, waiting, calling. Follow my voice."

"The Dark Seduction is over. It's on with the Surrender part? That's a real thing?" she gasped.

His finger pressed against her lips to quiet her. Simultaneously, his other hand reached downward to further open her legs.

As his ravenous mouth returned with a new fervor, Jesse felt the sting of the sharpness of his fangs on her lips, and the warmth of her own blood on her tongue.

Lance entered her inferno slowly, with his mouth on her mouth, feeding on her heat.

His love was scintillatingly hot, and tight. He hadn't realized how cold he'd been all this time, until confronting her fire. Each inch he gained inside her moist folds was met by a dozen shudders, and startled sounds of delight that stuck in her throat. Her hands tore at his shoulders and back. Her hips raised to meet his, instinctively urging him on.

It had been so long since he'd been intimate in this way, he didn't want to hold back much longer. He didn't want to be gentle or take his time. Jesse was a fierce soul. Her own impatience screamed at him for culmination almost before things had really begun. And in truth, slowness shouldn't have mattered. There should be endless time in the future for pleasure and exploration. But nothing was a certainty, Lance reminded himself.

What if this was to be their first and last time together? If his reasons for doing this were too selfish? If the vow he was breaking in her honor—a vow he had never once undermined—would send him, and Jesse with him, to hell? If they were to be damned?

Just in case, he should prolong this moment, stretch it out, since it might indeed be their last…

Jesse wasn't going to let that happen, he realized. She was not to be deterred from satisfying her hunger. Letting loose a throaty sigh, she wrapped herself around him, met him with a scalding wave of moisture that sent him to the edge and held him suspended there.

Suddenly, he was afraid. Frightened out of his mind. What if this didn't work? What if the rumors about this kind of union turned out to be myth? What if he hurt her again? Lost her?

She might not open her eyes.

She was rubbing against him now, urging him on, tugging him toward ecstasy, needing him as much as he needed her, and trusting him to get her through this.

He felt the chaos coming. Not just imminent orgasm, but something beyond the physical…circling, fluttering, suspended, with the smell and taste of night, splashed with blood.

Thirst.

"God, Jesse…"

Lance's insides contracted, sending his hardness deeper into her. A cry slipped from Jesse as she dug into him with her fingers.

His fangs ached. His body spasmed as thirst began to overtake him. He kissed her again, long and deep, and drew his hips back. Then he thrust into her plushness,

spurred on by the flames in her embrace and the sound
of her heart revving. She wanted this. He owed her.

He repeated the action several more times, pressing
himself into Jesse, locked to her with his body and his
mouth. Jesse accepted it all.

Their bodies merged fully, meaningfully, bathed in
the hazy red light of a nearly extinct, partial blood moon
streaming through the open window.

Sacrifice was the song that moon sang.

Bite! Jesse's soul cried.

His final plunge reached the core of Jesse Stewart.
She screamed her pleasure, and the sound echoed off
the walls. The bed shook. The apartment shuddered on
its foundation. And the thing that had loomed in the
periphery careened down through him and into her, as
unrighteous as it may have been, wickedly insatiable
and hungry. The result of his broken oath.

And now for your soul, my love.

Covered in a light sweat, writhing with the burn of
a need reaching its zenith, Jesse turned her head on the
pillow...

And Lance sank his teeth into her neck.

Liquid filled his mouth, dispersing his senses, threatening to overwhelm. But he had to hold it together. He
had seconds, if that, to drain her to her heart's final beat.
Seconds, while she burned...pulling from her not too
much, nor too little. Taking her blood and her life force
into himself. Bringing her to the brink of death, where
nothing but sparks existed on a gray, mountainless plane.
After which he would give all that blood, mixed with
his own, back to her. Along with her soul.

Hang on, my love.

He drank, drawing deeply, and watched her life
unfold. He saw it all, and ached with the loneliness she

had endured. She did not cry out. Her muscles twitched, then convulsed in helpless waves, but she did hang on.

Her pulse dwindled to three faint beats.

Two.

No rise of her chest. No visible breath.

No more pain.

Lance brought his head up quickly, spoke clearly. "You must come back to me, Jesse. That's the deal."

Using his fangs, he tore open his wrist, opened Jesse's mouth gently and dribbled fluid from his open vein onto her pale, lifeless lips. He laid his bloody wrist over her mouth. His other hand pushed against her chest.

Drink, Jesse. Now. Do this for me. For us. He sent his demand into her via his blood. He willed her to heed, pleaded with her to obey this one last thing.

Bless her, she heard. Her bloody lips accepted his offering. Her soul, lighter now but still fierce, and so very lovely, slipped back in through her mouth.

Chapter 22

Jesse ran.

Through the dark streets of L.A., her gun drawn and steady in her gloved hand, its chambers loaded with silver bullets. The soft creak of her leather pants masked the sound of her low whistle.

Above her, on the rooftop to her right, her lover stood with a confident grace, his leanness outlined by the light of a full moon. As always when she saw him, his beauty took her breath away. But breathlessness wasn't a problem these days. And no vampire trying to get away with biting someone in her territory could outrun her anymore.

Plus, she had added another secret weapon to her arsenal. A friend.

On the ground, fairly close, an answering growl rumbled through the night like a charging freight train.

"Come on, wolf," she muttered. "Get this monster and I'll buy you more muffins than you can possibly eat."

She caught soft laughter from above and glanced that way. Tonight, Lance looked the part of the knight he'd once been. She'd seen several of his lifetimes in the heat of passion, though she often tasted the presence of secrets he still withheld.

Lance was formidable up there on the roof, in his dark pants and leather duster—all that leather a precaution against the silver intended for a rogue vampire invading their space.

She'd promised him a trip home as soon as this pervert was dust. They'd take Stan along. Nadia would like that, even if Carol wouldn't be so keen on the separation.

Everyone deserved a vacation now and then from their secrets. Some freedom. The exception being the monsters, who were presently nearly nonexistent in this part of Los Angeles, thanks to no small thing some called the Night of Dark Surrender, and to her own kind of rebirth.

And thanks to the gorgeous immortal who taught her things, day by day, and who had shared what he held so dear with her, in the name of love. Bad things, and good things. How to come back from death. How to move through shadows, and survive the light. What it took to control the cravings and the ever-present thirst. But then, she was used to issues of control after a lifetime of dealing with it.

She was still a fighter.

Her new images? Buzzwords? Death and rebirth, willingly accepted. Sex and intimacy. Timeless, un-ending love beyond imagination, and beyond boundaries.

Strange new liaisons. Friendship. Purpose. Guardian angels…the new, unspoken platform for her company.

She and Lance were two souls entwined. Night souls, reborn of darkness, but allowed to live in the light. Massing their strength to help others in need. Keeping the monsters in their places. Understanding that forces of good can overcome evil in the darkest of circumstances, if the heart is pure. And understanding that love can conquer even the most heinous of prejudices, in the end.

Way too many things to have learned in six short months.

"Boss?"

"Hey! You changed back," Jesse said, cruising to a stop.

"Cloud cover," Stan said. "Plus, he took all the fun out of it."

Jesse looked up to find the rooftop empty. She grinned, showing, she knew, a gleam of fang.

"Mind if I ask what he does with the crazy bloodsuckers he catches?" Stan asked.

"Do you really want to know?"

Stan shrugged. "Nope. Sometime you'll tell me about this, though. What happened, and how you do anything around those." He pointed to her mouth.

Jesse nodded. "Sometime."

"Well, I suppose I'll be off, then, since it's after midnight," Stan said, his voice lowering to a bass register.

"Home?"

Stan's turn to grin. "Carol and I have new sheets."

Jesse laughed out loud.

Stan glanced up at the moon, emerging again from the clouds. "Secrets aren't always bad," he said.

"Yours was a whopper," Jesse admitted.

Stan's grin widened. He stretched his shoulders and his thick neck, then gave a bark of impending transformation, heralded by a disgusting popping sound from the vicinity of his spine. He asked gruffly, "Does he still wear those poofy shirts?"

Then he was gone…

And another body, the epitome of magnificent mysteries…golden hair gleaming in the moonlight like a halo…eyes the color of a Slovenian lake…fangs hinting at his own special kind of lust, and just now tipped in red…pushed her into the side of the closest building, pressed his body suggestively to hers…and smiled.

* * * * *

nocturne™

COMING NEXT MONTH

Available April 26, 2011

#111 GHOST STALKER
The Trackers
Jenna Kernan

#112 THE BEHOLDER
The Nightwalkers
Connie Hall

REQUEST YOUR FREE BOOKS!

2 FREE NOVELS PLUS 2 FREE GIFTS!

Harlequin®

nocturne™

Dramatic and Sensual Tales of Paranormal Romance.

YES! Please send me 2 FREE Harlequin® Nocturne™ novels and my 2 FREE gifts (gifts are worth about $10). After receiving them, if I don't wish to receive any more books, I can return the shipping statement marked "cancel." If I don't cancel, I will receive 4 brand-new novels every other month and be billed just $4.47 per book in the U.S. or $4.99 per book in Canada. That's a saving of at least 15% off the cover price! It's quite a bargain! Shipping and handling is just 50¢ per book in the U.S. and 75¢ per book in Canada.* I understand that accepting the 2 free books and gifts places me under no obligation to buy anything. I can always return a shipment and cancel at any time. Even if I never buy another book, the two free books and gifts are mine to keep forever.

238/338 HDN FC5T

Name _____ (PLEASE PRINT)

Address _____ Apt. #

City _____ State/Prov. _____ Zip/Postal Code

Signature (if under 18, a parent or guardian must sign)

Mail to the **Reader Service:**
IN U.S.A.: P.O. Box 1867, Buffalo, NY 14240-1867
IN CANADA: P.O. Box 609, Fort Erie, Ontario L2A 5X3

Not valid for current subscribers to Harlequin Nocturne books.

Want to try two free books from another line?
Call 1-800-873-8635 or visit www.ReaderService.com.

* Terms and prices subject to change without notice. Prices do not include applicable taxes. Sales tax applicable in N.Y. Canadian residents will be charged applicable taxes. Offer not valid in Quebec. This offer is limited to one order per household. All orders subject to credit approval. Credit or debit balances in a customer's account(s) may be offset by any other outstanding balance owed by or to the customer. Please allow 4 to 6 weeks for delivery. Offer available while quantities last.

Your Privacy—The Reader Service is committed to protecting your privacy. Our Privacy Policy is available online at www.ReaderService.com or upon request from the Reader Service.

We make a portion of our mailing list available to reputable third parties that offer products we believe may interest you. If you prefer that we not exchange your name with third parties, or if you wish to clarify or modify your communication preferences, please visit us at www.ReaderService.com/consumerschoice or write to us at Reader Service Preference Service, P.O. Box 9062, Buffalo, NY 14269. Include your complete name and address.

HN11

With an evil force hell-bent on destruction,
two enemies must unite to find a truth that turns
all-too-personal when passions collide.

Enjoy a sneak peek in Jenna Kernan's next installment
in her original TRACKER series, GHOST STALKER,
available in May, only from Harlequin Nocturne.

"Who are you?" he snarled.

Jessie lifted her chin. "Your better."

His smile was cold. "Such arrogance could only come from a Niyanoka."

She nodded. "Why are you here?"

"I don't know." He glanced about her room. "I asked the birds to take me to a healer."

"And they have done so. Is that *all* you asked?"

"No. To lead them away from my friends." His eyes fluttered and she saw them roll over white.

Jessie straightened, preparing to flee, but he roused himself and mastered the momentary weakness. His eyes snapped open, locking on her.

Her heart hammered as she inched back.

"Lead who away?" she whispered, suddenly afraid of the answer.

"The ghosts. Nagi sent them to attack me so I would bring them to her."

The wolf must be deranged because Nagi did not send ghosts to attack living creatures. He captured the evil ones after their death if they refused to walk the Way of Souls, forcing them to face judgment.

"Her? The healer you seek is also female?"

"Michaela. She's Niyanoka, like you. The last Seer of Souls and Nagi wants her dead."

Jessie fell back to her seat on the carpet as the possibility of this ricocheted in her brain. Could it be true?

"Why should I believe you?" But she knew why. His black aura, the part that said he had been touched by death. Only a ghost could do that. But it made no sense.

Why would Nagi hunt one of her people and why would a Skinwalker want to protect her? She had been trained from birth to hate the Skinwalkers, to consider them a threat.

His intent blue eyes pinned her. Jessie felt her mouth go dry as she considered the impossible. Could the trickster be speaking the truth? Great Mystery, what evil was this?

She stared in astonishment. There was only one way to find her answers. But she had never even met a Skinwalker before and so did not even know if they dreamed.

But if he dreamed, she would have her chance to learn the truth.

Look for GHOST STALKER by Jenna Kernan,
available May only from Harlequin Nocturne,
wherever books and ebooks are sold.